PENGUIN · SHORT · FICTION

"Not that the story need be long, but it
will take a long while to make it short."
— Henry David Thoreau

Learning by Heart

Margot Livesey was born in Scotland and grew up there
in an isolated part of the country. She attended the
University of York in England and, after extensive
travel through Europe and North Africa, emigrated to
Canada. She now divides her time between Toronto,
Boston and London.

Although her stories have appeared in various magazines, this is Margot Livesey's first collection.

LEARNING BY HEART

Margot Livesey

Penguin Books

Penguin Books Canada Limited, 2801 John Street, Markham, Ontario,
Canada L3R 1B4
Penguin Books Ltd., Harmondsworth, Middlesex, England
Penguin Books, 40 West 23rd Street, New York, New York 10010 U.S.A.
Penguin Books Australia Ltd., Ringwood, Victoria, Australia
Penguin Books (N.Z.) Ltd., Private Bag, Takapuna, Auckland 9,
New Zealand

First published by Penguin Books Canada Limited, 1986

Copyright © Margot Livesey, 1986

Canadian Cataloguing in Publication Data

Livesey, Margot, 1953-
Learning by heart

(Penguin short fiction)
ISBN 0-14-008157-7

I. Title. II. Series.

PS8573.I89L42   1986   C813'.54   C86-093419-5
PR9199.3.L565L42   1986

For Merril and Roger

Acknowledgements

Earlier versions of some of these stories appeared, sometimes under different titles, in the following magazines: *The Fiddlehead*, *The Antigonish Review*, *The Wascana Review*, *The Dalhousie Review* and *California Quarterly*.

An early version of "Obituary" appeared in *Prism International*; the story was included in *The New Press Anthology: Best Canadian Short Fiction* #1.

I am grateful to the Ontario Arts Council and the Canada Council for their support.

Contents

Obituary

Obituary

Whenever I visit a museum and see one of those orange and black Attic vases, around which the figures pursue each other in an endless faded procession, I remember my father, who held in great regard mummeries and funerals. His whole interest in life lay in death and the rituals surrounding it, and, like a character on a vase, he remained poised always, for as long as I knew him, in the same attitude. If he had lived in that age, he would have appeared frequently in funeral scenes, as a mourner or bystander, even a rather solemn flautist, following the priest and the bier to some dark cave where the dead kept house. I can imagine him driving a good-humoured bargain about fares with Charon; the latter shaking his shaggy head and saying, "A man must live," while my father, notebook in hand, confronted him with the accounts.

Probably he would have been happier in that world, which paid closer attention to death than we do now, but, given his generation, he had done rather well for himself, indeed accomplished something rare, by professionalising his passion

and becoming the obituary writer for the local paper, an un-
salaried position which he pursued with conscientious zeal.
His real work too was bound up with mortality, for he owned
a small shop where he sold and repaired watches. In this
room, the size of a small cupboard, my father sat behind the
glass display case containing his selection of stock, new and
used, and worked busily on the tiny innards of old watches.
He wore a black apron to protect his clothes, and every
morning, almost as soon as he sat down, he would screw into
his left eye a black loupe. So permanent was this addition to
his vision that even when it was not in place his features, in
memory, were dragged a little to one side.

He closed the shop early on Saturdays, and almost every
Saturday afternoon during the summer months he and I
walked slowly up the hill to the local Nursing Home. For
these visits my father wore his second-best suit and carried
his silver-handled cane, which he did not use during the
week. Never passing up any opportunity to gather material
for his obituaries, he would stop beside one garden and then
another. While he conversed with the gardeners, questioning
them closely about the more elderly members of their
families, I would hop up and down on the edge of the pavement or dissect a rose or two. Finally to my delight we would
reach our destination.

The Nursing Home was surrounded by a wrought iron
fence. I would swing a few times on the gate before running
along the path and ducking past my father to open the green
door. Crossing the threshold, I entered a new world. Even on
these summer days, when many windows stood open, there
was an initially overwhelming odour of antiseptic. After a
short time in this intense atmosphere I could distinguish the
many smells that it smothered: meat and boiled vegetables,
the rather heavy perfumes favoured by the nurses, the wax
on the floors, the disinfectant in the toilets, the flowers, the
talcum powder and old skin, the dust and the death.

My father went first to pay his respects to the Matron,

whom I thought of as old but who was probably at that time no more than fifty. She was a large woman with grey hair. I remember her wrists, nipped in like tucks at the end of her plump, blue-sleeved arms, and her small, very white hands. I have heard people complain that geriatric nursing is depressing, but certainly this was never true for Matron. What mattered to her, as to my father, was the quality of death. Together they would discuss for hours who had made a good death, who had exceeded their expectations and who, perhaps surprisingly, at the last moment, cringed. While they talked, I would find the tea trolley and follow it on its route.

My father had a curious status as a visitor. Wearing black, seen by the patients as a harbinger of doom, come as it were to measure them for their coffins, ready or not, one might have thought he would meet with resentment. But somehow he had achieved the status of an old favourite whose peculiar habits were viewed as merely harmless eccentricities. He endeared himself to the patients by memorising the football results to tell them, by reading aloud from the local paper, by relaying gossip and running errands. In addition, for many of them he provided an important service; he was their chronologist, the one person on whom they could rely to listen to their history and give it sense and shape before the end.

The more lively of these elderly people called him "The Crow" and there was something bird-like about him as he zig-zagged around the ward, his cane pecking on the bare floor, searching for likely prospects. He approached the patients, male or female, hat in hand, making a brief side-step to confirm the name on the chart which hung at the end of the bed. If they were asleep, or had their eyes closed, then he would stand for a moment, his head on one side, as if listening for signs of life: the tricky beating of the heart, the swelling of the lungs. Presently, he would cough softly and ask, "How are you, Mrs Archibald?"

The patient would make some indistinct sound. "Not too good, I see," my father would say. "Shall we just make sure we've got everything straight?" As he spoke, he would reach in his pocket and produce the black notebook, which never left his person. "You were born in Tunbridge Wells, isn't that right? In 1868. That makes you eighty-two, doesn't it? Not a bad age, certainly more than three score and ten. It's amazing how many people do pass on in their seventies, almost as if they decided to." He would talk on in this fashion, mixing his philosophy with dates and facts, undeterred by the silence, until at some point Mrs Archibald would sit up and announce triumphantly, "I'm planning to live to be a hundred, so you can stay away from me, you old Crow."

My father was rarely startled by these transformations. "Good, you're feeling a little better. It was Tunbridge Wells, wasn't it?" In nine cases out of ten the patients, forgetting their irritation, would embark on their life story. Even though my father attached himself like a limpet only to facts, and regarded praise and blame as mere digressions, adding no substance to the narrative, he was in their narrowed world the only listener upon whom they could depend.

By these weekly visits my father kept his very thorough files up to date. He loved every aspect of death, the talk of last throes and last words, the discussion of caskets and coffins, the choice of hymns and funeral orations, where the reception would be held, the cost of the baked meats. His interest extended just the other side of death to the will, with all its surprising possibilities, and also to post mortems, which he considered another kind of Last Testament. But he found the minor vicissitudes of health quite boring and was not one to talk about illness in a hushed voice. Illness was interesting only when it was fatal; to watch someone slowly slipping out of life, either hanging on or letting go, that was his preoccupation.

In winter when it was cold and the hill up to the Nursing

Home seemed too long and steep, we would go round to the undertakers instead. My father's relationship with these men was an ambivalent one. He shared with them a common interest but at the same time viewed their activities with some disapproval; he felt that their services encouraged a certain disrespect for the dead. There were only two in our town, Mr Campbell and Mr Sullivan, but I don't think that there was any rivalry between them, except in the details of their craft. When my father was appealed to as a judge of such matters, he was always careful to remain impartial. They were probably united in regarding him as indecisive.

Mr Sullivan's shop had a plate glass window with his name in gold letters and a display of a grey tombstone with a bunch of red plastic roses in front of it. Behind the tombstone stood panelling which concealed the interior from passers-by. Inside there was a wooden counter with a blotter and an ashtray, a clock, a calendar and a couple of hard wooden chairs. It was not particularly comfortable but there was a certain incipient homeliness, as if, at any moment, a cup of tea might appear. My father, here too a privileged visitor, always had one to sip during his tour of inspection, and as he talked he would stir his tea endlessly, accompanying the conversation with the soft clinks of teaspoon on china. he and Mr Sullivan would assess a corpse, like a couple of soothsayers scrutinising a liver.

"Well, he's neatly turned out, Mr Sullivan, but this suit isn't up to much. Surely it isn't his best? I've seen Mike at a couple of funerals quite nicely dressed."

"I think she's keeping the suit for the son. He's nearly of an age now when he'll need it, and they are dear."

"Still," my father would say quite sternly, "she should understand the occasion. This is his big day. Look at these shoes, they've got a good shine on them, but didn't she realise that everyone would see the soles? I never noticed the play on words until Mr Campbell pointed it out; of course his sister-in-law is a Catholic."

My father would pursue one of his favourite topics, the stinginess of women in the face of death. Women, he claimed, were guilty of a lack of respect for the dead, they often seemed to consider the living to be more important. Mr Sullivan, who must have heard this lecture almost as often as my mother and myself, would nod, until at last my father turned his attention back to the body. "Now I look closely at the feet, they don't look so good. You've got an awfully funny angle for that left foot."

"We tried but you know that's how he was, he limped, especially when he was tired. Remember at his father's funeral how slowly they had to walk because of Mike?" To nudge my father's memory one had only to mention a funeral and his vagueness vanished. Once or twice I even heard him refer to my birth as being the day before the former minister's last rites.

While this conversation was going on, I too would look at the body, but more perfunctorily unless, as sometimes happened, the person appeared greatly changed. Then I drifted off to play with Mr Sullivan's various tools. As a child I took my father's hobby for granted, and although he was almost completely oblivious to me, I enjoyed accompanying him on his rounds. I even, in my own way, tried to emulate him.

I had a little cemetery in the garden where I buried what dead animals I could lay my hands on, mostly birds or mice that the cat had proudly deposited on the kitchen floor. I wrapped them in handkerchiefs, gently deposited them in a hole with some of the words I could remember, threw on earth, and had my dolls celebrate the whole event with cups of tea. Each grave was marked with a small cross made from two twigs tied together. This was my equivalent of a stamp collection, and I felt no squeamishness at all in handling the bodies. Where appropriate I also buried relics with them, things they would need in the happy hunting ground, favourite toys, pictures of dangers and pleasures cut from magazines. On the long-standing graves I planted flowers, and in the case of family pets I remembered the anniversaries of their deaths.

My father never commented on this as far as I recall. I did overhear him once saying to my mother, "Perhaps she'll be a vet when she grows up. She seems to have leanings that way." Maybe that was a comment. The first couple of times I buried a pet my mother thought it was sweet. Then when it became apparent that I was interested in any corpse, not just a dearly loved one, her attitude changed. It was not in her nature to forbid me; she only tried, without success, to divert my attention.

On Sundays we had to go to church, although my father did not, on the whole, see eye to eye with the minister and had considerable reservations about the teachings of the church. Christmas he loathed. The Easter period I think he viewed with mixed feelings: until Good Friday events were definitely going his way, but Easter Sunday left him uncertain. He was not sure that this was what he wanted; it was one thing to seek death, another to make it seem as if it had not occurred. But he did, I know, believe in the physical resurrection of the body, for he often made remarks which reflected the idea that in heaven we would all be whole and comely and athletic. Because of this he deplored cremation, although, as our town was too small to boast a crematorium, it was not an immediate threat. He felt that cremation made it difficult to connect everything up again and stripped the dead of all the things they would need in the after-life, for certainly one would need one's best suit in heaven. Later, when I attended a service at a crematorium, I thought he would also have hated the efficiency, the soft-footed attendants, the well-oiled doors, the lack of personal reference to the dead. At our church it was obvious when the bearers were struggling with a heavier person and when they could march with a good swing. We all knew who was dead.

On funeral days there would be a service in church. Then we would go out into the graveyard, following behind the coffin. My father, to his chagrin, was debarred from the activity of a bearer by reason of his weak heart. The turf in the churchyard was so green and smooth, each grave was like a wound. While the coffin stood on a plinth beside the open grave, the minister would say, "Man that is born of woman hath but a short time to live, and is full of misery. He cometh up and is cut down, like a flower; he fleeth as it were a shadow, and never continueth in one stay." That part of the service always made me shiver, it sounded so black and final. The coffin would be lowered and we would give thanks for the occupant's relief from this world. Soon the nearest and dearest would have to hurry off to organise the reception, and it was my father who lingered when everyone else, bar the gravediggers, had left. After a few moments of silent contemplation, perhaps a reverie or an assessment of the flowers, he would nod and turn away.

The reception, his only kind of party, would be held either at the home or at one of the two small hotels, The Cross Keys or The Green Plum. There would be sherry, ham, slices of tomato, shortbread, rolls, hard-boiled eggs, scotch eggs, cheese. My father took upon himself the part of chief mourner; he passed from guest to guest with a soft, dry handshake and the ordinary condolences of which he was a master. "He had five younger brothers and he outlived them all, so he hasn't done so badly." Often it was the case that he knew more about the dead than anyone else present; in a low voice he would impart information and make sure that everyone had the facts straight. "No, he wasn't decorated during the war. He was cited for helping to improve the drainage in the trenches." I, meanwhile, in a dark skirt with a white blouse and white socks, would sit on a chair near the food and eat, with discretion, as much as possible.

I thought of death as a kind of blessing, and never understood my mother's murmured regrets, until one winter there was a death more shocking and violent than the elderly fading to which I was so well accustomed. I had not realised that death can rip open the quietest life, man is indeed cut down like a flower and grief can be a rampant lion. Through the middle of town, just behind the High Street, ran the river. The year I was nine it froze solid and everyone turned out to skate or to enjoy the novelty of walking across the ice. When darkness came, at about four o'clock, a big bonfire was lit on one bank and a pub, ambitiously called The Waterman's Arms, sold hot chocolate. There were a few days of unusual jollity. Douglas Brown was the only son of rather elderly parents who kept a farm outside the town. He was three years older than I, so I only knew him by sight; he had gap-teeth, which he displayed in a wide grin, and curly brown hair; he was always getting into scrapes. One afternoon, when there were only a few people around, he skated too far downstream and disappeared. The current was swift, and he must have been immediately swept away beneath the ice. I imagined him still dimly able to see the daylight, pressing his face to the cold, rough ice as he had pressed it to the windows of so many shops and houses in the village, his mittened hands trying desperately to find the latch that would let him back into the world. My father told me all the details of the search for the body, and I was fascinated to learn that there was a place, near the mouth of the river, where the police could usually rely on finding their corpse. I pictured a sand-bank around which beautifully dressed bodies floated and socialised. But Douglas never appeared at this gathering; his body could not be found.

Eventually, the funeral was held anyway. The church was full to overflowing, but my father, an old hand, had come early and secured a ringside seat, from which he could covertly observe the family. I had never seen him so full of zest. The Browns occupied the front centre pew. The mother sat silent, holding a handkerchief over her face; the father stood beside her, his features set like iron, the blue stubble gleaming just beneath the surface of his freshly shaved skin; their two daughters sobbed; other relatives stood by, stoically partaking of the limelight. The minister preached as best he could, in the face of such grief, about life everlasting, how only the good die young, and how God needed messenger boys and Boy Scouts in heaven. The sobbing continued un- abated, and my father's face gleamed with disapproval. Douglas had been the town hooligan, an unreliable messen- ger and a menace to the scoutmaster, but the minister refused to confront these facts. It was not that my father believed in speaking ill of the dead, but he did not think that death was an occasion for false praise; his obituaries were remarkable for their accuracy.

We retired to the grave. This time the coffin was so light that the bearers had to resist swinging it high over their heads. I wondered if there was anything inside it, a picture, a lock of hair, any sign to show whose corporeal being was meant to be enclosed in that dark wooden space. The icy spell was over and it was a cold, damp day. The grave- diggers must have grumbled heartily as they worked, but the grave was smaller than usual; for them that surely was a kind of blessing. As the ritual of laying to rest unravelled, the mother burst into loud sobs and hurled herself upon the empty coffin. She lay there, begging death to admit her, un- til her husband pulled her off. While the minister intoned, disposing of all possibility of life, the mother's sobs went on and on, relentlessly, like the water dripping off the church eaves. My father told me that if they found the body they would break open the grave and place it inside. But even if this did not happen, he explained, God had already found Douglas and transferred him to heaven. God did not need a funeral to alert Him to death, or to identify the body. I thought he should have said all this to Douglas's mother.

Much to my father's disappointment, there was no recep- tion after the funeral. He and a few other people, obviously at a loss, drifted off to the pub. Presently he came home, smelling of whisky, for a lunch of shepherd's pie and peas. As he ate, he described the funeral to my mother. In dispassionate tones he recounted every detail of the Browns' grief; such lavish displays of emotion were foreign to his nature and irrelevant, he thought, to the real nature of death. "People wouldn't get so upset if they had the corpse lie in at home. Then they could see for themselves that it's nothing so terrible." "Not much use in Douglas's case," my mother murmured over her knitting, and my father gave her a sharp look before continuing.

He remembered the death of his father, a gardener at a big house, who had died of a heart attack while hauling the roller across the lawn. Another gardener and the bailiff had carried the body home to the cottage. From her kitchen window his mother saw the two men approaching with the body slung between them like a heavy sack. She went to meet them, walking slowly, wiping her hands on her apron, while the boy who was my father ran ahead. His father was still warm; he touched his hand. They asked where she wanted him and she said on the parlour table and then bustled ahead to wipe it with a duster and pull the chairs away. The two men hoisted him up and laid him down. They did not offer consolation nor did she seem to expect it. She at once began to undo her husband's boots. She stripped him and washed him and dressed him in his best suit, all in silence, almost dreamily. Then she went off to cook dinner up at the house, which was her job. It did not occur to her that such exceptional circumstances would allow her to absent herself. She left her son behind with the injunction to watch his father, and so he did.

The curtains were drawn to protect the carpet, but there must have been enough light to see by. If he wanted to address the body directly, my father could pull up a chair and stand on it. He was quite unafraid. He was accustomed to his father's taciturnity, and death merely accentuated this quality; their companionship had long lain in silence, rather than in conversation. In the evening the neighbours came to keep my grandmother company in her vigil, and my father was banished to the edge of the circle. The grown-ups sat around the table on six matching chairs, almost as if they were sitting down to consume my grandfather. On the third day, when the coffin was ready, they took him to church and buried him. I imagine my father as the kind of boy who had few friends, set apart even then by something odd in his nature. For a brief time he had enjoyed his father's almost undivided company; now he was lonely again. He longed to repeat this feeling of closeness, but there seemed no possibility. His mother was in good health and, in spite of his entreaties, she never remarried; he remained an only, solitary child.

My father thought the modern methods of dealing with the dead were impersonal and disrespectful; death was not sufficiently honoured. For surely, if we did hold it in respect, we would not relegate it to tradesmen, but would keep it in the family. In this context it was important for him to remind people of his amateur status with the local paper. It meant, he said, that he did not owe anything to the paper, he was his own master and people respected him for it.

Gradually my mother, never very noticeable in her prime, began to fade; she coughed more, grew thinner, sat occasionally with her hands idle and talked even less than before. My father's interest in her revived, and he became solicitous and attentive. For quite a while, I am not sure how long, he refrained from calling the doctor, then, perhaps thinking that this was a mistake in strategy, went ahead and called him, first ensuring that my mother looked her best for his visit. I was in the garden when the doctor came, and out of curiosity followed him into the house. My mother was up, dressed as always in a flowery dress with an apron over it and a cardigan; she was seated by the fire. Doctor Sanders shook her hand and asked how she felt. She said she felt fine. My father offered the doctor a cup of tea and said she had a bit of a cough. I watched with interest as the doctor opened his bag and got out his shiny metal stethoscope. He listened to my mother's chest, then, seeing my curiosity, allowed me to do the same; through the rubber ear-pieces I heard only a dull, undifferentiated roar. The rest of his visit passed in conversation, and only when he came to depart did he offer some medical advice: she should keep warm and rest. My father saw him to the garden gate and they talked for a few minutes, but that could have been about the doctor's passion for fast cars, rather than about my mother.

People said that my father looked after my mother with devotion. He cooked, cleaned, and did the shopping on his way to and from work. Rather than taking a sandwich with him for lunch, he came home and made something for my mother and me. I went to school and did not think much about it. Looking back I can discern my father's excitement, how my mother became daily more dear to him, more exquisite. He cleaned the parlour at least once a week. My mother, I think, was past caring; certainly she did not resent but enjoyed her husband's renewed attention, even if she sensed that it stemmed from a delight in the process of corruption. Nor did she seem to mind his conversation, which typically went something like this: "Old Simon died last night. Do you remember him? He used to run that little newsagents on the bend in the High Street. Eighty-two he was and still digging the garden when he caught a chill. He was dead in a couple of days, chilled to death you might say. No family at all." And so on. It was such a part of him that perhaps neither of them noticed its inappropriateness.

The only person who remonstrated was my Aunt Theresa, who lived near by. I think she saw straight away what was happening but when she tried to rouse my mother, she encountered a gentle, obstinate optimism. She hinted to my father that his motives were questionable, but he stood up for his devotion, confident of my mother's support. It was the same when the doctor, at last, tried to get my mother to go into hospital. My parents presented a united front. My father, secure in his knowledge that no help was possible,

argued nobly to be allowed to continue to care for her; the
Nursing Home would only frighten and depress her. My
mother said she was much happier at home. Finally the doctor said, well, wouldn't the child be upset by the whole business. I was called in from the garden. My father asked, "You
want Mother to stay at home, don't you?" I, carefully
coached, said, "Yes, I want her to stay. Where else could she
go?"

At last she died, wasting peacefully until the very end. My
father cried, but not I. He would not let me out of the house
that morning, in case I should tell anyone, for he knew that
Aunt Theresa and the neighbours would come round and
assume to themselves the prerogative to wash and lay out the
body, which he so dearly sought to do. He had my mother's
best dress already clean and pressed hanging in readiness;
while I ate breakfast, he polished her smartest shoes. I
helped with the buttons and the underwear; her body was
still warm and supple. When she was finished, we both kissed
her.

Only that evening did he let me go and spread the news.
Aunt Theresa and the neighbours came gladly to watch with
him, for they remembered the custom. My father had
already written her obituary and sent it in promptly. At the
funeral we occupied the star pew, as opposed to our usual
one; I had a new black dress, and even a hat. The minister
preached his usual sermon about the dearly loved sister
whom we had lost but God had gained, how many people
would remember her for little selfless acts of kindness, and
would miss her; all the usual, irrelevant things to which I
paid no attention, although I could feel my father fidgeting
with annoyance beside me. Once again he felt that the
minister's inaccuracy trivialised death. At the grave, as always, he cheered up, and by the time we got to the reception
at The Cross Keys, he was glowing. For this one time he was
the hero.

After my mother's death, my father grew depressed. He

was older now and needed a more powerful loupe. In the evening while I did my homework he often sat, careless of the watch lying open for repair on the table before him, gazing at the pendulum of our grandfather clock as it swung back and forth. The intimacy of my mother's demise had made ordinary obituaries remote and unexciting; death had abandoned him, and he felt the slight deeply. He would ask me how I was feeling, but I always felt fine and was rosy and well. Gradually he began to realise that the only death he had to look forward to was his own. All his life he had anticipated events on behalf of other people. Now, for the first time, he began to study himself; like an old soothsayer, he plunged in his hand and drew out his own liver. His great fear became that he might die suddenly, hit by a car, or struck by lightning, removed to oblivion in one moment, unable to savour the experience, to understand it at last. He grew nervous and was careful crossing streets.

When I left home, he lived alone, too blind to mend watches but still writing obituaries. He could no longer tackle the hill up to the Nursing Home; instead he gathered information assiduously in the local shops, at church, at The Cross Keys and The Green Plum, and almost every afternoon he visited one or both undertakers and examined their handiwork.

I am sure that my father knew when death was coming. He had spent a lifetime listening for the signs in others; now that he had turned his hearing inwards he could not fail to recognise the rumours whispering along his arteries, echoing in his heart. Everything was well prepared. He had laid in a large supply of tinned food, and stopped the milk and papers, telling people that he was going off to visit me. On his bedside table there were books and a radio, but I imagine that in those last days my father had better things to do; he must have been busier than he had ever been, waiting, watching, listening, for his old friend; I know at last he saw him face to face. Two days later the body was found; nearby, on the polished mahogany desk which stood at my mother's side of the bed, lay his own scrupulous obituary. By the time I heard the news he was already safely ensconced at the undertakers. If only they had told me sooner, I would have washed him, and laid him out, and sat with him in proper state.

Now I am too old to bury pets; my friends are young and do not die. Occasionally, driving through some small village, I see a crowd in the churchyard. I stop and stand at the back, to watch and hear those lovely words rattling around, but it is not the same. The dead are unknown; my father is not there to inform the occasion; it is, as he predicted, impersonal.

Umbrellas

Umbrellas

We meet quite often hurrying around London. I will be pushing my way through the crowds in a pub in Covent Garden when a voice behind me will suddenly say, "Julian, what are you drinking?" Or sometimes walking along Cork Street or New Bond Street, I will see his familiar figure in a gallery talking to one of the pretty women who run such places. Last spring I bumped into him in the rose garden at Regent's Park, and in the summer I saw him among a group of teenagers, peering salaciously over the fence of the Ladies' Bathing Pool. So it was something to be remarked upon that I hadn't seen Henry for almost two months. I was sitting on the top of a bus that passed near his house, debating whether to get off and go and call on him, when I saw him coming out of his local off-licence. I jumped up from my seat and got off at the traffic lights. Henry was walking in the oppposite direction to the bus. I ran to catch up with him and, as I got closer, called his name. He stopped and waited.

"I haven't seen you for ages," I said, clapping him awk-wardly on the arm. He was holding a bag of bottles in each hand.

"I've been working like a dog," he said, "for the show."

I realised at once that of course the forthcoming exhibition explained his disappearance. We turned into Henry's street. Almost every house on the street is a squat, and Henry often boasts that he is the only person for miles around who works. "I used to be a Bohemian," he tells people. "Now I'm a pillar of society." Amidst the general shabbiness his house stands out by virtue of its unboarded windows.

He led the way inside. It was cold and neither of us took off our coats. Henry opened a beer and began to paint while I perched on a radiator to watch. His easel was set up to catch the afternoon light. He was fiddling around in one corner of the canvas which was only faintly sketched in, and as he worked, he talked. "Have you seen Blond's new show? Last time I went there I met an art student called Susanna. She made me want to do a painting of Susanna and the Elders; I feel I'm certainly of an age to capture that aura of prurient interest. Curious to be inspired by a name; not how I usually go about things. She was furious at the idea of appearing in a realistic painting. I knew a Judith once but she didn't inspire me at all, no wickedness in her."

Henry went on to discuss the effects of women's names on their characters and dispositions. He often rambled on in this fashion while he worked; I knew better than to reply. I watched him shaping the paint on the canvas and looked out of the window at the sky, which hung over the roof-tops like a dirty sheet. Finally he set his tools aside and asked, "Did you say you'd seen Blond's new show?" I said yes I had but I was tired of their stable of artists. Henry laughed and made a joke about my militant reviews. Although for the most part he agrees with my opinions, he rarely misses an opportunity to make fun of my reviews; in his eyes critics are not so much the handmaidens of art, as the whores. I began to talk about one of Blond's major artists, but, before I could get out more than a few words, the phone rang.

"Would you answer that?" said Henry.

I found the phone at last, under a jacket in the kitchen. "Where's Henry?" said a woman's voice. While he was out of the room, I studied the picture he was working on. Two figures in the foreground, a woman with abundant hair and a much larger man, were wrestling or embracing. It was night-time and light shone into the room from an open doorway, through which a crowd of people peered. The clothes of the main figures swirled around them in a frenzy. I heard Henry say several times, "I'm working," and then, "well, you'd better come over." By the time he returned, I was back on the radiator; he doesn't like anyone to look at his unfinished work. He said nothing, but in a perfunctory way began to wipe off his brushes. He left the room and came back carrying his hat.

"Let's go for a drink," he said.

"Didn't I hear you telling that woman to come over?"

"Are you coming?" He was already at the door.

In silence we walked down the stairs and along the street. We turned into a passage between two houses and came out on the tow-path of the canal. The water was very dark and, at that time of day, shared the general seediness of the neighbourhood. A mattress was floating on the far side.

"A good place for an assignation with a naiad, if there are any left in these urban waters," Henry said.

The opposite side of the canal was bordered by sheets of corrugated iron, behind which rose a building surrounded by scaffolding. We walked next to the road with its elegant terraces. These presently gave way to a new estate which boasted an unpleasant, modern little pub, where five minutes after opening time we were seated over our beer. We had the place to ourselves.

"I've decided to change my life," Henry announced.

"You're going to retire to a monastery," I said.

"Almost. I'm going to get married."

At various times Henry had been married, but it had always seemed accidental. His wives had arranged everything, including, when they could no longer stand it, the divorce. Henry had seemed relatively unmoved by these experiences; he behaved in exactly the same way whether he was married or not. It was not therefore particularly surprising that he should marry again, but that he should announce it so deliberately suggested that something out of the ordinary was about to occur. I asked who the bride would be.

"I don't know. I have to look around."

I said that it sounded as if he'd gone mad. Henry grinned. "No, it's quite the reverse. For once I'm planning my life intelligently. Recently I was looking at Rembrandt's self-portraits and it's obvious that he understood himself, unlike me. I've never done a drawing of myself, not even as a student. If I did attempt one, there would just be a vague outline. No depth. No details."

As I listened I realised with some surprise that what Henry said was true. Although he was completely absorbed in his own concerns, he rarely thought about himself; nor did he have doubts or second thoughts. His present behaviour was a perfect example. It's just possible that I might invite someone to my house and then go out, but I would be obsessed by the whole business, quite unable to conduct a conversation. Henry, however, seemed to have entirely forgotten the reason for our abrupt departure.

"Anyway the point is that I don't pay much attention to myself and that prevented me from seeing what must have been apparent to everyone else for ages: I'm growing old."

"We all are," I said. "I was forty-nine in June."

"It's not just a matter of years, Julian. I'm old as a painter, painting has made me old. I see signs everywhere, in my clothes, in my paintings, in my body. Look at my hands."

He held out one hand over his glass of beer and I saw the first faint spots of age. "I don't see how getting married will help," I said.

"It'll give me money, I hope. I've never had any. I sell a few paintings, and occasionally I get commissions, but there's always been only this much," he pinched his thumb and forefinger together, "between me and the people who sleep on the embankment."

Several of Henry's women had supported him, but never in a very lavish fashion: I said something to this effect.

"Ah, but this time it's going to be different. I'm going to marry a rich bitch. The best thing would be a wealthy lunatic; I've never understood why Rochester didn't thank heaven daily. However, if worse comes to worst, I'll even marry someone young and attractive, so long as she'll support me. Of course, I would have to guard against coming to dote on her."

"You don't think that whatever you do, it'll end in divorce? Like all the other times?"

"I wasn't trying then. I thought if the woman wants to marry me, let her. I just didn't care. Christ, how many times have I been married? There was Anne, and Clarissa. Then there was that Italian woman; she was the closest thing to an idiot: being screamed at in the language of Dante was heavenly. That makes three. I was married to Rosemary, wasn't I, because you were a witness, and of course Caroline. That's five altogether. It would seem I'm a marrying kind of man, and yet most of the time I've been unmarried, and I've nothing to show for any of it. Well, this is going to be different. I'm going to plan things carefully, like a campaign."

I was trying not to laugh. The whole thing sounded absurd, but then Henry asked me a series of questions which made me realise how serious he must be. He leant slightly towards me and said, "Do you have any suggestions? Isn't Christina quite wealthy? Doesn't she know someone suitable? Never mind the imbecile part — that may have to remain a fantasy."

"I can't think of anyone offhand. I could ask her."

"Yes, do that," Henry said. "It might save me a wild goose chase."

I began to laugh. In a few months I would remind Henry of this conversation and he would see the joke as well.

"Christina *is* wealthy, isn't she?" he repeated, like a tax accountant seeking a precise figure.

"Not in the Rothschild class, but by our more modest standards she's well off."

"You're rather lucky, you know. I've always thought you were a miserable son of a bitch when it came to women, but now I wonder if you haven't done quite well. Better than I have, anyhow. I'm just at the stage when I have to stop myself running after pretty girls. That's why we had to leave before Susanna came round, because I could feel that I wanted to stay. At least I can rely on marriage to save me from turning into a dirty old man."

"Not necessarily," I said, and he grinned. I looked at the clock above the bar and saw that I had to go. I drained my glass.

"Don't forget to ask Christina," Henry said as he went over to get another drink.

On the way home I thought about what he had said. His repetition of Christina's name inevitably made me nervous. On several occasions women with whom I had thought I was in love had succumbed to Henry's charms. Of course I had been angry, but mostly with myself; I had facilitated these affairs by talking constantly about Henry and what a genius he was. This hadn't happened now for a number of years, but still, his sudden interest in Christina made me uneasy. Although, he always seemed pleased to see her, he had never before asked a single question about her, or even mentioned her name when we were alone. I knew if he decided to pursue her, he would not let considerations of friendship stand in his way.

For a moment as I stood in the hall I thought that no one was home, but then I heard the sound of splashing; Christina shouted hello. My anxiety disappeared. I went into the kitchen and poured us each some wine. When I pushed open the bathroom door and stepped inside, I was instantly blinded, my glasses befogged by steam. I carefully put down the wine and removed them, whereupon I could see Christina's head and shoulders above the green foam of her bath. I was reminded of Henry's remark about naiads. I kissed her and handed her a glass of wine.

"Oh, lovely," she said. "Look how cold and slippery it is."

"I'm sorry I'm late," I said, and sat down on the toilet to tell her about my meeting with Henry and his plans for matrimony.

"Really, is he serious? That's a joke."

"What about Audrey?" I asked.

Christina sat up in the bath and stared at me. "You're just the sort of man who'd have plotted to get his sister married to Henry VIII. I hope you didn't mention her name."

"Of course not. But you are always telling me that she wants to get married. And she is well off."

"She wants to get married to someone she loves who loves her. Doesn't that go without saying? Can you imagine throwing her to Henry. We might as well give them a gas oven for a wedding present."

"She could do a great deal worse than love Henry. He's working on something very interesting at the moment, and he might be touched by her innocence, as well as her money. I don't see that it's such a bad idea."

"Julian, I wouldn't sacrifice someone I loathed to Henry, and I'm very fond of Audrey."

"Don't get upset. I promised Henry I'd ask and I have." I placated Christina and left her to finish her bath. She was one person to whom I hadn't presented Henry in a favourable light, and I was relieved to find that, like an innoculation, the bad impression seemed to have taken. I went into the bedroom. put on the heater and sat down to wait. In a few minutes she came in, wrapped in a towel and drying her hair with another.

"I've been thinking," she said, her voice muffled by the towel. "I could buy one of his pictures if there's one we like. It might be a good investment and it would help Henry. Isn't that a good idea?"

"Yes, I'd love to have one of the Biblical pictures he's done for this show. I'm going to take a look at the show the day before the preview. You could come along."

I went over and embraced her. In spite of the heater, she shivered and said, "It's cold in here. I'm going to get dressed in the bathroom." Reluctantly I watched her leave the room.

The week before his exhibition was due to open I went to see Henry again. We had talked on the phone, and for once he seemed to be fretting about the reception of his work. In the past he had always disdained success; in fact it had almost seemed that the more severely he was criticised, the more convinced he was of his own genius. But now, perhaps because he had decided he was growing old, he seemed to feel that this was his last chance to be famous. I too was feeling nervous about the exhibition; the relationship between artist and critic tends to be strained at the best of times. As Christina had said, if I was going to be Ruskin, then Henry had to be Turner and who knew if he was up to it.

On the easel this time there was a scene with two figures embracing on a flight of stairs that looked like Henry's stairs.

"It's the Prodigal Son," he said. "The framer is pestering me for it night and day but I don't feel it's quite finished. Of course no one ever notices these things."

"I will, now you've told me."

For a moment Henry looked at me as if uncertain what to make of my remark, then he smiled. When he did not speak, I blundered on and asked how the pictures were to be framed.

"Let's go out," he said. "Is it cold?"

"Damp."

He left the room and I noticed for the first time that it was even messier than usual; paintings were propped up against every available piece of wall, and the drawings, which were normally kept in a folder, were scattered around the table and floor. On one end of the mantelpiece there was a large jam jar holding a bunch of chrysanthemums. As the implications of all this registered, so did the fact that I was hearing voices from the bedroom. A moment later Henry came out wearing his coat.

"You have company?"

"Yes, Susanna is living with me."

"She's forgiven you about the Elders?"

"The Elders?"

Looking back at Henry as I walked through the door, I tripped over an umbrella that was leaning against the wall. I stooped to pick it up and, holding the clammy folds, offered the handle to Henry. He shook his head and waited for me to answer him.

"Your picture," I said, replacing the umbrella.

"Oh, yes. Once she saw it among the others she understood what I was doing, that it wasn't personal. Women take everything so personally; they have no conception of the grand design."

By the time he had finished this speech, we were out in the street. I asked where we should go and Henry suggested that we walk to the Fields. His conversation seemed peculiarly unfocused, but I assumed he was preoccupied with the painting. I turned up my collar against the drizzle and stuck my hands in my pockets. I felt ill at ease and began to talk about the exhibition of Spencer's work at the Royal Academy.

"I loathe the Academy," said Henry. "I do hope I get a chance to turn them down before I die; merely intending to isn't the same thing at all."

"I have no influence, but if I hear rumours I promise to aid and abet them. Tell them you'd be delighted and all that." I couldn't stop myself talking in this unnatural way.

We stood aside to permit a woman with a pram to keep the same course. She was humming to herself and seemed oblivious to the cold. I remembered reading in the newspaper how for years people had assumed that Sherpas did not feel the hardships of the Himalayas. Now tests had shown that they felt cold and hunger to exactly the same degree as the men whose bundles they carried. As we walked along, talking desultorily, I found myself thinking that Henry really was older; perhaps he was less able to sustain the physical effort of standing all day in a cold room, laying on paint.

After a long pause I said that I had asked Christina about prospective wives but she didn't know anyone suitable.

"That's all right. If you write me the rave review I expect, then wealthy women will flock to me."

As we walked back in the direction of his house, it became clear that Henry wasn't going to ask me in. I couldn't help being rather disappointed, for I was curious about Susanna. At the same time I wasn't surprised, because I knew that Henry often preferred to keep his women in the background. We parted at the bus-stop; I waited in the door of the launderette until the bus came.

I arrived home and met Christina just coming in. Over tea I told her that Henry's interest in matrimony seemed to have vanished.

"Luckily for him," she said. "I was all set to rescue any woman I saw him make the faintest gesture towards at the preview."

"You sound like a knight, all ready to charge around help-ing damsels in distress," I said, trying to tease away her anger. I had been going to tell her more about my visit to Henry; instead I began to talk about Mark, with whom I'd had lunch. Probably I had been insensitive in mentioning Henry's plans in the first place; I had wanted Christina not to like him, so I could not complain if she was now unsympathetic, especially when she herself was exactly the kind of woman he had in mind.

On the day before the preview I met Christina after work, and we walked over to the gallery together. In spite of the rain, we paused outside. It was already dark and the pictures glittered on the walls. Betty, the owner of the gallery, was standing before one of them as if lost in thought. I've always loved looking into lighted rooms at night. When I was young it took the place of other, more expensive forms of entertainment. This room, furnished with Henry's pictures, seemed the perfect setting for something exotic and wonderful.

I tapped on the window and Betty hurried to let us in. I was relieved to discover that she was alone.

"I'm sorry," she said. "I was dreaming. These are wonderful, aren't they?"

Indeed they fulfilled all my hopes. There were ten large pictures. The subjects were stories from the Bible: some famous ones, like Samson and Delilah, some that I had never seen before, like Jezebel falling down into a pack of hounds. I waited to hear what Christina thought. She came up to me and said without smiling, "Maybe he's better than Turner."

"Have you decided which one you want?"

"No. I hadn't expected it to be so difficult. I've never really been much of a fan of Henry's work, but these are great."

I said that I was glad it was not my decision. We walked around together, looking at the paintings and trying to remember the stories. Then I went to talk to Betty. Presently Christina came over and said, "If it's all right, I'd like to get two: Elijah and Delilah. They're both wonderful and I can't choose between them."

While she discussed the details with Betty, I went to look

again at the two pictures. Elijah was high up on a mountain, with immense clouds heaving around him and ravens, very black and sinister, dutifully bringing him food. The painting of Samson and Delilah was the one I had seen on Henry's easel when I went to visit him several weeks before. Delilah had, I now saw, already cut off Samson's hair, and he was fighting with her to get it back; so immediate was the loss of his famous strength that apparently they were evenly matched, and none of the onlookers came to Delilah's aid.

We said goodbye to Betty and went out into the street. I asked Christina if she would like to go and call on Henry. I felt so elated that I wanted to be with him at once, to congratulate him, but she said she wanted to wait until tomorrow. "I can't do justice to my feelings now," she said. It was still drizzling. Christina was wearing her hat, and I turned up the collar of my raincoat. We went to the Dog and Duck for a quick drink and discussed the review I would write.

The following evening the gallery was packed, and in the midst of the crowd was Henry looking like the lion of the occasion. His beard was freshly trimmed, his clothes were clean. For once he was wearing something colourful, a red waistcoat with a denim shirt and jeans, rather than the dark baggy suit, his habitual garb for gala events, which one of his wives had so saturated in mothballs that you could always detect Henry's presence by their pungent odour.

I went over, planning to congratulate him, but before I could speak he said, "Julian, come and meet Susanna."

He led me to where a girl was talking to an elderly man whom I recognised as an occasional critic for the *Financial Times*. She looked about seventeen; her hair stuck up in stiff, erratic spikes and her eyes were caked with make-up.

"Hello," she said in a surly voice when Henry introduced us.

"She's my Abishag," Henry said. "Do you know the story of King David and Abishag? I won't enlighten you. Nowadays I know the Bible well enough to teach Sunday school."

He patted Susanna and, bearing the critic with him, disappeared into the crowd.

I began rather awkwardly to search for a topic of conversation, but Susanna broke the silence by saying, "Christ, what a lot of old farts Henry knows."

Uncertain as to whether this comment applied to myself, I offered to get her another glass of wine.

"No, I'm already pretty smashed. So what do you do?"

I told her, expecting that at any moment she would interrupt with an abusive comment, but she seemed genuinely interested and asked my opinion of a number of well-established artists. I began to think there was something refreshing in her acerbity. She was talking about Francis Bacon when the crowd shifted and suddenly I could see over her shoulder all the way across the room to the picture of Samson and Delilah. In the spotlights the paint glowed. Delilah's hair, hanging around her shoulders like sheets of gold, emphasised Samson's impoverishment, and she looked as if she were about to sink her teeth into his arm. The lower part of Samson's body was hidden. Standing in front of the picture were Henry and Christina. I had always thought of Henry as short and Christina as tall, but now I saw that their faces were on exactly the same level; they were gazing into each other's eyes. Neither of them was speaking, Christina's jacket was the same shade of red as Henry's waistcoat and Delilah's dress.

Susanna was still talking. I caught the phrase "Henry's work." I nodded.

A new group of people had arrived and blocked my view. Interrupting Susanna in mid-sentence I said, "Will you excuse me? There are a couple of people I ought to talk to."

"Don't bother about me," she said. "I'm going to give the paintings another go."

I had taken only a couple of steps, however, when Betty took my arm and said, "Do you know Miles? He tells me you once gave him quite a favourable review."

While Miles rambled on, I kept searching the room. At last I saw Henry's red waistcoat; he was engrossed in conversation with a rather distinguished-looking man and Betty was mediating between them. I saw Christina's scarlet jacket quite near by; she was talking to two women, neither of whom I recognised. When she saw me looking, she raised her hand in a kind of salute, and after a few minutes she came and stood beside me. I introduced her to Miles. "Didn't Julian talk about you in one of his reviews?" she said, and he brightened up considerably; obviously I had not been sufficiently attentive.

Together we talked to a few more people, then we were ready to depart. I said, "I must speak to Henry before we leave."

"Let me come and thank him too."

"No, I'd be embarrassed if you were there. I'll just be a minute."

I could sense her watching me as I made my way to Henry. I drew him aside from his current audience. "Henry, I know you think my reviews stink," I could feel myself growing hot, "but that's because the work stinks. This is really wonderful, the best show I've seen in years." I thought he would interrupt, but he stood listening quietly until I finished my flustered speech.

"Thank you," he said. "Don't think me unappreciative." Then, to my amazement, he embraced me. He let me go and, turning back to the people he was with, said over his shoulder, "Give my love to Christina."

I found her at the door, sorting through a pile of umbrellas. Finally, in exasperation, she selected a large black one, and we went out into the street.

"Henry sent you his love," I said.

"That was unnecessary. I spoke to him just a little while ago." She was fiddling with the catch of the umbrella.

"Yes, I saw you," I said, trying to sound neutral.

At last the umbrella opened; Christina held it over us. "Which way shall we go? Do you remember that poem, 'The rain is raining all around, It falls on field and tree'?" She linked her arm through mine, and we started walking.

" 'It rains on the umbrellas here, And on the ships at sea,' " I concluded. Almost oblivious to the rain I walked closely beside her.

Jean and Little Aunt

Jean and Little Aunt

Jean came into the kitchen slowly, sniffing. Little Aunt, who was standing at the sink scrubbing the knives with a cork dipped in scouring powder, knew the purpose of these decisive inhalations; her sister was trying to discover if she had been smoking.

"Those stairs will be the death of me," Jean said. Little Aunt only nodded. Jean made this remark every day although, at the age of seventy-four, she seemed as strong as ever. Little Aunt was five years younger, and this had put her at a disadvantage with her sister all her life.

Jean put the black bag full of groceries down on the table and went to hang up her coat in the hall. Little Aunt rinsed off the knives and dried them firmly. She was listening to the clack of heels on the linoleum. There was always a danger that Jean would suddenly decide to open the door of the box-room, where until five minutes ago Little Aunt had been sitting on a trunk, having a quick cigarette and reading her book *Love in Second Place*. Quietly she put the knives away in the cutlery drawer and lifted the kettle off the hob onto the fire.

Jean came back in and closed the door. Seeing that she looked no more disapproving than usual, Little Aunt relaxed.

"Mrs Duff gave away our paper again," Jean said as she made her way round the table to her armchair. Like a hen settling onto its nest, she sat down, arranging her skirts and covering her knees with a rug.

"Did you have to go to Murphy's then?" Little Aunt asked.

"No, she had one left, but what if she hadn't? I've been going there for forty years and she can't remember to put by a paper for me."

"What about my *Woman and Home*?" Little Aunt ventured in the hope of distracting her sister from this perennial grievance.

"It doesn't come out 'til Friday."

"Oh, I forgot."

"You'd forget your head if it wasn't screwed on. Goodness knows what would happen to us if you did the messages. We'd never have a decent meal again."

Little Aunt managed to stop herself from pointing out that they hadn't starved in December when Jean had been in bed with the flu. She warmed the pot and measured in the tea-leaves: a spoon for each of them and one for the pot. While they drank their tea, she did her knitting. She was making a pair of socks for Cousin Kenneth, whose new wife could neither knit nor sew. As she worked, Jean related the gossip she had picked up at the shops.

"Goodness gracious," Little Aunt murmured at appropriate moments in between counting stitches.

Jean put her cup and saucer back down on the table and moved her head from left to right. "Where have you put the newspaper?" she said irritably.

"It's right beside you." Little Aunt stood up and pushed the *Edinburgh News* across the table. She put the sock back in her knitting bag and got up to unpack the groceries. There was tinned ham; all Little Aunt had to do for dinner was to make potatoes. She was over at the sink, peeling them, when from behind the newspaper Jean said, "It's a good drying day, Peggy. You won't want to miss it." For many years Jean had been the only person to call her by her Christian name. Everyone else, relative or not, knew her by the name her brother's child had invented: Little Aunt. By now she even thought of herself this way.

Jean's comment made her sigh. She had not been planning to do any washing today. She wanted to get back to Alma, the heroine of *Love in Second Place*. Alma was rowing across a loch with Colin, the son of her employer, and the situation between them looked very promising. She put the pan of potatoes on the fire and went to organise the washing.

In the bedroom she sat down on the pink candlewick bedspread and allowed her mind to drift. When she was nursing at the Glasgow General there had been a surgeon named Colin, with sandy hair and blue eyes. One Christmas he had surprised her under the mistletoe. But then in the spring she'd gone home to take care of her father, and by summer Colin was engaged to the staff nurse. She hadn't thought of him in years.

She stood up and carefully smoothed the counterpane. For the thousandth time she wished she could have her own room. There seemed no reason to keep the sitting-room cold and empty, but Jean was adamant. "No, Peggy," she would say. "We couldn't manage without a sitting-room. Besides, what do you need your own room for?" And Little Aunt could not explain. Although there had been an interval of almost forty years, it sometimes seemed that she had always shared a room with Jean. As a little girl, night after night, she had struggled to stay awake and listen to her older sister's endless stories, and even now scarcely a night passed without Jean waking her. "Peggy," she would say, "are you awake? Do you remember the time I dropped all my school-books in the burn?" Sleepily Little Aunt would search her memory, casting her mind back fifty, sixty years, and then, when it was clear that they were both wide awake, she would suggest a cup of tea and shuffle off to boil some water.

She collected her pyjamas from under the pillow and went around to fetch Jean's from the side nearest the door. Alan, silver-framed on his mother's bedside table, accorded her a mournful stare, just as he had done when alive. The photograph had been taken when he was nineteen, the year before he died of TB, and she could see the marks of illness already there on his face. Of all the people in the family who had died he was the only one she had never nursed. Until almost the last moment Jean had refused to acknowledge that he was ill, and then she was much too proprietary to share him. In front of his portrait, like an offering, stood a jar of mauve cough-drops. Little Aunt lifted the lid and popped one into her mouth.

Back in the kitchen the potatoes were boiling over while Jean heedlessly scanned the newspaper through her magnifying glass. Little Aunt moved the pan to one side of the fire, then she got out the basin and began to wash the clothes. The piece of green Fairy soap was so small that it kept slipping through her fingers; in the soapy water her hands were the colour of beetroot.

Carrying the basin full of wet clothes under her arm, Little Aunt let herself out of the flat. Even at midday the stairwell was dark and gloomy. She hated every corner of the grey stone which separated her so completely from the outside world. The only other place she had ever lived where she had to go up and down a stair was the nurses' hostel, and that was when she was young and fleet and could run up and down as often as she pleased. Here she always needed an excuse to go out, and even when she had one she sometimes could not face the thought of climbing back up three flights.

She fished the key out of her apron pocket and unlocked the door to the green. Jean was right; there was a good breeze. Almost all the space on the clothes-lines was already filled with the jeans and T-shirts of Mrs Sangster's endless children. Little Aunt wrung out the clothes and hung them up close together. On the far side of the green, purple primulas were opening. In the next garden the daffodils would soon be out. She lingered for a moment watching the pigeons circle the steeple of St Columba's church. Although it was cloudy she could tell it was going to be fine later; there was already enough blue sky to make a pair of sailor's trousers.

As soon as dinner was over the sisters began to bustle around; they were going into town. Jean, who had an appointment with the optician, insisted on changing into a clean blouse, and Little Aunt had to help her with the buttons. She herself simply took off her apron and put on her ordinary navy hat and blue tweed coat. Together they walked down the stairs, along the road to the main street and down the hill to the bus-stop. All the way Jean held on to Little Aunt as if afraid that she might wander off. When Little Aunt tried surreptitiously to shake her sister's grip, she only seemed to hold on tighter.

The bus came, a number seventy-three; they got in and sat down. Jean took charge. "Two to Hanover Street," she said. She had the correct money ready in her glove. The conductress adjusted the ticket machine and cranked out their tickets. Watching that smooth, unsmiling dark face, Little Aunt thought of the time, many years ago, when she had gone to Egypt. The family had disapproved, but they couldn't stop her because she had been invited by Nora, their only wealthy relative, to come out as a nursemaid for her children. Almost as soon as the boat left Glasgow, most of the other passengers succumbed to seasickness, but she turned out to be an excellent sailor. She quickly became friends with the first officer, and he promised to come and see her next time he was in port. But she had been in Alexandria for only six weeks before the threat of war brought her back to Glasgow, and the first officer had never replied to her letters. In her memory he had come to look very like the sailor on the packets of Players cigarettes. She still had a photograph of herself standing in front of a pyramid. It was a windy day and she was using one hand to hang onto her hat and the other to hold down her skirt.

The bus clattered over the cobblestones and drew up at their stop. The conductress gave them a hand down, first Jean, then Little Aunt. Little Aunt was determined to walk by herself; she hated measuring her steps to those of her sister. "Do you always have to clutch at me?" she asked.

Jean ignored her question and took her arm. "Everything changes so fast, I can't keep up with it," she said disapprovingly, and started walking.

Willy-nilly Little Aunt fell in beside her. Presently, in spite of her irritation, she started looking eagerly around. She was staring at a bright red fire-engine in the window of a toy shop when she was brought up short. A boy hurrying in the opposite direction had collided with Jean.

"Watch where you're going, young man." Jean glared at him and reached to straighten her hat.

Little Aunt looked in amazement at the boy's short bristling hair and black leather jacket as he walked away.

"Young people nowadays have no manners." Jean spoke loudly. She was puffed up with righteous indignation.

"He was in a hurry. Come along," said Little Aunt. Privately, she sympathised with the boy, who had been doing no harm. Jean never bothered to look where she was going.

They arrived at Dr Wishart's in good time and sat down in the waiting-room. Little Aunt got out her book, but Jean began to tell her about Mrs Sangster, who lived downstairs. Mr Sangster had disappeared and Miss Proudfoot had seen a man leaving the flat late at night. Little Aunt was longing to read.

At last the receptionist called "Mrs Watson." "Your turn," Little Aunt said, giving Jean a nudge.

Jean levered herself to her feet and stood for a moment, as if gathering herself together, until the receptionist took her arm and said loudly, "This way dear."

Alone, Little Aunt settled down to read. Alma and Colin had reached the shore and were having a picnic by the side of the loch. Suddenly Colin announced that he was going to Australia for a year. In an effort to conceal her disappointment Alma reacted coldly, which Colin mistook for lack of affection. Little Aunt was absorbed. She would have given anything to be Alma. The only man she had ever been rowing with was her brother. She gave a little jump when the receptionist spoke to her.

"Miss MacEwan? The doctor would like a word with you."

Reluctantly Little Aunt put her book away. She expected to be taken to join her sister in the darkened room where Dr Wishart unfurled his charts and pressed strange machines against one's face, but instead she was shown into a small, well-lit room with a large desk and two chairs.

"He won't be a minute," the receptionist said, and closed the door.

While she waited Little Aunt looked at the certificates on the walls. There were five of them, each with a different coloured seal; the only thing clearly legible among the ornate black letters was the doctor's name: Arthur Edward Wishart. Suddenly Dr Wishart himself appeared through a door behind the desk, which Little Aunt had assumed was a cupboard.

"Miss MacEwan," he said and shook her hand. His black suit echoed the authority of his certificates, and his eyes, slightly enlarged by glasses, seemed capable of extraordinary vision. "You live with Mrs Watson?" he asked.

"Yes." She nodded.

"Since I saw her last year, there's been a marked deterioration in her sight. She is now virtually blind in her left eye, and the right is very weak." He looked grave and tugged at his moustache. "You must have been aware of this."

Little Aunt shook her head. No, she had not been aware, not at all. She thought of the steady certainty of Jean's progress as she went forth daily to do the messages. Of course, she did use a glass to read the paper, but at the same time she was always complaining that this or that needed cleaning. Was it possible that she was only guessing? Little Aunt tried to imagine Jean blind, with a white cane, dark glasses, a dog. It was impossible. She waited to see what Dr Wishart would say next.

Words swarmed from his mouth and buzzed around the room. He couldn't risk an operation, given her age, but perhaps her condition would stabilise, it sometimes happened, although they mustn't allow themselves to get their hopes up. He spoke softly and soothingly, and the more he said, the angrier Little Aunt felt. When Cousin Kenneth remarried, Little Aunt, with only her tiny pension, had found herself homeless. Reluctantly Jean had taken her in, and ever since had treated her like a servant, and made her feel beholden. Little Aunt, knowing that she ought to be grateful for the roof over her head, had agreed to everything. Now, suddenly, she understood that all along the boot had been on the other foot. Here was Dr Wishart telling her that it was Jean who needed her, not the other way round.

"Your sister absolutely refused to read my charts or answer my questions. And she didn't admit to having the slightest difficulty with anything except fine print." He shrugged. "It's obviously an asset, her confidence. There's no point in my destroying it, is there?"

Little Aunt, as if the word was being squeezed out of her, said no.

"Well," he said, hurrying to finish, "I've given her a prescription for new glasses. They'll help fractionally. If there's anything I can do, please don't hesitate to get in touch." He came around his desk to shake her hand again and show her out.

For a moment Little Aunt stood in the doorway of the waiting-room and watched her sister. Jean was sitting with her handbag on her lap, slowly turning the pages of a magazine. She seemed to give each page serious consideration before turning to the next, and yet, Little Aunt thought, if Dr Wishart was right, she was seeing only a blur of shapes and colours. As Little Aunt approached, she looked up and said, "Ah, there you are."

"What are you reading?" asked Little Aunt. She could not resist the impulse to force a confession.

"Rubbish," Jean replied briskly, getting to her feet.

Outside in the street the sun was shining. Jean stopped and said, "As we're here anyway, I'd like to pay a visit to Alan."

"It's not that warm, and we'll be late for tea. Couldn't we go some other day?"

"I haven't seen him in over a year, since I went with Cousin Kenneth," Jean said stubbornly. She turned in the direction of the cemetery and stood waiting. Little Aunt looked away and for a moment savoured a delicious feeling of power. If she refused, Jean was helpless; there was nothing she could do; she was at Little Aunt's mercy. It was she, Little Aunt, who would decide whether they were going to visit Alan.

"Come on," Jean said, and took a couple of steps.

Little Aunt gave in. She would bide her time. When they reached the corner, she asked if they shouldn't go and buy some flowers and guided Jean to Rankins, where the air was sweet and heavy.

"What shall we get?" Jean said.

"I don't know. They all look lovely to me. You choose." Now that she knew, Little Aunt could see how cunningly Jean contrived to keep her secret. It was that cunning which made her cruel.

"Can I help you?" a shop assistant asked. She must have been a schoolgirl. Her fair hair was tied back with a pink ribbon which matched her uniform.

"Yes," said Jean. "I want some flowers. Something cheerful."

"How about daffs?" The girl stooped and picked a bunch out of the bucket on the floor. "Lovely, aren't they?"

Jean nodded and the girl went over to the counter to wrap them.

"Ask them for a jar," Jean said, as soon as the girl's back was turned.

"They have them at the cemetery, plenty of them," Little Aunt told her. It was just an excuse to tell the girl about Alan. Jean always wanted everyone to know that she wasn't an old maid; she preened herself on having had both husband and son. But this would be the last time, Little Aunt thought grimly. When the assistant came back with the wrapped flowers, she asked in a low voice if she could let them have a jar.

"A jar?" the girl said, obviously puzzled.

"We're on our way to the cemetery," Jean announced. "The flowers are for the grave of my son."

The girl hurried away, and came back with a green metal container which she proffered tentatively.

"Thank-you," said Little Aunt quickly, before Jean could speak.

They walked in the direction of the cemetery. At the bottom of the hill up to the church, they passed a greengrocers with a display of fruit and vegetables outside. A box of shiny purple plums reminded Little Aunt of Alan. To celebrate his tenth birthday, Jean had taken him and Little Aunt to the beach at Cramond. It was the year after Mr Watson died of a heart attack. Little Aunt had brought a ball and a small bat, but there was no question of Alan being allowed to play. All afternoon he had to sit, fully dressed, on a bench beside his mother. From time to time as she wandered around gathering shells, Little Aunt looked over at them. Jean was feeding Alan plums. Whenever she gave him one, she held out an open paper bag and waited until he obediently leant forward and spat the stone into it. Remembering Alan made Little Aunt even angrier. She had known dozens of people cured of TB — with proper care he could have been one of them. But Jean was so stubborn, she wouldn't listen to anyone. He just needs to pull himself together, she kept saying. She had said the same sorts of things when Little Aunt had pneumonia.

The cemetery was behind St Margaret's church. Keeping firm hold of Little Aunt, Jean led the way down the main path at a steady pace. The graves were laid out in straight lines, and the endless grey Aberdeen granite headstones all seemed identical to Little Aunt. At last Jean stopped in front of one of them. "Go and get some water, Peggy," she said.

Without saying a word, Little Aunt went. The tap was in the far corner behind the gardener's shed. She could have reached it in a minute by walking over the grass, but she took her time and kept to the paths. All the things she would say to Jean jostled around inside her head. She would take over the shopping; she would smoke if she pleased; she would use the sitting-room as her bedroom; she would read in the mornings; and sometimes, in the evenings, she would go downstairs to sit with Miss Proudfoot. She wouldn't be ordered about any longer.

Little Aunt hadn't been to the cemetery for several years and she had forgotten how awkward the tap was. She placed the green tin on the ground and with both hands wrestled the faucet open. The water gushed out, splashing her legs. She bit her lip and almost swore. As she bent awkwardly to pick up the overflowing tin, something glittered on the edge of her vision. The high brick wall which surrounded the cemetery was topped with shards of broken glass, green and clear, sticking up like jagged teeth. Catching the sunlight, they seemed to wink at her, as if mocking her servitude. She carried back the tin, walking directly over the grass.

Jean was rubbing at the tombstone with a large white handkerchief and grumbling about the dirt.

"It's the city," Little Aunt said tartly, setting the tin of water on top of the stone.

"Here, you arrange the flowers." Jean put the handkerchief back in her pocket.

Little Aunt picked up the daffodils and unwrapped them,

crumpling the paper into a tight ball. Without even taking off the elastic band, she stuck the flowers into the tin and placed it on the ground, directly in front of the stone. For the first time she focused her eyes on the words that were engraved there: Sacred to the memory of John Campbell Grahame, 1923-1978.

"Alan would have been forty-four this year," Jean said. "No age at all, and here am I, an old woman. You know, Peggy, sometimes I can scarcely credit that I was married and had a son. When I remember them, what I remember is photographs. But I can still recite the names of every boy and girl in our Sunday School class. I always sat in front of Ian McCloud."

As Jean talked, Little Aunt looked first to the right and then to the left; not the next grave, but the second to the left was Alan's. She began to shake; she had proof, absolute proof, of Jean's infirmity.

"Do you remember Miss Chisolm and that daft hat?" Jean was saying.

Little Aunt trembled on the verge of speech; triumph swelled inside her. She imagined Jean roosting at home as she went out to do the messages. She would become friends with Mrs Duff at the newsagents, and Jimmy at the butchers, and Mrs Carlisle at the fishmongers; they would chat with her and tell her the best things to buy. Jean's voice rose and fell; she was talking about all the prizes she had won. Suddenly Little Aunt remembered her first day at the school. Her hair was so tightly braided that her head ached; she was almost paralysed with fear. When Miss Chisolm asked her a question, she couldn't have answered for all the tea in China. She longed to be thousands of miles away, to be invisible, to be buried ten feet deep. But then Jean had leaned over and whispered the answer and she had mumbled it and Miss Chisolm had nodded approval and gone on to the next girl. Later Jean had told everyone what an idiot Peggy was; it was a very easy question. Little Aunt looked at her sister. There she stood, havering in the sunlight, her hat cock-eyed and the stout black shoes which Little Aunt had polished only the night before already grimy. All Little Aunt's life, for better or worse, Jean had been there. And she understood that if she spoke, everything would be different. The tombstones swayed before her eyes, and she closed them to ward off dizziness.

"You won a prize once for good attendance," Jean said.

Little Aunt opened her eyes. "Don't you think we ought to be getting home?" she asked, picking up her handbag.

Jean did not seem to hear. "Do you remember Jamie running away to enlist?" she said. She took a step towards the stone, as if to give it a final polish.

Little Aunt's arm shot out; she grabbed her sister's shoulder. "Jean, it's almost four. I told Miss Proudfoot she was welcome to a cup of tea." She was gabbling, saying the first thing that came into her head.

"Why on earth did you do that? The woman's nothing but a nosy parker."

"She probably won't come. You know how she is." Little Aunt retrieved her sister's bag and placed herself in front of the stone, as if shielding it.

"Well," said Jean, "I suppose we'd better go and carry out our social engagements." She turned her head from side to side, searching for her bag. Little Aunt handed it to her.

They stepped onto the path and, linking arms, moved slowly in the direction of the gate. The church bell struck four. As they walked a sudden gust of wind swept through the cemetery. In unison the sisters raised their free hands and held on to their hats.

A Story To Be
Illustrated by Max Ernst

A Story To Be
Illustrated by Max Ernst

Sweet-smelling Alexander grew to manhood surrounded by three hundred servants, who guarded him as carefully as the Chinese guard the bamboo that flowers only once in every hundred years. He lived in a palace which had a thousand rooms and then a thousand rooms again, and he had a bear named Aman which he rode through the splendid halls and corridors without ever having to retrace his journey. When evening came, he climbed in between golden sheets and gazed up through a glass ceiling at the stars. A story-teller sat at the foot of his bed, and long after Alexander's eyes closed, the soft voice continued to tell amazing adventure stories without apparent end. At the first fluttering of colour in the sky a second voice took up the tale.

Outside, peacocks cried and flirted in the courtyards and leopards lounged in the trees. The courtyards opened onto formal gardens which stretched down to a lake where an orchestra played. When a breeze rippled across the water, the boats seemed to move in time to the music, as if performing a gentle minuet. On the far side of the lake were orchards and a large farm. Beyond all this was a wilderness so enormous that if Alexander rode Aman for a whole day, by nightfall he would be less than half-way to the walls which encircled his land.

This was Alexander's kingdom. Everything he could see from the highest tower was his, and for many years he was perfectly happy. But as his height increased so did his curiosity about what lay outside the walls, and on his eigh-teenth birthday he demanded that the immense wooden gates be opened. When he cautiously urged Aman across the threshold he found himself in a village utterly different from anything he had ever seen. He looked at the small thatched huts with wonder and announced that he did not want to go back to the palace, he wanted to see the next village, and the next. His guardians, foreseeing this moment, had already hired a young man to be Alexander's companion and guide on a grand tour.

Bruegel had a pale, slightly freckled face and reddish hair cut close to his head like fur. He wore exquisite handmade shoes and closely fitting vicuna shirts to match his large grey eyes. The guardians had chosen him from many applicants because he was an aristocrat. Like Alexander he was the son of a great king, but, born out of wedlock, he had never been acknowledged by his father. In accepting the position as Alexander's tutor, Bruegel hoped to recover to some extent his birthright, becoming a participant in that life from which he had been banished.

Bruegel and Alexander left the palace together and trav-elled from one city to the next, from Constantinople to Athens, from Cairo to Paris and London. They stayed in the best hotels. Bruegel had a map of the world and they would pore over it, picking their next destination. Alexander chose on the basis of the colours of the map, the sounds of the names, the stories Bruegel told, for Bruegel had been every-where. By the time Alexander decided they should go to New York Bruegel had metamorphosed from his servant into his close friend. He gave to Alexander all the love and devotion for which his family had had no use.

The sun was just coming up as their plane reached the east coast of America, and the towers of the World Trade Centre hovered mysteriously above a thick layer of white cloud. Alexander made the plane go round and round until he had had his fill of these gleaming apparitions. From that first moment he was thrilled with the city. He wanted to go everywhere. People stared in wonder at the two princes in their raw silk suits, eating foot-long hot dogs at Nathan's, or watching with complete incomprehension a night game at Yankee Stadium, or swooping and shrieking on the rides at Palisades Amusement Park. Never for a moment did Alexander miss Aman or the palace or the story-tellers.

Life passed swiftly, sweet as a young girl on roller skates.

Every day Bruegel was awoken by Alexander climbing onto his bed, already dressed and eager for fresh adventures. But one morning there was no sign of him. When Bruegel knocked on his door, a small voice bade him enter. Alexander had pulled the bedclothes all the way up to his chin. Against the satin pillows his face looked paler and smaller than usual and the perfect roundness of his cheeks seemed less full. Bruegel studied his friend at a distance and noticed something which no one had ever seen before: Alexander was frowning.

"What is the matter?" Bruegel asked.

Alexander did not answer. Instead he stretched out his arm and moved his hand in and out of the bar of sunlight which lay across his bed.

"Are you ill?"

"I'm not sure. I just don't feel like doing anything."

"Don't worry. You're probably exhausted from yesterday. After all, we'd never been hang-gliding before."

Reassured by his own words, Bruegel settled down to entertain his friend, but, as the day progressed, Alexander only seemed to grow worse. During the days that followed he refused even to do things he could do in bed, like listen to music or watch a film. Bruegel could not bear to see him this way. He exercised all his skill and concentration to devise new amusements, but Alexander did not show the slightest interest in even the most fanciful suggestions. Ever since leaving the palace, he had been skimming along like a seabird over the water: what could be done to restore his graceful, darting passage?

At a loss, Bruegel began to take long walks around the city. One day he was sitting in a bar near Washington Square when a girl walked in; she was quite tall and dressed entirely in black. Everyone stopped talking as she crossed the room. She ordered a drink. Her eyes were as grey as Bruegel's, her hair as short although more golden. Bruegel thought of the lions he had seen in Africa, swishing through the long grass, hypnotic in their ease and energy. Not knowing quite what he was doing, he stood up. As he approached, she watched him steadily in the mirror above the bar. Standing beside her, looking back at her reflection, Bruegel said, "I want to talk to you."

She said nothing but did not stop watching him.

"I want to make you a proposition."

She shook her head and he caught sight of the glittering studs which covered her ears.

"It's not the usual kind of proposition. You might find it intriguing." He said nothing more, only looked with utter seriousness into her reflected eyes. She finished her drink, then turned towards him and said, "I'm meant to be meeting someone here. We'll have to go."

They left the bar and began to walk along the street; neither of them spoke. After a short distance she turned down a flight of stairs and led the way through a heavy door into a dimly lit, red room. At the bar she ordered two vodkas, which she carried over to the corner table. "I'm Zoie," she said, and looked at him expectantly.

Bruegel hesitated, for it was not easy to say what he wanted. "I have a friend whom I think you could help. He imagines he's ill. He stays in bed all day long, refusing to get up. All the things he formerly enjoyed now fail to bring him pleasure.'' Bruegel was silent for a moment; when he spoke again, it was in the sad tone of someone breaking bad news. ''He is extremely wealthy. There's really no limit to what he can do. He bears a charmed life.''

''Is that so bad?''

''In a way. Just as airplanes reduce vast distances to a matter of a few hours, his wealth eliminates the usual distance between desire and its object. Everything comes to him so easily, he has nothing to hope for.''

''What makes you think I can help?''

''I don't know. I have an intuition.''

''But how? I don't have special powers.''

''I think you do.'' For the first time Bruegel looked directly at Zoie, and she looked back. There was absolute silence, the air between them quivered; like an audience in the moment before the prima donna begins a famous aria, they were suspended. At last Bruegel said softly, ''I would like to arrange for you to meet Alexander.''

''Well,'' she said, ''this *is* an unusual proposition.''

''No, wait. I know what you're thinking. But I want you to keep your distance. That's the point. If he had something to wish for, something unobtainable, I think that might restore his health.''

Bruegel laid out the rest of his plan and told Zoie what he thought would be a reasonable salary. She shrugged her shoulders. Later he learned that the enormous sum he had offered only persuaded her that the whole episode was nothing more than an elaborate way of asking her for a date. When all the arrangements were made, she shook Bruegel's hand and left.

On the agreed day, Bruegel set to work to persuade Alexander that he ought to get up for a few hours. At first he would not budge. Bruegel waved his favourite clothes enticingly.

''Come on,'' he said. ''Manuel is keeping our table.''

Grudgingly Alexander put on his midnight blue silk suit. Their helicopter carried them to the roof of the Panorama Lounge. They sat at their usual table by the window drinking champagne and raspberry juice. Zoie was nowhere to be seen. Bruegel, seated with his back to the bar, kept turning his head to scan the crowd. Alexander fidgeted and complained that he was too ill to be out of bed. But suddenly his manner changed and he touched Bruegel on the arm. "Look," he whispered.

Bruegel glanced around and saw Zoie. She moved through the crowded room separate and distinct as a high-wire artist fifty feet above the ground. Again she wore black, and yet she glowed like a firefly in a dark garden.

Trying to sound calm, Bruegel said, "How about another drink?"

"I don't want another drink. I want to talk to her."

"A woman like that is sure to be expecting someone."

Alexander got to his feet; he took Bruegel's hand. "I must talk to her," he said pleadingly. "Tell them not to let anyone else in."

Exhilarated by the success of his plan, Bruegel hurried off to find Manuel. The manager insisted that he could not possibly close during business hours, until Bruegel crushed a thousand dollar bill into his hand. Then he volunteered to shut the doors for ten minutes. In half that time Alexander had successfully introduced himself to Zoie; they left the restaurant before it reopened.

Next morning Bruegel was woken by someone blowing in his face. It was Alexander, already up and fully dressed. He told Bruegel that Zoie had taken him to Washington Square and introduced him to a fire-eater. "The skin on his chest and arms was like a lizard, all dry and scaly," he said in wonder. All day long he made exuberant, silly jokes which both he and Bruegel found hilarious.

In the following weeks Bruegel watched happily as his beloved friend sprang back to life. Alexander talked inces-

santly about Zoie. She was fabulous. She took him to places
he had not known existed. He wanted her to live with them
in the hotel but she only laughed at the suggestion. She was
very secretive: she refused to say what she did or where she
lived. Whenever Alexander watched her ride away on her
black motorcycle, he was afraid that he would never see her
again.

After she left Alexander, Zoie often met Bruegel in a bar
or a diner. He would ask how the evening had gone and she
would tell him briefly, but if he tried to ply her with questions she teased him into silence. "I didn't come to talk about
Alexander," she would say. "I came to see you."

At first these visits made Bruegel uneasy; he worried about
Alexander finding out and feeling slighted: it was one thing
for Zoie not to spend time with him because she was aloof
and mysterious, quite another for her to be spending time
with Bruegel. But gradually the pleasure he found in Zoie's
company and the absolute confidence he had in her discretion allowed him to look forward to meeting her; their relationship seemed to guarantee Alexander's happiness. Zoie
took him for walks around the city; or Bruegel would perch
on the back of her bike while she drove at tremendous speed
out to Long Island or down to the docks. Months passed and
they became lovers. Bruegel thought that now everything
was perfect.

Under Zoie's influence Alexander abandoned his suits
and began to dress entirely in black. It made him look, to
Bruegel's eyes, oddly endearing; his face and neck seemed
more sweetly rounded and his eyes, which had before been
the colour of lapis lazuli, now seemed darker. In the run-
down night clubs to which Zoie took him he no longer
seemed quite so out of place. They met with increasing fre-
quency and there was no indication that Alexander's affection was in any danger of diminishing.

One night Zoie took Bruegel to the roof of an apartment
building near Central Park. They walked to the edge of the

roof and stood side by side, leaning against the parapet, looking down. In the zoo, far below, shadowy forms moved restlessly among the rocks and trees.

"Do you love me?" Zoie asked.

"Of course," said Bruegel.

"Do you love me very much?"

"Yes, very much."

"And Alexander?"

Bruegel was puzzled; it went without saying that he loved Alexander. He nodded, and pulled himself up to sit astride the wall.

"How much do you love him?" Zoie persisted. She came and stood in front of Bruegel so that she could look into his eyes, and he understood that he must take her question seriously. He flipped through his mind, like an oriental cashier sending the beads of his abacus whizzing back and forth, in an effort to discover the sum of his love.

"I love him like . . ." Bruegel began, but he could think of no simile worthy of his affection.

"More than," she paused, as if debating what to suggest in comparison, "more than yourself?"

"Of course, but that's not saying a great deal."

Zoie's face was shadowed. An animal howled in its cage; after a moment another answered. "I don't know what to do about him," she said. "I don't want to continue with our arrangement."

Bruegel stood up and put his hand on her shoulder. "There's no need. You've cured Alexander and he loves you. Of course you must love him." He felt dismayed by his own selfishness; it had not occurred to him that he had been keeping her and Alexander apart.

"That isn't what I meant." Zoie ran her hand over her face as if to wipe away the expression. "I thought you loved me," she said, offering each word separately, as if she were handing him shells she had found at the edge of the sea.

"I do. That's why I'm so sure that you can make Alexander happy."

Zoie looked at Bruegel; in the dim light he could see the glint of her pupils. She stood motionless, without speaking, as if hoping for some gesture from him, but what it could be, he did not know. He waited for her to tell him, but she said nothing. After a long time, she leaned forward and kissed him quickly on the lips.

He saw her only one more time. The following evening she came back to the hotel with Alexander, and from the courtyard Bruegel watched them soaring upwards together in the gleaming glass elevator. Knowing that they would at last be lovers he felt a grave kind of happiness. In the early morning he waited for Zoie to visit him, but he was not surprised when she did not come. It was several days before he realised that she had disappeared.

Alexander missed and mourned her. He did not understand why she had left nor why Bruegel could not find her. Bruegel tried everything. He left messages with every motorcycle dealer; he placed advertisements in all the newspapers; on clear days he had a fleet of small planes writing endless messages in the sky above Manhattan. At enormous expense he hired scores of detectives, but none of the women they produced were remotely like Zoie. In the shifting city many of the places to which she had taken him had already disappeared, but he went to all the ones that remained. He made his way through the crowds of people asking anyone who would listen if they had seen her, but the answer was always the same. Alexander too looked everywhere for her. Whenever he and Bruegel entered a restaurant he scanned the room hopefully, and walking down the street his head swivelled from side to side searching the faces of pedestrians. Sometimes, late at night, unable to sleep, he woke Bruegel and together they went out hoping that they might meet her.

And in this way half a year passed.

When it became clear, even to Alexander, that there was
no hope, he decided to return to the palace. He assumed that
Bruegel would be coming with him, and Bruegel was glad to
be taken for granted.

They took a plane from New York to Tel Aviv via London,
then a flight to Lahore where they boarded a train to the
north. At the last railway station they hired a carriage. When
there were no more roads, they left the carriage and went on
with the horses. The gates of the kingdom opened as they approached; they were expected and the way was lined with
flowers. That night as he lay between his golden sheets,
listening to the story-teller, Alexander felt, in spite of the loss
of Zoie, a kind of peace.

Everything at the palace seemed the same. The servants
looked no older, and the bear Aman, who had died during
Alexander's absence, had been replaced by his son, also
called Aman. There was only one change. The furthest wing
of the palace was now occupied by a number of guests,
mostly students, whom Alexander and Bruegel had met on
their travels and to whom Bruegel had persuaded Alexander
to offer sanctuary. Each guest had a unique talent: one could
communicate with animals, another could read minds, a
third had the power to move plants by his singing. To an exceptional degree they were all clairvoyant, and by a con-
certed effort they could make a comet come closer to the
earth. But after a fierce storm ruined a day's skiing for Alexander, Bruegel forbade all such group activities.

Bruegel had visited the palace only once before, when he
had come to collect Alexander. Now he was enthralled by the
sauntering leopards, the gentle servants, the wild orchids,
the exotic rooms. Alexander taught him to ride Aman's
brother, Atar, and together they passed many days riding
their bears through the palace and the gardens. In the evenings after dinner the students entertained them, performing
plays and illusions and joining the palace musicians in

elaborate concerts. They taught Aman to say his master's name and levitated Bruegel up to the library ceiling.

But then one day when the two friends were sailing, a sudden shower surprised them, and as they changed their clothes in the boat-house Alexander said, "Wouldn't a cup of hot chocolate taste wonderful?" And later, at dinner, after the roast plover was served, he said he would have preferred lobster. The following evening, watching a mime show put on by the students, he had a craving for a baked potato.

Bruegel, sensitive as a seismograph, was alarmed. The students had successfully cultivated artichokes, tomatoes, and several kinds of herbs in the palace greenhouse, but some plants were beyond even their powers of persuasion: potatoes remained recalcitrant, coffee and cocoa shrubs refused to flower. Seafood, of course, was out of the question. Bruegel himself was quite satisfied with the palace cuisine but, hoping to assuage Alexander's appetite for the unobtainable, he began to spend long hours with the chefs. He planned lavish menus — his artichokes stuffed with a fricassee of peacocks' hearts and goats' cheese were a great triumph — and for a time Alexander seemed content.

One morning at breakfast, Alexander announced that today as a special treat he was going to take Bruegel to visit the gold mines on the far side of the lake. There had been a storm the night before, and the day was astonishingly clear. Side by side Aman and Atar padded along over the wet grass. If only Zoie were riding beside us, Bruegel thought, but he did not say this to Alexander; in some mysterious way it had been decided between the two friends that her name should no longer be spoken. Suddenly Alexander interrupted his reverie. "Do you hear anything?" he asked.

In addition to the rustling of the trees and the breathing of the bears Bruegel could hear a distinct musical note. The entrance of the mine came into view. Beside it sat a small, dark man who was steadily striking a golden gong almost twice his own size. "The sound guides the miners back to the surface," Alexander explained.

Servants tethered the bears and Alexander led Bruegel down the main passage. Except for the glimmer of lights from the side galleries, where the ore was loaded onto the backs of tiny ponies, it was dark. The sound of the gong grew faint. Bruegel was nervous. Alexander seemed to forget that he was now fully grown and led Bruegel through smaller and smaller openings. At last, in a particularly narrow passage, he stuck fast. He did not seem upset but suddenly announced that he was hungry. It took Bruegel ten minutes to tug and squeeze him free.

Perhaps it was hunger that made Alexander querulous; on the return journey he complained ceaselessly about the slowness of their progress. "If I had a motorcycle this whole trip would take less than ten minutes. I could visit the mines every day." All the way home he was full of grievances and plans.

At a concert a few days later Bruegel noticed that one of the students, Patrick, was missing. He leaned over and whispered to Alexander, "Patrick must be sick."

"No, he's running an errand for me."

"What's he doing?"

"Fetching a Moto-Guzzi bike."

"But Alexander, what use is a bike here? There are no roads."

"We'll make some. You'll see."

Bruegel was dismayed. To make even one road was not a simple matter, he thought, and one road would never be enough. Alexander would demand alternative routes. In its wake the bike would bring all kinds of paraphernalia at present quite unknown in the palace. Atar and Aman would be retired and the leopards caged. Everything would be transformed, but to no purpose, for within a short period of time Alexander would again be dissatisfied. The more he thought about these changes, the more distraught Bruegel became.

Late that night he made his way to the dormitory where the students slept. He tiptoed from bed to bed, telling them to come to the green marble bathroom. When they were all present, yawning and blinking in the moonlight, wrapped in their blankets, Bruegel asked softly if anyone knew where Patrick was. No one knew. He had left the day before without a word.

"Didn't he say anything to you, Mikhail?" Bruegel asked Patrick's closest friend.

"No. He just disappeared."

"Well, I want you to get him back as quickly as possible. Sit down now and will him back or whatever it is you do. I want him home by tomorrow. And listen, this must be a secret, an absolute secret, between you and me. No one must ever know, not even Patrick."

The students sat down on the floor. As Bruegel walked towards the door, a slow, humming vibration filled the room; he felt the hairs on the back of his neck prickle.

At dinner next day the chilled mango soup had just been served when the door opened and Patrick appeared. His clothes were dirty and torn, his dark hair was awry and thick with mud, his beautiful skin was heavily bruised, his expressive eyes were drawn to mere slits, the fullness of his cheeks was gone and his mouth was grotesquely elongated as if someone had stood behind him and tugged at each corner. Worse still, his nose, which must have taken the brunt of the onslaught, was flattened beyond recognition. He looked as if he had been rudely pulled through a thick hedge at high speed. He tried to sit down, but collapsed. For a moment everyone at the table continued to stare. Then the four nearest students jumped up and carried him out.

I should never have told them to bring him back so fast, Bruegel thought. Why had he not realised that a force that could attract a comet would have a devastating effect on a human being? He looked across the table at Alexander and said, "Shall I go and see how he is?"

"No. The students will take care of him. I told them to get a doctor. I hope he has my bike."

Bruegel knew he should say something, but before he could speak the main course was served and Alexander had turned away to talk to Mikhail. Bruegel was unable to eat a single mouthful of the pheasant with apricots and almonds.

As soon as dinner was over he hastened to the dormitory. Patrick was lying on a bed, apparently unconscious. Several students were nursing him. Mikhail came in and drew Bruegel aside.

"I suppose you've guessed what happened. We didn't know the danger; we just brought him back as fast as we could."

"Do you think he'll recover?"

"We'll do what we can to make him better."

"But will he be all right?"

"Eventually, yes."

Bruegel stayed awake most of the night. He felt full of remorse. In spite of Mikhail's reassurances it was hard to imagine that Patrick would ever recover his former grace. This, however, was not the greatest cause of Bruegel's distress. He had thwarted Alexander because he believed his own judgement to be superior; it was a clear abuse of his special position of trust. He decided he must confess, no matter what the consequences. In the morning, as soon as it grew light, he tiptoed to Alexander's room and lay down beside him. The story-teller was describing a kingdom that lay deep underground. Alexander asked about Patrick.

"He's still unconscious but Mikhail says he'll be better soon."

"So long as he recovers, that's what matters."

"Alexander," Bruegel said abruptly, "it was my fault. When you told me that you'd sent Patrick for a motorcycle, I asked the students to bring him back. I am sorry. I shouldn't have interfered."

"No, you were quite right. It's a stupid idea to have a bike here." Alexander set his clockwork dragon marching across the bed, and followed its progress. "How did they do it?" he asked.

Bruegel had been lying flat on his back, glaring up through the glass ceiling. Now in his relief, he turned to face Alexander and tried to explain. "Their individual powers are somehow enhanced when they work together, and they can do amazing things. They themselves don't fully understand their own strength, and they brought him back too fast. Are you sure you're not hungry?"

"No, you needn't worry. I shouldn't have complained about Aman, I love the way he rolls along. Look, I'll show you something. 'Here is the church and here,' " he said, holding up his two forefingers, " 'is the steeple. Open the doors and see all the people.' Zoie taught me that." Alexander sat up cross-legged in the bed. "Now you do it."

Clumsily Bruegel tried to imitate Alexander's gestures. As he unfolded his hands it suddenly occurred to him that, through his blunder, he might have discovered a way to find Zoie.

He began to have long conversations with Mikhail. They went for walks together, talking late into the night, discussing whether the students could influence someone whom they had never met. Bruegel was concerned that they take every precaution and not make the same mistake they had with Patrick. After several weeks of consultations the students began to meet nightly in an effort to summon Zoie.

The days passed and Alexander did not speak of her again; he seemed preoccupied with building a skating-rink and Bruegel decided not to tell him what was going on. But all the peace that Bruegel had found in the palace was gone. Now that he was no longer resigned to Zoie's absence he missed her more than ever; he could imagine no greater happiness than joining her and Alexander every morning. While the story-teller talked they would lounge between the golden sheets, feeding each other on mangoes, strawberries, *petits fours*, and planning their day. As the weeks went by, however, his hopes waned. It was ridiculous to expect that she could find her way across half the world. Supposing that the students did have an effect on her, surely it would be only a slight twinge which she could easily dismiss. But there was no evidence that even that small success had occurred; it was beyond the students' powers to determine if they were making any progress. Bruegel wondered if he should ask them to stop; only then would he be able to relinquish the tiny painful hopes he still cherished. And yet he did not want to give up hope. Every day he climbed the tower and looked across Alexander's kingdom, hoping to see in the distance, walking over the fields, a slender figure in black.

One morning as he sat in his bath Bruegel heard laughter. He was rippling his limbs back and forth through the warm, foamy green water, and at first the bubbles of sound seemed merely an echo of these lazy movements. He scarcely differentiated the two until the servant who was pouring water down his back suddenly spoke.

"Don't you know me?" she said.

Slowly he turned around, and there was Zoie. His memory of her, wearing black, riding a motorcycle through the streets of the city, had been so vivid that he had not recognised her standing over him with a jug of water. Her hair now hung below her shoulders, and she wore a crimson dress.

"Zoie," he said. He pulled her into the bath and her skirt floated around them. He kissed her over and over. When he came to the tiny snake tattooed on her left shoulder, his last fear vanished.

"You're really here," he said between kisses. "I thought you would never come."

"You don't know how I've missed you," Zoie said.

"Alexander will be ecstatic."

Zoie stopped his words with a kiss. Then she spoke. "Listen, I want to tell you something wonderful. I didn't come alone." She pulled slightly away from Bruegel and, turning her head, called, "Phoebe."

At the sound of her voice, a small child emerged from behind the curtains and walked unsteadily to the side of the bath.

Bruegel was astonished. He sat up and looked at the little girl. She stared back at him with wide grey eyes. Her hair stood up in little golden spikes, as Zoie's once had, and she wore a dress the colour of honeysuckle. He reached out and touched her cheek; it was softer than silk. Phoebe giggled and put her hand to her face to feel the wet imprint of his fingers. Then she sat down and began to play with the mechanical bird that perched on the edge of the bath.

"She's beautiful," Bruegel said, smiling at Zoie. "Whose child is she?"

"Mine."

"Yours," he said incredulously.

"And yours."

Zoie moved to kiss him again, but Bruegel stepped quickly out of the bath. He pulled on a robe and went and stood with his back to the room, gazing out of the window. Outside Atar padded back and forth, but Bruegel did not see him, nor the orchards, nor the gardeners. He was looking into the far distance, where he could see his two friends rising swiftly upwards in a glass elevator.

"Mine? No, she can't be mine," he said, pausing heavily after each word. He whirled around to confront Zoie. "She's not mine."

"Bruegel," Zoie said, climbing out of the bath.

He could not look at her face. Ignoring her outstretched hand, he bent down beside Phoebe and said decisively, "Let me take you to your father."

The little girl looked towards her mother, but before Zoie

could speak, Bruegel took her hand, and led her through the arched doorway. They turned down the long corridor. He was all ready to pick Phoebe up and carry her, but with tiny rapid steps she trotted along at his side.

Something caught Phoebe's attention. Following her gaze, Bruegel saw that it was the large blue china elephant which stood to one side of the corridor. She raised her arm and pointed. "Look, Father," she said.

Bruegel stopped. He stared down at the golden aureole of hair. Within his grasp her small hand tugged at his.

Suddenly, in the interval between one heartbeat and the next, he heard a sound, sweet as a thrush's song. Alexander was singing to himself, a tune that they had heard in a club in New York.

Bruegel tightened his hold on Phoebe; together they went on more swiftly than before. His robe billowed behind him, and Phoebe's bare feet made a soft pattering on the floor. Only as they reached Alexander's door did Bruegel dare to glance back. In the doorway Zoie stood watching them. Her red skirt clung to her legs; water dripped from the hem and formed a pool around her feet.

The Acrobat's Grave

The Acrobat's Grave

"Just made it," the guard said, as I climbed onto the train. He spoke with a certain relish, as if he enjoyed the thought that I had almost been left behind. In one smooth movement, we pulled out of the station and passed under the Castle Rock. He helped me prop my bike against the wall and asked if I was an American. I shook my head and told him I was Scottish born and bred. Why would he think I was an American?

"In the summer there's always swarms of American girls taking their bikes around by train," he said. "It gets to be a real nuisance. How far are you going?"

"Ballinluig. Then I'm going to cycle up to Glen Lyon. I have today and Monday off for Easter."

"What a pagan country this is. When I was a boy we spent weeks getting ready for Easter. It was a big to-do. Here it just means time and a half." His Irish accent was pure and strong, but he said he'd lived in Edinburgh for the past twenty-seven years. Pointing to a tea-chest, he invited me to sit down.

"How old do you think I am?" he asked. He was standing very straight, his feet slightly apart, swaying gently with the movement of the train. Even in the dim light, his eyes were bright blue. When he saw me studying him, he winked.

"I don't know."

"Take a guess," he insisted.

"Fifty-four," I offered, to be on the safe side.

"Sixty-three," he said, triumphantly, holding himself even straighter.

"Really? That's amazing. How old do you think I am?"

He tilted his head and looked at me for a moment. "Twenty-nine?"

"Not bad. Twenty-eight."

He nodded, obviously pleased with the accuracy of his guess. "During the war I was in the army," he suddenly announced. "When I finished my training, I came home on leave. My two older brothers were already overseas and my father was alone. The first night I was back, the doctor came round and told me Dad was dying of cancer, that he hadn't a snowflake's chance in hell of lasting more than a couple of months. So what was I to do? There was no one else to nurse him."

He glared at me. I shook my head, helplessly. "I stayed absent without leave. For two months I only went out at night because I was scared stiff they would come and take me away. The day after the funeral, I went to the nearest army post and gave myself up. I was sentenced to eighteen months in prison; when I got out the war was over."

"How dreadful," I said.

"At least I survived. My brothers both died in France." He looked at me. "You're much too young to know about these things."

I didn't know what to say. I wanted to get away, so I asked if he would like something from the buffet. He said he was well provided for.

I got some coffee and sat down in the carriage next to the buffet car. The sky was burly, grey and overcast. Although it was not actually raining, it looked as if it might at any moment. When I was little I always expected terrible things to happen on Good Friday — storms, earthquakes, the sun to grow dark and never shine again — and even now it was a day on which random events took on the force of significance. Probably the guard, like some ancient mariner, told his sad story to anyone he could get his hands on, but I could not help thinking that the way in which his tale reflected on my journey was more than just coincidence.

I was going to Glen Lyon to find out what I could about my father's family, who lived there for generations. My father himself had grown up in Glasgow, sent away from the glen after both his parents died young; he had died before I was two. Our house had been full of photographs of him: at school, in the army, getting married, at my christening. As a young girl I had studied these pictures closely, willing them to give up the secret of his personality, but the bland official poses had soon defeated my curiosity. It was only since my mother had died, last Christmas, that I had developed this craving to find out about him. When she was alive I had seldom taken the trouble to question her, and now I regretted this lack of interest, which had allowed her to take to the grave everything that she knew. Coming to my father's birthplace seemed the last possible way of being close to him.

As the train pulled into Ballinluig, I hurried back to the guard's van. He handed me down my bike. "Have a good holiday," he said. I waved to him and checked that my panniers were secure.

In spite of the clouds the rain held off, and I made good time on the narrow winding roads. I reached the village by late afternoon. A couple of dozen stone houses, some of them still with thatched roofs, were strung along the road. There was a church, a school, a post office with a bright red call-box out-side, and a pub called The Four Feathers. I stopped at the post office and went in.

The man behind the counter was reading a newspaper. He looked up with a surprised expression, as if a customer was the last thing he expected. I explained that I was look-ing for a place to camp. He said he would ask his wife, and disappeared between the strands of the bead curtain at the back of the shop. I examined the display of birthday cards. They were all very specific: Happy Birthday Dear Mother/ Father/ Brother/ Sister/ Grandpa. I was moving on to the more distant relatives when the man came back.

"Just as you come into the village," he said, "there's a foot-bridge across the river. On the far side there's a good place to camp and you won't be bothering anyone."

I thanked him and he looked at me doubtfully.

"But you'll not be alone?" he said.

"Yes. Don't you think it's safe?"

"Oh, safe, yes, quite safe. But still a lassie camping all alone. I don't know."

I told him I would be fine and asked for a pint of milk. The transaction seemed to please him, and we parted on good terms. I found the bridge without any trouble; it was made of iron and just wide enough for me to walk across beside my bike. On the far side of the river Lyon there was a mossy plateau surrounded by beech trees. I unpacked my panniers and spent the next half-hour struggling with the lurid orange tent I'd borrowed from my next-door neighbour. By the time it was up, a little lop-sided but secure, I was cold and miserable. My friends were right: the whole idea of camping in April was ridiculous; I would go home in the morning. I abandoned any idea of cooking and decided to spend the evening at The Four Feathers, where at least it would be warm.

As I came through the door into the pub, everyone in the room stopped talking. There were perhaps a dozen people, and I would have turned tail and fled if the bartender had not called "Come in, come in." When I went over to the bar he introduced himself as Todd. I asked for a lager and lime and two packets of crisps.

"I hear you found yourself a good place to camp," Todd said. "Are you here to look at the stones?"

"The stones?"

"The standing stones," said a voice behind me. "You passed them on the road."

I remembered now that I had seen a small group of stones at the edge of a field a few miles outside the village. I turned and saw a bundle of a man sitting in the corner by the fire. He was wearing an old, voluminous tweed coat which hung unbuttoned over another coat; inside these two, I glimpsed a third. He motioned me to come and sit beside him. I carried over my drink and he stretched out his red and dirty hand. "I'm Grantie."

"Chris," I said.

"I hear you're staying by the bridge. The same as that other fellow."

"What other fellow?"

"The American. We called him the acrobat."

I asked why and Grantie explained that this man used to play on the swings in the school playground, swinging upside down and doing all kinds of fancy manoeuvres for the local children. Apparently he'd been a stunt man, for television.

"What was he doing here?"

"No one knows. He was a queer one. His family had come from round here and he wanted to take a look."

This seemed to be my cue. I told Grantie the reason for my visit and asked if he'd known my grandfather or my father.

"What did you say their names were?"

"Dunbar, Michael Dunbar. He married a woman called Alison Strachan from Aberfeldy, but she died in childbirth. My father was David Dunbar. He was just a little boy when he left."

"Michael Dunbar," Grantie said slowly. "So you're Mike's granddaughter. Well, well, who'd have thought it." He paused and I waited anxiously to hear what he would say. "We never saw much of him in the village because he lived along the glen at Coultry. Sometimes in the summer when I was minding the sheep up on the hill, he'd come by in the evening and chat for a while. He taught me how to set snares and guddle for fish. In the autumn he worked as a gillie. He had a rare talent for stalking and he could walk faster up a hillside than any man I've ever known. I can see him like it was yesterday." Grantie shook his head, as if still amazed at my grandfather's speed, and drained his glass. I asked him what he was drinking. Whisky, he said, and then seemed a little flustered. Perhaps it was the idea of a woman buying him a drink.

When I came back with the drinks, Grantie lifted his glass and said, "Slanch." Then he began to talk about himself. He lived in a house at the back of the village, the same house where he was born. After his father died, he had lived there with his mother, and since she died, his sister Valerie had come home to take care of him.

According to Grantie, Valerie was mad as a hatter. She had plastered the house with pictures of the Royal family. Everywhere he looked, they were waving at him. And she pestered him about getting an indoor toilet. They had a perfectly good one round the back. But now Valerie was sick and in the hospital and she blamed everything on the outside privy. Grantie sighed. She was his flesh and blood after all. He nodded sadly and got to his feet.

"I'm obliged to you," he said, and shambled out.

I watched a group of men playing darts. From time to time Todd would emerge from behind the bar and make a decisive thow. I felt rather woozy; my upper lip was tingling, always a sign that I had drunk more than I should. I knew it was time to go.

Outside it was very dark, there was only one street light in the entire village. I blundered along, hoping that I was going the right way. Gradually my eyes adjusted to the dark; I found the bridge without difficulty. The noise of the water was loud, and leaning over the rail I saw occasional flashes of white foam. Through my feet I could feel the slight vibration of the water tumbling over boulders in the dark.

When I reached the tent I couldn't be bothered to undress. I took off my boots and jacket, slid into my sleeping-bag, and, without a moment's pause, shifted into sleep.

The shrill scolding of a blackbird woke me; for a befuddled moment I thought the bird was inside the tent. The sun was shining brightly through the orange material, and my watch said five past eight. I got up and washed in the river. The water was cold as glass. As I made tea and porridge on my little gas cylinder I decided to visit Grantie.

I walked across the bridge and along the road to the post office. The man with whom I'd spoken the night before was again behind the counter. He greeted me like an old acquaintance, told me that his name was Mr Findlayson, and asked how I'd slept.

"Like a log," I said, and explained my errand.

"A gift for Grantie," he said. "Well, he always needs tobacco. Or what about chocolates? He has an awful sweet tooth." He indicated a couple of boxes of Black Magic on the top shelf. They looked as if they had been there for several years, and I felt a moral obligation to buy one. I chose the less squashed of the two and thanked him. The box just fitted into my jacket pocket.

It was only after I had left the shop that I realised I had forgotten to get directions. I stood in the road indecisively, not knowing which way to turn, yet reluctant to go back to Mr Findlayson. Glancing over my shoulder, I saw a figure watching me through the window. I started walking hastily towards the school. There was a row of swings in one corner of the playground. This must be where the acrobat played, I thought. A small girl was idly swinging back and forth. I opened the gate and walked over to her.

"Hello," I said.

She gave me a shy, toothy smile.

"What are you doing?" I asked.

"Just playing."

"What's your name?"

"Kate Sylvester."

"How do you do, Kate Sylvester," I said, holding out my hand. "I'm Chris Dunbar."

Kate put her small, soft hand in mine. "How do you do, Chris Dunbar," she said, stumbling over my surname.

"Very well, thank-you. Would you like me to give you a push?"

She nodded and got back on her swing.

"Hold on tight," I said, and began to push her. Her flaxen hair flew and she giggled with pleasure. I swung her as high as I could until I got tired. Then I sat down on the next swing and waited for her to come to a halt.

"Do you know Grantie?" I asked.

She nodded.

"Can you tell me where he lives?"

Arms whirling, she launched into an explanation; I saw she was too young to know how to give directions. I asked if she had time to show me the way and she said yes. We walked to the far end of the village and Kate pointed to a track going up the hill: Grantie's house was at the top. She turned and ran back in the direction of the playground, calling over her shoulder, "See you later, alligator." I walked up the hill carrying the chocolates and avoiding the cow pats.

Grantie's house seemed to disappear into the hillside: the grey stone was covered with ivy, the slate roof was green with moss. The windows were dark, without curtains, and the old uneven glass gave back a reflection of the sky. The front door had once been painted red; it looked as if it was never used. I kept walking, past a cluster of ragged buildings, to the back door.

I knocked. Nothing happened. I knocked again and then shouted, "Hello, Grantie. Are you here? This is Chris."

There was no reply. Except for the hens scratching in the dirt, the place seemed deserted. I had no idea what to do next. As I was turning away Grantie appeared round the corner of the house. He was adjusting his trousers.

"Hello, hello, hello," he said.

"Good morning. I'm sorry, I didn't mean to disturb you."

"Don't worry. I took my time, the same as usual. It's a grand day."

I agreed.

Grantie took out his pipe and began to fiddle with the tobacco. I wondered if he would invite me in, but he showed no sign of budging. "What's your line of work?" he asked.

"I'm an information officer for an advertising company," I said. Grantie did not look up. "I do research, keep files, answer questions."

Grantie sucked his pipe, musing. "An information officer. Now tell me something, does that mean you're well educated?"

The question took me aback. I didn't know how to answer. What did educated mean to Grantie? "Not really. I went to university but I wouldn't say that made me well educated."

Grantie mumbled something, rubbed his whiskers and looked at the ground. As he began to speak, I understood that these were signs of embarrassment. "I was thinking to ask you a favour. Would you write a letter for me? I have an above-average brain but what with one thing and another I never went to school much."

I said I would be glad to write a letter, several letters, and asked if he would like to do it right away.

"Maybe, maybe. I wonder if there's paper. I think Valerie has some. She's a great one for reading and writing." He led the way to the back door and held it open for me.

The small stone scullery was jammed with bottles, and the smell of whisky made me want to hold my breath. Grantie wiped his boots on the mat and urged me forward. We

moved into the kitchen. It was a low, dark room. Pictures of
the Royal family, torn out of women's magazines, covered
the walls, and a calendar showing the Queen on horseback
was propped up on the mantelpiece. On either side of the
fireplace stood an armchair, and behind one of them I saw a
pile of unopened letters.

I got the chocolates out of my pocket and put them on the
table. Grantie rummaged in the drawers of the dresser;
finally he produced a small pad of lined paper. He found a
pen in the toby jug on the mantelpiece. I had been thinking
that we were going to write a business letter, but it turned out
that he wanted to write to his sister.

I sat at the table, pen in hand, while Grantie walked round
and round the room. Each sentence took a long time because
as soon as he had said something Grantie would say no, no,
don't write that, she'll take it all wrong. After many hesita-
tions we wrote:

> Dear Valerie,
> I've been thinking that sometimes I was too harsh. God
> knows I've nothing against the Royal family, English
> papists though they may be. I hope you will overlook
> anything I said that upset you. I didn't mean it. It seems
> no time at all since you were bringing me my tea up the
> hill and now there's only the two of us left. We must get
> along as best we can.
> Do you remember Michael Dunbar who lived at
> Coultry? He was a grand poacher. This is being written
> by his granddaughter. Her spelling is better than mine.
> The hens are upset. They're not used to a man feeding
> them and don't lay as well. Come back when you can.
>
> > > Your brother,
> > > Grantie

As we laboured over the last few sentences I gradually
realised that Grantie was taking the exceptional step of writ-

ing to Valerie because he was sure she was dying and would
not be back to feed the hens.

"Why don't you go and visit her?" I asked, when I discovered that she was in Perth Infirmary, only an hour's drive
away.

"I've never been more than a day's walk from home and
I'm not going to start gallivanting about now," he said
sternly.

I didn't question him further. I had the feeling that I was
making him uncomfortable. Instead I asked if he could tell
me how to get to my grandfather's house at Coultry. For an
answer he led me outside and pointed up the hill. In the distance I saw a white cottage.

"Some painter chappie lives there now. His wife has a
bairn every year, regular as clockwork. The midwife usually
stops in for a dram on her way home."

"What's their name?"

"Patton. Are you going to call on them?"

"Yes. Would you like to come with me?"

"I've too much to do to squander the mornings," he said
reprovingly. He agreed, however, to go for a walk with me in
the afternoon, and said he would come by my camp. Without thanking me for either the letter-writing or the chocolates he went back into the house.

I set out up the rough track. Over and over came the faint
call of a cuckoo. Once I was past the forestry plantation, the
track dwindled to a path. The hills were vivid and subtle in
the sunlight and the grass was heavy with dew. I walked
across rough fields, clambering over stiles and fences. The
closer I got to the house, the more it looked like the kind I
used to draw when I was little, with four windows, a chimney
and a door. There was blue smoke trickling out of the
chimney, and as I crossed the final field a dog began to bark.

I climbed over the stile and walked round the side of the
house. The dog, an elderly collie, stopped barking as soon as
it saw me and began to wag its tail. I knelt to pet it and looked

around. Probably little had changed since my father was a boy; the only sign of modern life was a red tricycle lying in the mud. I gave the dog one last pat and knocked on the door. As I stood waiting I went over what I would say to the Pattons. A long time passed. Without quite intending to I tried the latch and, when it yielded in my hand, stepped inside.

I was in a stone-floored kitchen. The walls were whitewashed. The stove was shrouded in piles of washing and there were pots and dishes everywhere. A doorway led through a small hall to the living-room. Here too the walls were whitewashed, but almost every inch was covered with brightly coloured paintings. Against one wall stood a piano. I wondered who had got it up the hill and when. It could easily have been there since my grandfather's time. I struck a key; there was a thin sad sound.

Upstairs were two more rooms. One for the parents and one for the children. I imagined it had been the same for generations. I thought of my grandfather in one room and my father in the other. Now the children's room was jammed with beds; there was scarcely a foot of bare floor. If the midwife made many more visits, they would need to install bunk-beds. I was standing at the window, looking out over the valley, when the dog began to bark. Suddenly I thought about what I was doing; I could be arrested as a burglar. I hurried down the stairs and let myself out of the house. There was no one in sight. I ran through the yard and scrambled over the stile, into the field of sheep.

Back down in the valley, the village was silent, and I met no one as I made my way to The Four Feathers. It too was empty, save for Todd who was sitting behind the bar eating his lunch: peas, mashed potatoes and some sort of pie. Perhaps he ate all his meals there. He nodded and without being asked, fetched me a lager and lime.

"How was your visit to Grantie's? Did he like the choco-

lates?'' Todd asked. ''Never any use here trying to keep a
secret,'' he added cheerfully. His son, William, had been to
the post office.

Todd knew why I had come to Glen Lyon and began to tell
me about all the Dunbars in the neighbourhood. There was
a Dunbar family in the village, he said, but they were
newcomers, had only moved in ten years ago. And there was
a Mrs Dunbar who cooked at the big house each year when
the laird came to shoot. I told him that I hadn't expected to
find any relatives; my father had been an only child, and
although my grandfather had had seven brothers and sisters,
they had all left the valley at an early age. But I had still
thought it would be interesting to see the place where they
lived.

Todd finished the last mouthful of his lunch and nodded.
''Like the acrobat,'' he said. ''I'm certain Grantie told you
about him. He's a wee bit crazed on the subject.''

''Yes,'' I said. I was about to ask Todd for his version of the
story when the phone rang and he disappeared. I waited but
he did not return.

As I walked back to my tent, I thought about my visit to
Coultry. It was odd, nothing had happened and yet I felt
satisfied just to have seen the place where my father had
lived as a small boy. I wondered how my grandfather had
managed all alone up there; perhaps he had tied his son on
his back and carried him across the fields and over the
moors. I imagined the wide-eyed baby watching the birds
wheeling in the grey sky, lulled to sleep by the bleating of
sheep and the lowing of cattle. How had it been for him to be
sent off to live with strangers in a dirty city?

I began to tidy up the campsite and came across the remains of an old fire with a couple of rusty tins lying beside it.
They must have been left by the acrobat, I thought. I picked
up one of the tins and looked at it closely, but the metal was
mossy with rust and the label had long since disappeared.
Then I laughed at myself for holding it tenderly, like some

piece of ancient pottery, and added it to my pile of rubbish.

I was sitting on a rock, reading the little guidebook I had bought, when the heavy clang of footsteps on the iron bridge roused me. There was a rustling sound: Grantie appeared between two beech trees.

Together we recrossed the bridge and followed the road past the houses and the track up to Grantie's house to the far side of the village, where I had not been before. On our right the hillside rose steeply; on our left the distance between the road and the river had increased and there were several small fields, one with cows, one with turnips, a third har-rowed and perhaps already planted. I was wondering what to say if Grantie asked about my visit to Coultry, but he did not mention it. He was explaining that his family had once owned all the land we could see.

Where the valley narrowed the fields ended and there was a small wood. Planted in the moss beneath an oak tree there was a white wooden board with the words "MacGregor's Leap" in black letters. I asked about it.

Grantie said that one of the MacGregors had escaped from the English soldiers by jumping across the river. He sat down on the stone wall beside the road while I went to look. I found myself standing fifteen or twenty feet above the water. The opposite bank was only a little lower, and the rocks over which the water spouted looked sharp as knives. I walked back to the road and asked Grantie if he was sure that the man had made it.

"I'm certain. Those men had the fear of God in them. They had wings on their heels. There was nothing worse than being caught by the English." Grantie spoke with complete authority, as if he had witnessed the event. "Up on the hills," he went on, "there's a cave where the chief of the MacGregors hid for several months. Then one day when his wife was down in the valley, buying food, she was caught by the Sassenach soldiers. They used to brand the women on the cheek with a red hot key. Clever buggers."

He stopped and was silent, until I prompted him.

"They agreed not to brand her if she would lead them to her husband. Next morning the MacGregor awoke to find his wife walking up and down in front of the cave. She said she was just taking some exercise. She was acting so strangely that he got up and took a look outside; he was a canny man, a fine man. When he saw the line of soldiers moving up the hill, he bolted out of the cave and was never seen again."

"What a bitch," I said.

"No worse than the others," said Grantie. "When I was a lad and went to the Sunday school we learned the verse, 'It is better to marry than to burn.' Either way it's grief and misery."

"Were you ever married?" I asked.

"No. Use your brain. I had my sisters and my mother. I didn't want for anything. What more could a wife give me except trouble?" He winked at me. "Now," he said, "I'll show you the acrobat's grave."

All thought of protesting Grantie's view of marriage was driven from my mind. "His grave?" I said.

"Yes, it's right near here."

"I didn't know he was dead," I blurted out, almost as if I was accusing Grantie.

"He died at MacGregor's Leap."

"But how? What happened? Did he have an accident?"

"I don't know. No one knows. I have an idea myself that he was trying to do the leap and didn't make it. It was me that showed him the place, and he had some kind of notion about it. He was a MacGregor, you know."

"But why would he try to jump the river? It makes no sense."

"He was a troubled man. Maybe it made sense to him."

We were walking along the road. After a few hundred yards Grantie turned into a spinney; the hill rose steeply above us. In a copse of young fir trees there was a small clearing. Several fallen gravestones lay under the trees.

Grantie showed me a mound with a small plain stone: Lee MacGregor, 1940-1983. I asked why they'd buried him here when there was a graveyard next to the church.

"This is the MacGregors' old burial ground. We thought this was what he would want. He had this fancy about the valley and about not belonging. When he died, we waited for someone to come, but no one came, so we buried him here."

That evening I did not go to The Four Feathers. I gathered wood and, using most of a newspaper, succeeded in getting a fire going. The flames cast spooky shadows among the trees, but everything seemed safe and familiar. I baked a potato in the embers, and cooked sausages.

I remembered Grantie telling me that he'd never been further than a day's walk from the village, and I thought how that must be, to have all your memories, layer upon layer, in one place; memories that included not just yourself but your family and your forebears. That was how it must have been for my grandfather too, although perhaps he was a little more adventurous than Grantie; after all, he had married a girl from beyond the valley, and had had brothers who emigrated. For me such a life was unimaginable. When my father died, my mother moved back to Roxburghshire to be close to her sister. We lived in a small village and she sent me away to boarding-school. When I finished school I went to university; gradually the intervals between my home-comings grew longer. Now my mother and most of her relatives were dead. I had friends, of course, but how could friends compare with that insoluble and indissoluble relationship between Grantie and Valerie. What would happen, I wondered, if I fell ill or had an accident. Suddenly, I experienced a feeling of acute vertigo, as if, any moment, I would lose my footing. No one would come for me, I was sure.

Next morning I decided to walk up the hill that lay behind the village. As I climbed out from beneath the trees the church bells were chiming in the distance. The heather underfoot was soft and springy, just growing green, and every few yards the grouse started up, uttering their strange barking cries. The plovers and curlews called softly and kestrels hovered overhead. Higher, the heather thinned; the grass was short and slippery with tiny yellow flowers. Several times I thought I had reached the top, only to discover, as I breasted the rise, that it lay still further on. I climbed up a boulder-strewn slope and at last reached the small cairn that marked the summit. I added a stone and looked around. The sky seemed larger. There was on all sides a panorama of hills and lochs. In the distance a dozen tawny deer stood grazing; even as I noticed them, they seemed to sense my presence and shifted uneasily. I imagined my grandfather burrowing through the heather towards them with endless patience. I sat down in the shelter of a rock and ate the cheese sandwich and the apple that I had brought with me.

By four in the afternoon I was back in the village. As I walked past the playground I saw Kate playing on the swings with another small girl. Noticing me, she ran over.

"Come and give us a push, Chris. Please," she begged.

"Okay. But not for long, all right?"

She grinned, and grabbed my hand. We walked over the grass together. I asked if the other girl wanted to go on the swings too. Kate twisted her fingers through her hair and said shyly, "Well, just little turns. She's too little to do it properly."

I began pushing them both, but the younger girl quickly asked me to stop. When her swing slowed down, she slid to the ground and ran off.

Kate waved and went on swinging as high as she could. Eventually the swing came low enough for her to jump. She waited while I collected my things and escorted me across the grass. When we reached the road she pulled a small silver Easter egg out of her pocket and handed it to me.

"Thank-you, Kate," I said. "I was wishing I had an Easter egg. Would you like a piece?"

She shook her head. "It's for you. See you later, alligator."

"Bye-bye."

Kate looked at me reproachfully. "When I say, 'See you later, alligator,' you're meant to say, 'In a while, crocodile.'"

"In a while, crocodile," I said obediently.

"Then I say, 'See you soon, racoon.'"

"I've never heard that before."

"Lee used to say it."

Trying to sound casual, I asked if she knew Lee. She told me that he used to play with her on the swings.

"What did you play?" I asked.

"We played at being in a circus. He swung upside down. He could swing all the way round. I was his partner. Like on a trapeze."

"Did you like him?"

"Yes. He spoke funny. He was nice." We had reached the post office. She gave me a big grin and said, "I have to go home. See you later, alligator."

"In a while, crocodile."

"See you soon, racoon."

I watched her run along the road and disappear into one of the houses. It was growing dark and I was ravenously hungry, but suddenly I wanted to see Lee's grave again.

I came to the field where the cows were. A black and white one was standing beside the wall; when I stopped to talk to her she tongued my palm in an oddly intimate way. The evening star was out and a small moon had risen over the head of the valley. Every time I took my eyes off the road and the hills, they seemed darker when I looked back. I worried that without Grantie I might not be able to find the grave, but every step of the way seemed familiar. The fir trees quivered in the evening breeze and in their branches small birds twittered furiously.

I bent down beside the grave and wished that I had picked some flowers to place on it. Then I thought that I would build a cairn. The remains of the dry-stone wall which had once surrounded the graveyard lay scattered among the bracken and long grass. In the growing dark I began to gather stones and to pile them up in a rough heap at the foot of Lee's grave. What I began, I thought, others would continue.

At The Four Feathers I ate two rather stale Cornish pasties. I told Todd it was my last evening and he insisted I join in the game of darts. "You can be on my team," he said.

Grantie cheered us on, and at closing time we were slightly ahead. Todd claimed I'd brought him luck and told me I mustn't leave without saying goodbye.

Outside it was raining, a fine, light rain that prickled against my face as I stood waiting for Grantie who had decided at the last moment to go to the toilet. All evening I'd been thinking about the acrobat. After a minute or two Grantie emerged, fumbling with his pipe. He accepted my company without comment.

"So what did you think of Coultry?" he asked, as we walked along.

"It was pretty," I said, "but awfully bare. It must have been hard to live up there."

"That's right enough. The Dunbars were always a wee bit different from ordinary folk. The truth is, they never had an inch to spare."

On either side of the road the cottages were dark. We passed the church. "Grantie," I said, "I don't understand about Lee. Why did he die? Was he trying to kill himself?"

"Wheesht. That's an awful thing to say about a man. We can't know that. Some people are born trying to kill themselves; maybe he was one of them. Maybe it was just an accident. My father almost scythed his foot off one harvest. No justice in that." We had reached the foot of the track up to his house. Grantie stopped and turned to me. "Whatever ails you, lassie," he said, "forget it. Now away home with you."

I stood watching as he trudged away into the dark.

"Good-night, Grantie," I called after him.

In the morning, I was up early to take down my tent and cram everything higgledy-piggledy into my panniers. I wheeled my bike across the bridge and up to The Four Feathers. While I was propping it against the wall, I saw a red-haired boy watching me through the window. As soon as he realised that I'd noticed him, he ducked out of sight. I reached the post office just as Mr Findlayson opened the door. He seemed delighted when I bought the other box of Black Magic and wished me a good journey with unusual energy.

This time Grantie answered my knocking almost immediately and invited me in for a cup of tea. I followed him inside but said I couldn't stop, I just wanted to thank him for everything.

"It was nothing," he said. "You must come back when Valerie's here. She has some grand stories about Mike, I'm certain of it."

"I'll be back in the summer," I said. "I'd love to talk to Valerie."

"Good, good. So I'll see you then. It's bonny here in the summer. You'll like it. Maybe you'll bring your young man with you."

"Maybe," I said. "If I have one."

"Get away with you. A lassie like you. They must be round you like bees round a honey pot."

"I wish. Was Lee good looking?"

Grantie stared down for a moment. "He was awfully dismal. He asked me once if I was lonely. It was him that was the lonely one. He'd travelled too much; he had no home. That's America for you."

"Some people like to travel."

"To my mind it makes no sense," said Grantie severely. "It just shakes a body up, and makes them want things they can't have. You'll be back, won't you?"

"Of course. And you'll be here."

"Where else would I be?"

He escorted me to the top of the track. "Bye-bye, Chris," he said, shaking my hand. "Haste ye back." He was still standing there when I reached the road. I waved but he made no sign.

The next day at work I searched the newspaper files. When I found no mention of Lee MacGregor in any of the larger papers, I took the afternoon off and went to the library to read through old copies of the *Perthshire Advertiser*. At last I found notice of his death; he had died almost a year ago. In a few bald sentences he was described as a forty-two-year-old American tourist from Colorado; he had earned his living by doing stunt work for television. While visiting Glen Lyon he had slipped and fallen to his death. There was no additional information. The photograph, when I studied it, dissolved into a mass of dots.

The Ring

The Ring

From moment to moment the vague rumbling grew louder and more definite. It seemed to Sara to come from underground, as if perhaps a river ran beneath the fields. But before she could voice this speculation the mystery was resolved. Glancing over her shoulder she saw a mass of soldiers round the bend and come pounding up the track. She and John stepped aside to let them pass. Boy after boy streamed by, dressed in khaki, gasping for breath, cursing, wiping the sweat from their foreheads. Sara tried to make out their expressions beneath the black berets. One youth with a fresh complexion distinguished himself by turning to look at her, but she had no sense of his personality; he looked as anonymous as the grey figures in uniform she sometimes saw crouching on the television screen. Two slightly older men brought up the rear, and as they went by she heard one say to the other, "Once round the Ring and back is six miles. That ought to do for a Saturday morning."

The sound of their passage died away, and John and Sara remained alone beneath the trees. They continued walking.

On either side of the farm track the fences were reinforced with hawthorn hedges; gorse and blackberry bushes grew against them like prickly fortifications.

"They look so young," Sara said, "more like Boy Scouts than soldiers." John was walking faster than before, as if in emulation of the soldiers, and she had to almost run to keep up with him.

"Most of them are probably straight out of a school in Liverpool," he said.

"It's still a shock when you actually see them. They don't look old enough to drive a car, let alone a tank." She stumbled in a pot-hole. "Do we have to walk this fast?"

Sara and John had driven down from London the night before to spend Guy Fawkes weekend with Kim and Martha. That morning at breakfast John had proposed a walk to the hill fort known as the Chanctonbury Ring. He and Sara paid frequent visits to Brighton but they had never seen the fort although it was only a few miles away. Everyone had welcomed his suggestion, but, at the last moment, Kim and Martha had quarrelled and stayed behind.

Sara was wishing that she had not borrowed Martha's brown golf shoes. Pebbles kept getting stuck in the spiked soles. This happened a few minutes after the soldiers had disappeared. As she balanced on her right foot and poked at the sole of her left shoe, Sara felt foolish. She would have liked to use her husband's shoulder for support, but he was standing a couple of yards away. She made a joke about needing a Boy Scout; he did not move.

"I don't know how Martha can wear these damned shoes." The pebble came free, and she straightened up.

"You could have brought your own," said John. He was already moving ahead.

"Yes, I could, but it's so tempting to rely on Martha."

Sara and Martha were the same size, and they were also remarkably similar. Both had small hands and feet and springy dark brown curly hair. Even their voices sounded the same, so that over the telephone or in a muffled conversation in the dark they could easily be mistaken for each other. Their resemblance had always delighted them both. When the two couples were first married, it had been a pleasantry between them that, as in a story from the *Arabian Nights*, the women could exchange husbands without either man being the wiser.

"Where's the fort?" Sara asked.

"Up on the right, I think. We're probably looking at it without knowing it." They walked across a cattle grid.

"What did you and Kim talk about in the garden before we left?"

"We discussed wind-surfing, *Twelfth Night* and herbacious borders." John stooped to pick up a stick. "And Martha, I suppose, regaled you with her triumph."

"She did talk about Simon," Sara said slowly. "But she doesn't regard him as a triumph. You know she only started seeing him because Kim wouldn't stop whoring around."

"I wouldn't call it whoring around."

"No? What would you call it?" She heard John draw in his breath, as if about to speak, but he said nothing. After a moment she said, "Have you seen his latest?"

"Yes. In fact I introduced them; she's one of my students. You've met her too, don't you remember? That time you turned up unexpectedly to have a drink."

"Oh, yes." Sara tried to sound as if she had only a vague recollection of the meeting.

She tugged the zip of her anorak an inch higher, and pushed her hands into the pockets. She and John had been invited down for the weekend to help keep the peace, but she feared that on the contrary their presence only aggravated the situation. At breakfast Martha had said, "We should have told you which kind of fireworks we were going to lay on."

They came to a wooden gate sagging on its hinges. On the other side the fields gave way to open country and the track

narrowed to a path. "Do you think this is the end for Kim
and Martha?" Sara asked diffidently.

"You mean will they get a divorce? I should say it's quite
likely."

As he spoke Sara listened not to his words but to the sound
of his stick, flicking through the grass, like a snake's tongue.
She thought about how friends show the possibilities, some
pursued, others ignored, of one's own life. Kim and
Martha's happiness, the endurance of their alliance, had
borne witness to the success of her own marriage. Now she
felt she did not know what the future might bring.

They reached a crossroads and stopped. Both to the north
and the south there were small summits, either of which
could be the earthworks of a fort. As they were trying to
decide which way to turn, they heard again the thunder of
feet and saw the soldiers approaching, at a slightly slower
pace. Again they stood to one side.

"I like the idea that they use barbarian ruins for army
manoeuvres," John said.

They began to climb up in the direction from which the
soldiers had come. Suddenly they were standing on the ramparts. Far below to the south lay the sea, with boats pinned to
it like butterflies.

"We're here," said Sara. "I had no idea a fort could be so
big."

"The guidebook said that this is one of the largest in
southern England. In some places the ramparts are still
twenty feet high and there are traces of a second and possibly
a third line of defence."

They walked along the path. From time to time John
dropped to his knees to examine a stone. As a boy he had
searched avidly for birds' eggs, fossils and tadpoles, with only
moderate success. Sara, who had never in her life collected
anything, was always finding things. The next time she had
to fix her shoe, she saw lying in the grass a stone the shape of
an arrowhead. She hurried after John and silently handed it
to him.

"Well done. This is a beauty." He fingered the stone and smiled. "Where did you find it?"

They retraced their steps and she showed him the place, as best she could remember. He began to examine the grass with minute attention. Sara stood watching. "You can have that one," she said.

"Thank-you. Are you sure?" She could tell that it was not the same as finding one himself. He slipped the stone into his pocket and stood up. "I wonder how long it took to make an arrowhead," he said. "I can't imagine having the patience to spend all day chipping away at a stone."

He suggested that they explore the centre of the fort, but Sara preferred to wait on the ramparts while he took a look around. She sat down beside the path and watched the shadows of the clouds moving across the sea. She wondered if there was anything which could absorb her, make her lose herself, in the way that the search for arrowheads seemed to absorb John. Ever since Martha had confided in her, she had been in a state of amazed confusion.

At the end of May Martha had telephoned. "I need some new clothes," she said. "I'm coming up to town tomorrow. Can you come shopping with me?"

Sara had protested that she couldn't take a day off work; she and John had only just come back from two weeks in Brittany. Several of her juvenile delinquents had got themselves into a mess in her absence.

"They'll survive without you for one day. Please, Sara. I need to talk to you." She had sounded so desperate that Sara had ended up agreeing to rearrange her appointments.

Martha had taken the nine o'clock train up from Brighton and the two women had spent the whole day toiling around the shops, trying on clothes. Sara was amazed and slightly horrified at the number of things her friend insisted on buying. Finally in the late afternoon Martha relented; they went back to the house after Sara had assured her that John would not be there. As they sat at the kitchen table drinking coffee,

Martha at last began to talk. "I can't stand it," she said. "Kim is in love."

Sara looked intently at her to see if she was just being dramatic. "How do you know?"

"I don't know: I suspect, I surmise, I smell it. I kiss him very deeply to see if I can taste this other woman. Of course it isn't the first time, but before he was always careless about his affairs. He didn't really mind if I found out. Now he's being very, very careful. After fifteen years he's suddenly turned into the ideal husband. And yet it's clear that he doesn't give a toss about me."

"Martha, that's not true. Kim loves you," Sara said, but Martha interrupted her protestations. She asked Sara to go to the pub where Kim often dropped in after work and see what the woman was like.

Sara was reluctant to spy on Kim, but looking at Martha, whose hands were clenched around her coffee-cup, she could not refuse. The first evening she spent an hour at the pub, reading a newspaper, before she decided that he was not going to show up. The next day she had barely sat down when he came in. Following him were two young women and, behind them, John. Sara was stunned; she had fully expected John to be safely at home. Both the young women looked around, perhaps to observe the effect of their entrance, but neither of the men seemed to pay the least attention to the roomful of people. Kim found a table while John made his way to the bar.

There was one moment when Sara might have followed Martha's plan and remained hidden behind her newspaper. Instead, with quiet haste she picked up her bag, jacket and drink and went over and touched her husband on the shoulder. He turned around. At the sight of her, his smile seemed to flicker briefly, as if there had been a temporary failure in the current of his affection.

"What are you doing here?" he asked.

"I was out talking to a client and thought I'd come by and say hello to Kim."

"Kim is popular today. I came along to see him too."

They carried the drinks back to the table.

"This is my wife, Sara," John said. "Sara, Rachel and Lisa." Sara nodded to the two women and sat down next to Kim.

In spite of Kim's determined impartiality, she knew within a few minutes that it was Lisa who was his lover. She never doubted this, although she could not have explained why he preferred one to the other. When she looked at the two women, who were both young and pretty, they appeared interchangeable, not only with each other but with every other young woman in the room. John and Kim talked to Sara with unusual animation, and she in turn politely questioned Lisa and Rachel. They were both doing graduate work in economics.

"What do you do?" Rachel asked. She nodded as Sara described her job, the various pressures the young offenders were under. On her index finger were several thin silver rings.

"I could never be a social worker. It must be terrible, always being burdened with other people's problems," she said, pushing back her hair and looking earnestly at Sara.

Sara had agreed. John had begun to explain how the Conservatives' attitude to unemployment made her job even harder. After twenty minutes, he suggested that he and Sara should be on their way, and Kim jumped to his feet saying that he had to catch his train.

Next day on the phone Martha pressed Sara for every last detail. Describing Lisa, Sara kept thinking about Rachel pushing back her hair and smoothing down her skin-tight jeans. "Martha, I don't think you've anything to worry about," she said. "If he had to see her every day, he'd be tired of her in a week."

"I wish that were true, but many men find younger women irresistibly fascinating."

"Maybe some men, but not Kim."

"All men are a little that way, even John," Martha

declared. A moment of silence slid down the fifty miles of telephone wires. "Oh, Sara, what shall I do?"

"I know it sounds unsympathetic, but I don't think you have to do anything. Kim really loves you. Even if he does have a crush on Lisa, he'll get over it."

"Kim gave me his own version. He and John just happened to be having a drink with a couple of students when you showed up which was a lovely surprise. I'm sure they were all on their best behaviour in front of you." Martha paused. "It doesn't matter, really it doesn't. Do you remember Lucy? How we were always saying that her husband was a model of devotion? Well a month ago he came home from work, packed a suitcase, and left. I know Kim would never do anything like that, but every day I'm afraid he may be gone when I come home. It's ridiculous. I'm like a child in the dark, pretending there are ghosts to frighten myself."

Sara did not let Martha know how distressed she had been to see John at the pub, nor did she confide in John the real reason she had been there. She couldn't trust him, she told herself, not to tell Kim in a moment of male camaraderie.

The wind rustled through the trees and long grass growing in the centre of the fort, but neither this faint sound nor the noise of a tractor pulling a plough in a nearby field seemed to disturb the quiet. Sara thought, I must keep still, very still.

John was coming back. He scrambled up the ramparts to join her, his feet slithering on the loose stones.

"Did you see anything?"

"No, at least nothing ancient. There were some old beer bottles and the signs of several picnic fires." Still a little out of breath, he stood beside Sara, looking out across the earthworks.

"Do you hear how quiet it is?" said Sara softly. "Listen. They say if we weren't so accustomed to it we'd be able to hear the sound of the earth rushing through space."

"Let's try it," said John, sitting down beside her. He lay

back and closed his eyes. Sara looked down at him, then out again to sea. In his presence she could hear nothing but the queasy murmurs of her own anxiety. Perhaps John too was not as relaxed as his easy pose suggested, for she saw his eyelids twitching.

After a few minutes he sat up. "Well, I did hear something, but I don't think it was the roar of the universe. It's probably the sort of thing you have to practise." He did up his jacket. "You know, there are three or four more forts around here, and just along the coast there are flint mines. These hills must have been swarming with people."

The ramparts sloped steeply down to a golf course. In spite of the season, several people, wearing brightly coloured clothes, were playing. Her father, Sara remembered, had always played right up until Christmas.

"With a good pair of binoculars we could see Kim and Martha's house from here," John said. "We should have got them to hang out a flag: white for peace, red for war."

"I wonder if they're still arguing."

"Probably." He picked up a stone and examined it closely.

"What do you think of Simon?"

"Simon?" John tossed the stone at a tree, and picked up another. "I can't take him seriously."

"Do you think Kim does?"

"I'm not sure. I think he finds him a bit of a joke." John looked at Sara. "He is awfully young."

"He's older than most of Kim's girl-friends."

"That may be true, but I don't see what he has to offer Martha." He turned and went on walking.

Sara remembered that when Kim first heard how old Simon was, he had accused Martha of robbing the cradle. Martha had met Simon a little over two months ago; she had been taking a short-cut through the old cemetery behind her office and had found him sitting on a tombstone. They had begun to see each other; in the early evening, while the sun

set behind the brick terraces, they would stroll together
among the graves. He was a puppeteer with a local puppet
theatre and should have had a girl-friend who wore antique
flowered dresses and rode a bicycle, not someone like
Martha. It was when Martha brought him up to London that
Sara first noticed that her friend had several grey hairs. At
once she knew that soon she would look in the mirror and see
some grey in her own brown curls.

They reached the east side of the fort, where the ramparts
had almost entirely crumbled away. Abundant, glossy holly
bushes grew among the remains. John had taken the
guidebook out of his pocket and was reading as he walked
along.

"Does it say how old this place is?" Sara asked, as she drew
level with him.

"There are several theories," he read. "It is possible that
the earliest building on this site was a Druidic temple built
around the same time as Stonehenge. Recent excavations
suggest that Chanctonbury was in use throughout the
Roman occupation until the Dark Ages."

As she listened, Sara was filled with a sense of how hopeless
it was to speculate about the past. She was not sure of what
had happened last week, even this week. And the people who
lived in the fort had been dead for so long that their bones
were now part of the chalk downs over which she and John
had walked this morning. She could not unravel the years,
any more than she could undo everything which had led to
the present situation with John. How was it that she had
begun to feel that the relationship between them was fragile
as a robin's egg. She could not remember when their intimacy had first been breached.

It was mid-afternoon by the time they returned to the car.
John drove while Sara looked through the guidebook. When
they were back on the main road he said, "I didn't mean to

sound so definite about Kim and Martha getting a divorce. Maybe they'll be fine. We should keep that in mind."

"What do you mean?"

"Well, we should be careful not to get too involved. I'm sure it helps Martha to know you're on her side, but if it all blows over, then it would be a great pity if you and Kim were no longer on speaking terms."

"I don't exactly see you falling over yourself to be friendly to Martha."

"At least in public I try to be impartial." John reached over and patted her hand. "I'm not criticising you. I'm talking as much to myself as to you."

They arrived at the house, and even before they opened the front door the sounds of argument were audible. In the tall building there was no place to hide from Kim and Martha's voices. John went upstairs to the bedroom. Sara went into the living-room; she sat down and tried to read an article in the newspaper about the situation of immigrant women in the Midlands. The words lay dormant on the page, she could not make them come to life. Looking out into the garden, she saw Simon coming through the gate. She opened the French windows and went to meet him.

"Hello. Martha borrowed my bike. I came to collect it."

"Maybe I could get it for you. I saw it in the hall," Sara said. But she was so relieved to be out of the house that instead of going back she sat down on the wooden bench under the birch trees. Beyond the roof-tops she could see the downs.

Simon sat beside her. For a moment they listened in silence to the shrill voices.

"I wish they wouldn't quarrel," he said.

"They've known each other for a long time," Sara responded defensively. She thought that if she had met Simon, with his pale skin and Beardsley hair, in a cemetery, she would not have believed he was real; even at close quarters, sitting beside her rolling a cigarette, he seemed insubstantial.

"But what's there to quarrel about? If they don't love each other, quarrelling won't bring it back, and if they do, then they should stay together and not quarrel."

Sara watched him hold the cigarette up and run his tongue along the paper. "I thought I understood from Martha that you and she wanted to live together," she said.

"Yes, we do, at least I do. But the important thing is that we love each other, that's what matters, and if we can't live together, well then, so be it. As long as we can still see each other."

Listening to Simon's calm speech, while Kim and Martha fought in the background, made Sara uncomfortable. She got up and walked over to the stone bird-bath, which she and Martha had found in the junk shop round the corner.

"You and Martha are so alike, it's hard to believe you're not sisters," Simon said.

From the way he looked at her Sara knew that he wanted her to touch him, was willing her to do so. She stayed still with one hand resting on the rim of the bird-bath. When the silence between them became too awkward, she said, "Yes, we're very similar. Meeting Martha was like having a sister for the first time."

"And your husbands are very much alike too, aren't they?"

"How can you say that? They're completely different."

"I wasn't thinking of their physical appearance," Simon said. "You and John aren't in such great shape either, are you?" He got up from the bench and came over and stood close to Sara. He bent towards her. Without thinking, she raised her mouth to his.

Sara moved away. There was a book lying on the bench and she picked it up. It was *Twelfth Night*. From the house came the muffled sound of Kim's voice. As Sara turned she glimpsed John at the bedroom window, but before she could

gesture, he had disappeared. "We walked up to Chanctonbury Ring this morning," she said.

Simon began to pick the dead leaves out of the bird-bath
and said that he had visited Stonehenge for the summer
solstice.

"Did the sun strike the heelstone or whatever it's meant to
do?" Sara asked.

"No, it didn't. It was cloudy, and besides you can't get in
nowadays. There's a big fence all round the circle. We'd
planned to climb over it, but the place was swarming with
policemen."

As Simon spoke, John opened the front door and came
down the garden. He walked over to Sara and put his hand
on her shoulder. "Avebury is more domestic than Stonehenge but not without charm," he said. "Have you ever
been there?" He proceeded to give a full description of the
standing stones at Avebury.

When he finished, Simon said, "Maybe one of you could
get my bike now."

Sara put down *Twelfth Night* and went to fetch the bike.
Simon took it from her at once and wheeled it down the path.

"Give my love to Martha," he said as he closed the gate.

John sat on the bench, staring after him.

"Did you see him kiss me?" Sara asked. She sat down at
the far end of the bench.

"Yes, that's why I came out. I don't think you should steal
Martha's boy-friends. Surely the situation is already difficult
enough."

"I don't think theft is the issue, only affection," Sara said.
"What about you and Kim stealing each other's girl-friends,
or do you call that sharing?"

"What are you talking about?"

"Women like Lisa. Look at all the trouble your generosity
has caused. It would have been much better if you'd kept
her to yourself." Sara was astonished by the words that
leapt from her mouth; it was as if she did not care what she

said. But some deep and final instinct for self-preservation
stopped her from mentioning Rachel.

"I don't know what you're talking about. Lisa is one of my
students, nothing more." He looked at her oddly for a moment, then said in a quieter voice, "Did you know Kim
almost left Martha a few years ago?"

"No, I didn't."

"He was in love with a woman called Gwen. Seriously in
love, and now it looks as if he may leave Martha for someone
who isn't really important to him. It seems all wrong."

"So you don't think Lisa is important?"

"No, it's just an infatuation. At the moment he thinks he'd
die if he couldn't see her, but if Martha didn't make a fuss,
he'd get over it."

"And then there'd be someone else, another pretty little
student. Why should Martha put up with it? She's thought of
leaving him too, but she's always believed that Kim couldn't
manage without her."

"And Kim of course believes the same thing about
Martha. So even their sacrifices are useless," John said
quietly. "Surely humans haven't always been this way? It
must have taken a hundred years to build the Ring, maybe
two hundred. The first people who started digging knew the
fort could never be finished in their lifetimes, but they dug
anyway. They believed that future generations would keep
faith with them." He turned to look at Sara. "How did we
become so fickle and inconstant?"

"Who are we to say that their sacrifices were useless?"
asked Sara, and her eyes were full of tears.

Later, as she lay in bed, with John breathing steadily beside
her, Sara thought about Simon. She remembered the old
joke about her and Martha; Simon had almost mentioned it,
hadn't he? Perhaps it was possible. She knew where he lived,
on a street on the other side of the cemetery. Martha had
pointed out the house. There had been three bicycles locked

to the railings and innumerable milk bottles piled on the doorstep; she would have to be careful not to fall over them. She would open the door and tiptoe into the hall. If she did meet one of the other inhabitants, she would, in all likelihood, be taken for Martha. The stairs would probably creak horrendously, as they had at home when she and her younger brother used to sneak down to the kitchen for midnight feasts. Simon slept at the top of the house — Martha had described his attic room — and she imagined there would be only one, inevitable door. It would open quietly. He wouldn't wake, but perhaps he would sigh in his sleep. She would undress in the dark and in a moment be in bed, in his arms. She must take care not to fall asleep. When the time came she would slide stealthily from between the sheets and fumble on her clothes. Before she left, she would kneel down to kiss him. He would say "Goodbye" and then a name; it should be Martha's but perhaps, even half asleep, he would somehow divine the difference and call her by her rightful name. As she lay thinking, wondering if she would not prefer him to recognise her, John turned towards her in his sleep and murmured something, a name, she was not sure what, Martha, or Lisa, or Sara, or something else altogether.

The Salt Course

The Salt Course

Norman's mother opened the door of the farmhouse. "Norman will be ready in a minute," she said to Marian. "Would you like to come in and wait?"

Marian shook her head. She wanted to go and look at the kittens. They lived behind the barn, and she was hoping that her parents would let her have one of them. Mrs Vine shut the door and Marian ran past the granary to the barn. The kittens were outside in the sunshine, lying in a furry, ginger heap beside their mother. Marian knelt down and played with them until Norman came round the corner followed by Tim, his younger brother.

Norman was ten, a year older than Marian. He had very blue eyes and a sharp nose. Since the day the Vines had arrived at the farm, almost two months ago, Marian had longed with all her heart to be his friend. He bent to pick up a black feather and squatted down beside the kittens. Tim sat down next to him and carefully patted the back of the smallest kitten. He was only six and not allowed to leave the farmyard.

"I've got something to show you," Marian said to Norman.

"What?"

"It's a secret."

"I'm not interested in your stupid old secrets. The last time it was just an old tree, and the time before that it was a hole under a rhododendron bush." Norman turned away and tried to get one of the kittens interested in playing with the feather.

Marian was determined to make him come with her. "Come on," she said. "Don't be a spoil-sport. I bet you've never seen anything like this."

"I bet I have," said Norman, but he stopped playing with the kittens and got slowly to his feet.

"Get your bicycle," said Marian.

Norman fetched his bicycle from the shed and Marian led the way up the drive to the main road. As soon as he saw which direction they were going Norman raced off and disappeared over the top of the hill. Marian knew it was hopeless trying to catch up with him on her battered old bike. She pedalled along sedately as if she didn't have the slightest interest in going fast. Beside the track to the piggeries, she saw Norman's bike lying on the ground. She stopped and put her bike down next to his. Norman was leaning over the gate looking at the pigs.

"Did you bring any bread?" he shouted.

"No." Marian shook her head.

"Stupid," said Norman. He picked up a long stick that was lying beside the gate and began to scratch the pigs. Marian climbed on the gate to watch. The pigs grunted and frothed with pleasure.

"Let me have the stick, Norman," she said, stretching out her hand.

"No." He reached to scratch the pig that Marian called Long John Silver because it had a black spot around one eye.

Marian turned her back to him. She leant as far over the

gate as she could and tickled a pig between the ears. Its skin felt like the bark of a tree.

Norman threw down his stick. "So where's the secret?" he demanded, as if expecting her to produce it from her pocket. "I've seen pigs before."

"You were the one who stopped," Marian said. For a moment she was tempted not to show him after all, but then she climbed down from the gate and went back to her bike. "Come on. Follow me."

She turned onto the road to the old mill, but before they reached the mill she stopped and called to Norman, who had raced ahead again, that they were there. She leant her bike against a chestnut tree and laid her sweater on the ground beside it. A flight of stairs built into the hillside led down through the woods towards the river. The stairs were so wide that Marian could lope down them in a special way she called galumphing. She galumphed down with great authority and waited for Norman at the bottom.

The path wound along through the trees. It was very muddy. Norman in his old gym-shoes slid all over the place while Marian skipped along, jumping from one dry spot to the next. As soon as she caught sight of the fence she stopped. In a moment Norman was standing beside her, staring. Marian watched him; she was sure he had never seen anything like this.

"What is it?"

"It's the salt course," Marian said. "No one ever comes here except me."

Beneath the tall conifers the various obstacles were laid out in a rough circle. Marian's father had told her that the assault course had been built by the local branch of the Royal Highland cadets, to help them keep fit, but no one had used it for years.

"Why is it called the salt course?" asked Norman.

"Because that's what it is."

"Well, it's a stupid name."

"No, it isn't. My father said that's what it's called,"
Marian said indignantly.

"But it doesn't have anything to do with salt."

"It's a different kind of salt. Look I'll show you what to
do."

She began to go round the course. There was a tall fence, a
row of rubber tyres, several barriers, a line of ropes, a pole
over a ditch, a climbing frame. Some things she couldn't do
very well but she hoped that Norman wouldn't notice. She
was trying to clamber over the fence when she saw that he
was no longer watching; he was swarming up a rope. She
abandoned the fence and climbed onto the pole. From this
vantage point she glimpsed between the tree trunks the glit-
ter of the river. The pole was only as wide as her foot, and
beneath it was a large, muddy ditch. A couple of times she
pretended to be about to fall, just for fun. Then when Norman turned to look she nearly did fall.

He tried to grab hold of the next rope, but it remained just
out of reach. "Pass me the rope," he shouted.

Marian jumped down from the pole, ran over and pulled
the rope towards him. When he had swung onto the next
rope, she started up the one he had just vacated. She was
good at climbing ropes.

"Here," said Norman, "take my hand."

Stretching to the utmost, Marian managed to reach him.
As soon as her fingers grazed his, Norman took tight hold of
her.

"Let's swing," he said, and together they began to sway
back and forth.

"Okay, now we have to touch feet too," said Norman.

Marian was afraid she would fall, but she uncurled her
feet from around the rope and dangled her leg tentatively in
Norman's direction. Her arm felt as if it were being pulled
out of its socket. Just as she was ready to give in, Norman's
foot touched hers.

"We did it," he said triumphantly.

It began to grow dark. Marian told Norman she had to go home. Without a word, he headed towards the path. He was at the edge of the course before Marian remembered that they had not done the most important thing of all. "Stop," she called. "We can't go yet. We have to swear."

"Swear what?" said Norman grumpily, but he stopped and stood waiting.

"This place is a secret," said Marian. "You have to promise not to tell anyone about it, ever, and not to come here except with me."

"It's dumb," said Norman. "Why should we swear?" But reluctantly he came over.

Marian took her penknife out of her pocket and opened the blade.

"Hold out your finger," she said. There was the briefest pause before Norman's hand shot out. Solemnly Marian scratched first his finger and then her own, until there was a small drop of blood on each. "Now, say what I say. If I ever tell anyone about the salt course, or come here without Marian, I will be eaten by wolves, and weasels will suck out my brains to the last drop."

Before she had finished speaking Norman was already half-way through the oath. Marian was not sure that he actually said every word, but she did not dare to ask him to repeat it.

"Now we rub our fingers together," she said. "This makes it a proper oath."

As she bicycled home Marian sang softly to herself. It was almost dark by the time she came into the kitchen. Her mother looked up from the onions she was chopping.

"Where have you been?" she said.

Marian was about to tell — her mother knew all about the salt course — but she remembered rubbing her finger against Norman's and swearing. "We were in the woods," she said, "and we went to see the pigs."

"Well, you look like you've been playing with them. You'd

better go and wash before supper." She looked more closely
at her daughter. "Weren't you wearing your red sweater?"
Marian looked down and remembered leaving it on the
ground. "Oh, I left it in the woods."

Next day as soon as she got home from school Marian
bicycled down to the woods. She was glad of an excuse to go
out; often during the week her mother made her stay in to do
her homework. The sweater was a little damp but she tied it
around her waist anyway. Although her mother had told her
to come straight home, she decided to go to the salt course,
just for a few minutes. Maybe she could get over that high
fence. She galumphed down the stairs a little more slowly
than the day before. When she reached the bottom, she
stopped to do up one of her shoes and for a moment she
thought she heard voices, but no, it was only the creaking of
trees in the wind. She skipped along the path and began to
make her way among the trees. Suddenly there was a flash of
yellow. Marian edged forward to the next tree; when she
leant against the trunk, it was sticky and sweet with resin.
Peering around it she saw, wavering a little from side to side
as he walked along the pole over the ditch, Norman in his
bright yellow sweater. He was talking to two boys who stood
below him. Marian trembled in anger. If there had been a
stone among the pine needles on the ground, she would have
hurled it at him.

She stepped out from behind the tree.

"You traitor, Norman Vine. I'll never speak to you again
as long as I live," she shouted, and before he could reply she
turned and ran blindly away, crashing through the under-
growth. He was a traitor, a dirty traitor. It was unspeakable.
Breaking a promise was bad enough, but when you'd sworn
it was ten times worse, a hundred times. On her bicycle
Marian wobbled furiously from one side of the road to the
other.

Every evening that week, as soon as she had finished her

homework, she went out to her secret spy hut and stayed there until her mother called her to supper. The hut was built of branches with heather and bracken woven in between. Even her father did not know about it. In the spring, when the roadmen were working near her house, she had spent many hours there, secretly watching their comings and goings. Inside it was dark and small; Marian lit a candle and ate some of the stale chocolate biscuits which she kept carefully hoarded in a tin. She sat on her heels and thought.

On Saturday it was very windy. Marian crouched over the handlebars of her bike as she toiled along the main road. She was glad of the wind; it would help her plan. Norman's mother was outside hanging up the washing. Tim was handing her the clothes pegs.

"Hello, Mrs Vine." Marian pushed open the garden gate.

"Hello, Marian, how are you? I expect you're looking for Norman?"

"Yes. Is he here?"

"No, he's at the piggeries." Mrs Vine hung up the last pair of jeans and picked up the clothes-basket. "Are you coming in?" she asked Tim, and he ran ahead of her.

Marian hurried to the piggeries. Norman was leaning over the gate, feeding the pigs crust by crust and scratching their ears. He did not seem surprised to see her.

She climbed up beside him. "Hello."

"How did you know I was here?"

"Your mother told me." Long John Silver let out a triumphant grunt as he pushed a smaller pig aside. "Listen," said Marian, "do you want to see a new secret?"

"I'm tired of you and your secrets. I'm busy." Norman threw a large slice of bread to the runt. He held the bag carelessly in his free hand. While he was still shouting encouragement to the smallest pig, Marian grabbed the bag and tipped the bread all over the pigs. They rushed forward, grunting and squealing.

"Why did you do that?"

Marian flushed. "I'm sorry," she mumbled. She was sure she had spoiled everything.

Norman looked at the pigs. Then, to her surprise, he shrugged and said, "Okay, show me your secret." Before he could change his mind, she ran over and picked up both their bicycles.

"Where are we going?" he asked as they pedalled along.

"To the log scales."

"What are those?"

"Wait and see."

It did not take them long to reach the scales, which were in a thick clump of trees close to the road. Marian led the way into the clearing. "Here we are," she said.

"I don't see anything," said Norman.

"We're standing on them." A layer of moss and rough grass made the iron door almost invisible, but when Marian stamped her foot there was a hollow ringing sound. Her father had shown her this place. He had explained how the scales had been used by woodcutters to weigh timber. Beneath the iron door, just below ground level, was the platform of the scales. Marian's father had opened the door and they had both climbed down to look at the mechanism. When she was inside Marian could just see out by standing on tiptoe. She pulled back the moss to show Norman the outline of the door.

"What is it? A dungeon?"

"Sort of. They're scales. You know, to weigh things."

"How do you get it open?" He bent down and pried at the door.

"We need a branch. You'll have to help me. I can't manage on my own," she said. She was proud of this part of her plan: if Norman didn't know that she could open the door by herself, then he couldn't blame her. It took only a moment for him to find a branch. Together they levered open the door.

"It's just like a dungeon," Norman said. His face was glowing with excitement. "Maybe there's buried treasure."

Without the slightest hesitation, he climbed down. As soon as his head was safely below ground level, Marian whipped away the branch. The door slammed shut on him with a tremendous clang. Marian stood listening; she heard only the sound of the wind high up in the trees and the cawing of rooks as they wheeled above their nests. Why didn't Norman shout for help? What would she do if he were dead? It would completely spoil her revenge. She wanted to open the door, just a crack, to make sure that he was all right, but she had told herself that she must leave him for at least half an hour. If she let him out right away, it would hardly count.

To pass the time, she decided to ride her bicycle up and down the hill on the main road. She rushed down one side and let the bike's momentum carry her as far as possible up the other side and then back again like a faltering pendulum. As she came to a halt, Norman's father appeared over the top of the hill on his bright red tractor. He stopped. Marian got off her bike and wheeled it slowly towards him. She tried to think what she would say if he asked where Norman was.

"Hello, Marian. I'm going to feed the ponies. Would you like to come?"

Without thinking, she nodded, and Mr Vine lifted her and her bicycle onto the trailer. They started with a jerk and went bouncing along the road. Marian stood up, enjoying the struggle to keep her balance. The field with the ponies was not far away; she could easily be back in half an hour.

When they reached the field, Marian climbed down to open the gate. The ponies trotted over and crowded around her, snorting softly. She was scared and wanted to get back on the trailer. But Mr Vine came over to protect her and showed her how to feed them.

"Look, keep your hand flat like this. Then they can't find any place to bite, even if they want to."

He held out his hand and Marian very cautiously held hers

out too. The first time a pony's head approached she hid her hand behind her back, but when she saw that the pony just looked at her in a puzzled way, she stretched out her hand again and allowed it to eat the hay. The pony's nose felt soft and warm, like her favourite kitten. She offered it another handful and then began to feed all the ponies in turn; she wanted to feed them the whole trailer of hay, handful by handful. She stood there, surrounded by horses, forgetting to be afraid.

"Do you want a ride back to the farm?" Mr Vine asked.

Marian let her hands fall by her sides. How long had she been gone? It was hours surely since she had left the log scales. What would have happend to Norman?

"I have to go," she stammered. It took ages for Mr Vine to lift her bike off the trailer. She rode down the hill, pedalling madly. Even before she came to a stop, she flung her bike aside and rushed through the trees to the log scales.

She knelt down and knocked on the door. "Norman?" she shouted so loudly that her voice cracked.

No answer.

"Norman?"

She grabbed the branch and levered open the door. Once she had it open about six inches, it rose up very quickly and Norman's head suddenly appeared. He was pale. His eyes seemed very blue. Marian dropped the stick and backed away.

"Why didn't you answer?" she said. "I was scared to death."

"Hold the door."

She came over and held the door open while Norman clambered out. Together, silently, they lowered it back into place. At the last moment Marian snatched away her fingers. As she stood up Norman turned and grabbed her by the throat. She could not believe it. "Stop it," she croaked. She tried to pry his hands loose, finger by finger, but just as she loosened one, another tightened. She felt the pressure of his hands behind her eyes, in her chest. It was completely different from fighting with her friends at school; it was frightening. She could not fight back in the normal way.

She was off balance. Norman pushed her down, knelt on her chest and began to bang her head against the ground.

"If you ever tell anyone what happened, I'll kill you," he said, between thumps. Although he was an inch shorter than Marian, he seemed suddenly huge. His face was no longer pale, but bright red.

"But I rescued you," she managed to say. The moss and grass made the ground soft, but still at each thud she felt as if her teeth were going to fall out.

"No you didn't," Norman shouted. "I could have got out perfectly well by myself."

"You liar. You couldn't get out without me," Marian gasped.

"Yes, I could. I was only pretending I couldn't get out, to punish you." He tightened his grip and gave an extra hard thump. "Promise not to tell."

Marian wanted to grit her teeth and be silent, but the words jumped out of her mouth, like frogs in the fairy tale. "I promise."

Norman let go. He looked at her fiercely for a moment, then turned and ran away through the trees. He was gone before she could catch her breath and remind him that he had broken his oath.

Marian rubbed her aching neck with both hands and gingerly got to her feet. Now that the grass was trampled flat the outline of the door was clearly visible. Under a fir tree she found a branch; she raked the grass until it stood up, then strewed leaves and twigs around. When the scales were once again properly camouflaged, she walked slowly out of the clearing.

Peter and
the Asteroids

Peter and
the Asteroids

Peter has never believed in keeping in touch — absence, he used to say, should admit no substitutes — so it doesn't surprise me that I haven't received so much as a postcard from him in the last two years. Occasionally friends visit America and bring back reports that he is coming home, but within a few days, or weeks, these rumours always disappear. After numerous false alarms I have developed a sceptical attitude, and if anyone but Peter's mother had announced his return I would have paid no attention. When she telephoned last Sunday I recognised her voice at once.

"Craig, Peter just called." She said that he was arriving on Friday and asked if I would go with her to Heathrow to meet him. We made the necessary arrangements, and, before I could ask any questions, she hung up.

I walked over to the window and looked out at the allotments across the road. Although dusk had fallen a few of my neighbours were still working busily among their potatoes, green beans and lettuces. The thought of seeing Peter again gave me a peculiar sense of happiness. I felt too restless to finish reading the Sunday papers and decided to go for a walk.

Outside it was cool and pleasant. The local cats were congregating on window-sills and doorsteps, getting ready for their nightly rounds; the evening star hung over the tube station. I walked across the Liverpool Road and down through squares and side streets towards Barnsbury. Last winter I wrote a poem about a conversation with Peter. It had just appeared in *The New Statesman*, and its publication now seemed like an omen, heralding his return with suitable mystery and discretion.

Peter's mother lives in a small village on the Thames, and one night while he and I were staying with her, we had decided to go canoeing. It was summer and the sky was bright with stars. Peter had been talking about epilepsy and why it was that the status of fits was no longer divine or even upper-class. He himself suffers from a mild form of epilepsy. Suddenly one then both of us saw a shooting star. Two aeroplanes, winking green and red, flew across; then a whole clump of shooting stars exploded.

"It's like Asteroids," Peter said. He was referring not to the heavenly bodies but to the video game, which can be played in many pubs. In spite of, or perhaps because of, the fact that the brightly coloured, flashing lights were liable to trigger a seizure, Peter had a passion for the game.

"The aeroplanes are the weapons and the stars are the targets," he explained.

"Whoever's playing is going to get a very low score," I said. Peter laughed and said the rules were different for celestial games.

As I walked back down the street every house I passed had lighted windows; only mine was completely dark. When I opened the front door I noticed a curious smell. It turned out that I had left the kettle sitting on a low flame. I placed it in the sink and it sizzled violently.

I sat down at the kitchen table. More than anything I

wanted to talk to Clove, but it was already rather late. I try to avoid giving the impression of prying into her evenings. We are no longer on either the very good or the very bad terms that license the intimacy of random phone calls. Besides, I wanted to tell her the news in person. I remembered that there was a beer at the back of the fridge, drank it, and went to bed.

In the morning I dialled the number of Clove's office. Since our divorce I am nervous about calling her, and the woman at the switchboard seems to take a special delight in mispronouncing my name. But when I got through Clove sounded friendly. Without the slightest hesitation, she agreed to have lunch. I dressed with special care. We had arranged to meet at twelve-thirty, but I aimed for twelve-fifteen. Clove used to accuse me of being the most unpunctual person she had ever known; I was anxious not to provide further evidence for this charge.

The windows of the Health Education Office, where Clove works, are full of depressing facts about sugar and cigarettes, so I waited near the newsagents directly opposite. The day was very hot and the narrow street was jammed with cars. Only the motorcyclists, sporting names like Pegasus and Express on their bright yellow T-shirts, made much progress. They sped past the stationary vehicles like messengers between modern generals. At last Clove appeared on the other side of the street. She was wearing a red skirt which buttoned down the front and a red and white striped shirt. As she advanced towards me, she too seemed to have an air of military success.

She kissed me firmly on the cheek. Smelling her familiar, spicy perfume and seeing the glint of red in her dark hair reminded me of the peculiar aptness of her name. She led the way to a restaurant behind Carnaby Street. We secured a corner table and lined up at the counter to choose salads.

"Separately or together?" the cashier asked.

"Separately." I began to search through my pockets.

"Together," said Clove. "Don't be ridiculous, Craig. You know I earn twice as much as you do." She held out a ten-pound note. In a moment the transaction was completed, and we sat down.

"There's too much green in here," I said, looking around the room. A petulant note which recalled our married days had crept into my voice.

"It's a health-food restaurant. The decor is supposed to remind you of nature," Clove said soothingly. "I've been reading about colours. They have a much greater effect on us than we know."

The colour of her office, she said, interfered with her ability to concentrate, and she had plans to repaint the house we used to share. It didn't seem to occur to her that there might be a special reason why I wanted to have lunch; I had to wait until she finished describing a particularly calming shade of grey before I could get a word in. Finally I said flat out, "Peter's coming back," and quickly looked down at my plate and then up at her again.

A kind of warmth suffused Clove; I would have liked to spread out my hand and hold it to her face. She sat back with a decisive motion.

"At last," she said in a triumphant voice. "I knew that someone as intelligent as Peter could never take America seriously. When did you hear he was coming?"

I told her.

"You don't sound very enthusiastic," she said accusingly.

"Of course I am. He's my oldest friend." Clove hates to be reminded of my prior claim on Peter.

"Well, I suppose you must be pleased, to want to have lunch with me. After all you could have told me over the phone." Her face was still flushed.

I started to protest that I hadn't seen her for ages, but she waved her hand and said it didn't matter. While she finished her rice salad, I went to get coffee. I had wanted to tell Clove about Peter because I knew that she would share my excitement, but now I found myself growing irritated. When I came back to the table I mentioned that I was trying to decide whether to look for a new flat. She nodded but she clearly wasn't listening. I sat down and stirred my coffee.

"Jack will have to go," she said. Since we separated, Clove has rented out my former study; Peter was the first lodger, and Jack moved in after he left. Without waiting to hear what I thought of this idea, she went on. "Perhaps I can give him a month's rent, in lieu of notice. But it's bound to be difficult."

Her assumption that Peter was coming back for good made me realise for the first time that there were other possibilities. "Clove," I said, "Peter may only be here for a couple of weeks. He probably won't need his room. You've said yourself, often enough, Jack is the ideal lodger. Don't do anything rash."

As if I had not spoken she asked when Peter was arriving.

"Sometime on Friday." I was anxious to conceal the fact that I was going to the airport to meet him; I didn't want Clove to come along. I pressed my teaspoon against the table as if testing my strength and wondered what to say if she demanded exact details. But to my surprise, she suddenly asked how I'd been getting on.

Trying to sound nonchalant, I told her about *The New Statesman*.

"How wonderful." She leaned across the table and kissed me. "I must buy lots of copies to convince my friends that you really were writing poetry all those years when I said you were. Lily will be pleased; she always had a soft spot for you." She sipped her coffee. "You know I sometimes thought you would have been better off with Lily. You were so at ease together."

I looked at Clove in amazement. It was absurd for her to complain about my being at ease with her little sister.

"You were probably her first date. You remember that time I was studying and you offered to take her to the Gon-

doliers? You both came home giggling and confessed that
you'd shared a bottle of wine."

"A half bottle of Soave," I corrected, "for which you lent
me the money. And after your exams I took you out to drink
champagne. I suppose you've forgotten that."

"No, I haven't forgotten. That was a very sweet thing for
you to do." She looked at me and smiled. "I didn't mean to
tease you about Lily. Have you told her about Peter?"

"No, why should I?" It was one thing to break the news to
Clove; quite another to tell Lily, whose relationship with
Peter had come to a stormy end at about the same time as
Clove and I split up.

"He is her husband."

"Not any longer," I said defensively. "They've been
separated for ages. She's been with Leon for over a year."

"You're awfully simple about such matters. If there's one
person Peter will want to see, it's Lily," Clove said in her
most resolute manner.

To hear her speak with such authority made me furious.
How could she possibly know what Peter would want? But
before I could remonstrate, she announced that Lily was
coming to dinner that evening and she would tell her then. I
asked if I could come too.

"No, I want to talk to her alone." As she spoke Clove got
briskly to her feet. In silence, I followed her into the street.

"See you soon," I said awkwardly.

"Yes." She fiddled with an earring and did not look at me.
"Peter's sure to bring us together." She turned and walked
quickly away.

I made my way slowly along Oxford Street through the
crowds of jostling tourists. Lunch with Clove had suggested a
wealth of possibilities neither acted on nor perceived during
our marriage. When we had faced each other daily across a
kitchen table littered with rough drafts of my poems, I had
found her stubborn confidence extremely irritating, but,
now that she had slipped through my fingers, it seemed en-

dearing. The idea of her repainting the house, which we had decorated together, gave me a sharp pang. These feelings surprised me. After all, I moved out of the house almost four years ago. But I suppose I've always been inclined to view our separation as temporary, a bad patch that we would soon get through. It was Clove who announced last year that she wanted a divorce.

At Tottenham Court Road I caught a bus. I got off near the library and went in to choose some records. By the time I emerged, school was out; as I turned into my street I saw the local children playing rounders outside my house. A ball curved towards me, and without thinking I caught it and threw it back. They yelled their thanks. Perhaps the little buggers will stay clear of my windows now, I thought.

I put on one of the new records, made myself a cup of tea, and sat down at my desk. I had no excuse for not working — a book review, long overdue, was waiting to be typed — but my mind kept wandering. It was frustrating to sit at home, knowing that only a mile away Clove was talking to Lily. I sharpened my pencils, changed the ribbon on my typewriter, retyped a paragraph and threw it out.

When Jack called at eight-thirty to ask if I would have a drink, I agreed at once. We arranged to meet at the Lord Nelson, a rather gloomy pub about halfway between my house and Clove's. As I walked over I kept thinking that in only a few days I would be sitting in a pub with Peter; we would spend the whole evening talking as we so often used to at Cambridge. There was no sign of Jack when I arrived, so I went to the bar and ordered a couple of pints. The barman, hearing my accent, asked where I was from.

"Bradford," I said.

He nodded complacently, and told me he was from Leeds. As I turned to look for a place to sit I saw Jack on the other side of the room. I waved and made my way to his table.

He took a pint from my hand. "Cheers," he said. "I didn't know you were from Bradford. I thought you grew up in

Yorkshire." I was amazed that he had been able to hear me.

"I sometimes say that because it's easier," I explained. When I first went to Cambridge I was embarrassed to admit I came from Bradford; it seemed the sort of place everyone made jokes about. Now I don't give a damn, but I must have been vague about my origins with Jack and of course he remembered every syllable.

He looked at me reproachfully. "You'd say anything so long as it's comfortable. No wonder Clove left you."

No one had ever seemed surprised by the failure of my marriage, but I was startled to hear myself criticised, albeit mildly, by Jack. His universal admiration has always got on my nerves. I looked at him more closely and saw that he was brimming with excitement. His rather close-set blue eyes appeared even larger than usual, and he had rolled up the sleeves of his T-shirt. Such a gesture of bravado could only indicate that he had something to tell me. There is something about Jack, a kind of harmless quality, which encourages people to confide in him. This, combined with an amazing knack for overhearing things, leads to his knowing many secrets. I had been assuming that Clove had thrown him out in order to have privacy for her dinner with Lily. Suddenly it occurred to me that he might have witnessed their conversation.

"Did Lily come over this evening?" I asked, trying to sound casual.

"Yes," he said, putting down his beer and leaning forward over the table. He had been in his room reading while the two sisters had dinner in the garden. I could easily imagine the scene; when that room had been my study I had often sat for hours gazing out of the window at the roses and small birds instead of writing poems. Jack launched into an account of the last time he had seen Lily. There was a note of gentle longing in his voice which made me uncomfortable. I listened impatiently, but I knew it was never any good trying to rush him. Finally he came round to this evening. Lily had apparently taken the news of Peter's return fairly calmly. "She said he was bound to come back for a holiday at some point."

"And what did Clove say to that?" I asked.

"She was sure he was coming back for good. You know how she is," Jack said. "She hangs onto an idea like a terrier."

This was true; Clove would rather die than change her mind. It was one reason our marriage lasted so long.

Jack asked if I wanted another. I nodded. He got up, spoke to the bartender and went off in the direction of the Gents. A couple had sat down at the next table. I could see the spindly boyfriend clearly, but the girl had her back to me. Suddenly, in a voice loud enough to fill the room, she said, "It was special for me and you fucking ruined it." Jack, who was coming back with our drinks, looked at the couple and grinned at me.

He put the glasses down neatly on the mats. As usual he had bought half-pints to my pints. "Cheers," he murmured, and ducked his head to take the first mouthful. Then he asked what Peter was like.

The question took me aback. It's much easier to describe a stranger than someone you know well. I flailed around and finally told the story of how Peter failed his logic exam. We were in our first year at Cambridge. Peter walked in late, read through the exam, and quietly got up to leave. The lecturer stopped him at the door and said that if Peter just wrote his name he would pass him, but he couldn't pass a blank piece of paper.

"That's amazing," said Jack. "Why would a lecturer do that?"

"Oh, he knew Peter was brilliant. Anyway his offer wasn't put to the test. Peter thanked him and walked out."

"He sounds mad," Jack said in an admiring tone of voice. I took a large mouthful of beer, and asked what else had happened between Clove and Lily.

"Well, she told Lily she wanted me to move out. That was a bit of a stunner."

I felt sorry for Jack, but he seemed almost pleased to be the focus of so much attention. He said Lily had told Clove she was being absurd: what on earth made her think that Peter would want to live in her house again, even if he was back for good. Clove countered by saying that Lily couldn't just ignore the fact that she was married to Peter.

As he described this exchange, Jack began to look embarrassed. "I'm not sure I ought to be telling you this. After all, you and Clove."

He trailed off and I said hastily, "Clove and I are good friends, more like brother and sister now. Nothing you could say would upset me."

"In that case," he said, and without further hesitation he told me that Lily had accused Clove of having an affair with Peter. "I don't know why I was so surprised. After all they were living under the same roof, and Clove is so attractive," he sighed.

However brotherly I felt, I wasn't sure I wanted to listen to Jack having wet dreams about my former wife. When I first found out about Peter and Clove I didn't speak to Peter for nearly a year. Jack was looking at me curiously, and I quickly offered to buy him another drink. From the bar I watched him staring at the couple next to us. The girl was leaning towards her boyfriend in an attitude of reconciliation. With her blonde hair falling across her face she looked quite appealing.

I put the mugs down too heavily and some beer slopped onto the table. In a mild attempt to annoy Jack I asked if it didn't make him nervous to listen to Clove and Lily talking about him.

"A little, but even Clove said she liked me; it was only for Peter's sake that she wanted me to leave."

"Did she admit to sleeping with him?"

"Not exactly. She just sort of smiled. Then she made a little speech about how she had no designs on Peter; on the contrary she hoped very much that he and Lily would be reconciled. That's when I decided to slip out and give you a call." Jack rubbed at a smudge on his white trousers. "What do you think?" he asked in a significant tone, "is there any chance of Lily and Peter getting back together?"

I shrugged. "I doubt it. Just because Clove is convinced that everyone is in love with Peter, doesn't mean it's true. He treated Lily appallingly."

I could tell that Jack was about to ask for details, but the barman shouted "Time." We drained our glasses and went outside. It had grown chilly and Jack, who had no jacket, began to shiver. I lent him my sweater and promised to talk to Clove about letting him stay. His reluctance to move out was not surprising; apart from practical considerations, something was stirring and he wanted to be part of it.

At home I made myself a cup of tea and sat in the kitchen for a long time thinking about Peter. One of the odd things about our friendship is that neither of us has any memory of our first meeting. Soon after we arrived at Cambridge we were firm friends, but how this came about is a mystery. The first thing I remember is standing in the Lady Chapel at Ely Cathedral listening to Peter talk about anti-Semitism. I already knew him well, but I had not realised before that he was Jewish. When I told him this, he said, "That's exactly what I mean. You've been bred to think that Jews don't exist." He was the first Jewish person I had ever known, and I remember looking at him in the clear greenish light of the Lady Chapel and thinking that he was a genius.

The morning after the conversation with Jack I slept late. In the middle of a dream about W.H. Auden, with whom, much to my own surprise, I seemed to be on good terms, I was woken by the phone. It was the editor's assistant wondering what had become of my review. Half asleep, I rashly promised that she would have it first thing tomorrow. As I got dressed I tried to reconstruct my conversation with

Auden; I was convinced he had told me the one thing I
needed to know about poetry, but all that I could remember
was sitting beside him sharing a bottle of whisky. I thought
that I must tell Peter about it. At one time he and I kept
dream diaries which we read to each other. Now I find that I
remember some of his dreams better than my own.

I sat down at my desk and stayed there most of the day,
forcing myself to work at the review.

Around six there was a knock at the door. Lily was standing on the doorstep. In her yellow jeans and Hawaiian shirt
she looked disconcertingly exotic.

"Lily," I said, and hugged her.

She hugged me back and took off her dark glasses. "Am I
interrupting?" she asked.

"No, no, not at all. Come in."

"Actually I wondered if you'd like to have dinner with
me?" She pointed to her little blue car, double-parked on
the other side of the street.

"I'll be two minutes." I grabbed my jacket, turned off the
stereo, and ran out to join her.

Like Clove, Lily suggested that we go to a health-food
restaurant, which made me wonder if I was looking seedy.
This one had wood panelling on the walls and the usual
masses of plants. I noticed as we sat down that Lily was wearing earrings shaped like leaves. If Clove was the most aptly
named person I knew, then Lily was the least. Instead of
being tall and pale and fair, she was small, with the same
dark hair as her sister and eyes so deep-set that they had an
almost oriental slant. In this pseudo-sylvan environment she
looked a little like Puck. She ordered watercress salad and
aubergine casserole, and I followed her example. We ordered a litre of house white. I filled our glasses. Lily raised
hers to me. "Congratulations," she said. "I loved your
poem."

"Thanks."

"It's about Peter, isn't it?"

"How did you know?"

"Oh, Craig, did you think you were being obscure? Who else besides Peter is crazy about Asteroids?" She smiled at me. Under Peter's influence she too had become an accomplished player. It was not uncommon to come across the two of them in some pub, whiling away the afternoon, watching the flashing lights and begging change from all their friends. Peter claimed that they had put Asteroids on their list of wedding presents.

Our waitress' beaded hair jangled as she placed our plates on the table. I topped up our glasses.

"This is all right," said Lily. "Sometimes the food here is so healthy it's inedible."

I nodded, although I thought the aubergine came close. After a few moments I said, "Clove told you about Peter."

"Yes. I find it hard to believe. I thought he was never coming back. Clove claims that she always knew he would; she's very pleased."

"And you? You were closer to him than anyone."

At my words, Lily seemed to shrink down in her seat. "I'm not pleased," she said. "I don't know what I feel: apprehensive? terrified? Clove was so strange yesterday. She wants to have everything ready for Peter and I'm on her list. She seems to think if she just keeps telling me I'm in love with him, I will be."

Her last remark reminded me of a comment Peter had made after we had seen a production of *Julius Caesar*. "On all sides," he said, "Caesar's death is foretold. He's in the prime of life, but everyone starts telling him he's about to die. In the end we can't help feeling that the prophecies are as much to blame for his death as the conspiracies." I was about to repeat this to Lily, but thought better of it.

She put down her fork and took a sip of wine. "Did you know that Clove and Peter were lovers?"

"Yes, but only when it was all over." I was anxious to establish my innocence.

"I wasn't sure until yesterday. Then when I asked her, she looked distinctly smug."

"I can imagine. Were you upset?"

"Yes, terribly. I feel like a real dog in the manger, I mean I don't have any claim on Peter, but somehow the thought of him and Clove is the last straw." She tried to smile, but I could see she was close to tears. She turned her face away and studied her plate.

I wanted to hug her. I said earnestly, "But it was never important to Peter, not in the least. When he saw how involved Clove was, he felt badly."

"That only makes it worse. If it wasn't important, why bother?" Lily pushed her plate aside and asked if I would like to finish her aubergine. She put her elbows on the table. "Why is Clove so determined to get Peter and me back together? If she's in love with him, it makes no sense."

I didn't know what to say. In spite of my protests to Clove and Jack I often catch myself having daydreams in which Peter and Lily and Clove and I live happily ever after. I mumbled something about Clove knowing that Peter wasn't interested in her but still wanting to keep him in the family.

"But that's bizarre," Lily protested. "You know, I think she spoke to Leon. When I told him about Peter, he didn't seem in the least surprised, and he was very cold with me. I don't know how she could be so disloyal."

I tried to be helpful. Leon has set several of my poems to music, and I like him. Also, as far as I can tell, he does seem to make Lily happy. I suggested that he was feeling insecure.

"I still think she told him," Lily said stubbornly.

"Perhaps she did. Maybe she swore him to secrecy. That would put him in a very awkward position; he wouldn't want to cause trouble between you and Clove."

I wanted very much to convince Lily that everything was going to be all right, and suddenly she seemed to believe me. She smiled and said, "You're so sweet, Craig. If only my girlish dreams had come true, I'd be married to you and living happily ever after."

I smiled back. For years Lily had been just Clove's sister; it wasn't until Peter started going out with her that I had recognised how attractive she was. Now I cursed my myopia. For a brief moment I imagined us living together, going for long walks and coming home to make love in a bed strewn with books. I looked around for our waitress to order more wine.

"She's busy," Lily said.

In the doorway of the kitchen, silhouetted against the light, stood our waitress wrapped in the arms of one of the waiters. The sight seemed to make Lily feel suddenly worse. "Craig," she burst out, "what shall I do?"

"Don't you want to see Peter?" I asked. "For old times' sake?"

"No. The old times were terrible. Why would I want to repeat them?"

"Maybe you and Leon should go away?" I suggested. "Get out of London for a few days. Then at least you wouldn't have Clove breathing down your neck."

"That is an idea," Lily said. "Maybe we could go and see Leon's brother in Devon." She looked at me pensively, and I was pleased to think that I had provided a solution to her difficulties. Clove would be furious when she found out.

Our waitress disengaged herself and, smiling lazily, came over to clear our plates. I ordered more wine. "It's a nice time of year to get out of the city," I said, as I refilled our glasses.

"Why don't you come too?" Lily asked. "You could sit and write poems on the beach."

I shook my head. "I was furious with Peter about Clove, but now there's nothing I want more than to see him."

My confession embarrassed me, but Lily seemed to understand. "I remember the two of you sitting up late talking," she said. "I used to go upstairs to bed and fall asleep to the sounds of your voices. And in the morning when I came down there would be books all over the living-room."

She smiled and excused herself. I sipped my wine and looked at the Japanese painting on the wall. When Lily and

Peter first moved to London, they had lived just round the corner from Clove and me. I was meant to be ghost-writing a book, and Peter was doing something equally nebulous. While our wives went off to their nine-to-five jobs we spent our days together, or at least what remained of them given that neither of us ever got up before noon. The idea was that we would do menial work during the day and then, at night, while the city slept, write our masterpieces. I don't remember writing a word of the ghost book, but I did produce poems at a great rate. Peter hardly ever worked as far as I could see, but within six months he had mysteriously finished a slim book about Shklovski.

I watched Lily threading her way between the tables; she looked like a yellow butterfly.

"It won't work, Craig," she said, as she sat down. "I can't run away from Peter — I'd only feel badly if I tried. He's not really a tyrant, even if Clove makes him out to be one."

"You don't want to have terrible rows with Leon," I said. I felt suddenly sad, as if I was losing Lily, but she, now that her mind was made up, seemed much more cheerful.

"It's wonderful to see you, Craig. It's silly how seldom we meet," she said, and began to tell me about a book on Mary Queen of Scots that she was editing. I thought how beautiful she had become. Only when the waitress brought our bill did I notice that the restaurant was almost empty. Before I could move, Lily had handed her a credit card.

"Lily," I protested.

"I'm taking you out," she said firmly. "To celebrate your poem."

We left the restaurant and walked arm in arm towards her car. As we waited to cross the road, she turned to me. "I keep thinking Peter may not show up," she said. "It would be just like him to have us all running around for nothing."

I stood on the curb and envisaged all the steps of his journey. On Thursday night while I go to bed as usual, he, in a land further from the sun, will be boarding a plane. Knowing his arrival is imminent, I will dream with special virtuosity, and he will sit by a window, open-eyed, watching the rushing darkness. In the early morning, as the coast of Ireland comes into his view, I will get up and take the tube to Heathrow. His mother and I will both arrive early. We will get coffee and talk until it is time to go and wait outside the doors; presently, amidst a crowd of strangers, he will appear. "No," I said. The final image still shone in my mind. "This time he's coming. I'm meeting his plane on Friday, at seven in the morning." As I spoke, Lily looked away. She tugged my arm, and pointed to the green light. We stepped out into the empty street.

A Small Price

A Small Price

The manageress frowned as she read my application. "Don't you have any local references?" she asked.

"I just came from Scotland last week." I could tell she was about to say no. Before she could speak, two women walked into the bakery, and she left me for a moment. I stared at a tray of éclairs and cast around desperately for something to say; renting a room had taken nearly all my money. Then I remembered my Aunt Irene telling me how she got her first job. "Couldn't you give me a trial?" I begged. "I'll work without pay for a week. Two weeks."

She hesitated.

"That way you can see what I can do."

She removed her blue-rimmed spectacles and slowly wiped them on a handkerchief. "All right, Kathleen," she said, "I'll give you a go. Come in tomorrow at eight."

I liked the sweet floury smell of the bread and the precise slap of the slicing machine, which reminded me of the machines in the knitting mill where Penny and I had worked last summer. But it was hard to keep straight the names of all the different breads and cakes, and every time I made a mistake the manageress seemed to be watching. I kept think-ing she was about to tell me to leave. Then on Saturday after-noon, as we were closing the shop, she smiled and said I was a good worker. I had a job.

All day it had been windy, and under the tree at the corner of Formosa Street the pavement was dotted with freshly fallen chestnuts. I stopped to gather them, splitting the prickly shells, looking for the biggest shiniest nuts, until the pockets of my jacket were full.

When I let myself into the house a woman was standing in the hall, going through the papers on the table.

"Hello," I said. "I'm Kathleen."

"Oh," she looked up at me, "you're the new person."

"I brought some cakes home. Would you like some?" I held out the bag. She looked inside, then told me her name was Isobel and invited me for a cup of tea.

Her room was across the hall from mine and exactly the same shape and size, but she had a pink bedspread, an armchair, a sofa and a TV. I sat on the sofa. Isobel talked. The previous occupant of my room had been a student. He had gone around barefoot even in midwinter and Isobel had often met him in the hall wearing only an orange bath towel. It was he who had painted the walls of my room in six different colours. Finally, thank goodness, the landlady had thrown him out.

"This is a nice quiet house," said Isobel, "but I wish I wasn't stuck on the ground floor."

I thought that was the one thing that made my room bearable. I could sit by the window and just by looking out be a part of things. "I was glad to find it," I said.

Isobel took another slice of Battenburg and told me that she worked at Sainsburys as a cashier. "I've been there five years and they still don't trust me an inch. You're not allowed to carry any money on you. Every evening before you can leave they search your bag. It's humiliating."

I said how different it was at the bakery. Isobel nodded. Her real ambition, she said, was to be a hairdresser. Her hair was the most notable thing about her; the mass of curls almost hid her thin, sharp face. She kept winding strands around her fingers to perfect their curliness. I could see her looking critically at my short straight hair. When I got up to leave she asked if I had any magazines that I could lend her. I hadn't quite finished with them, but I went and fetched my copies of *Honey* and *Seventeen*.

Back in my room I lined up the chestnuts on the mantelpiece, next to the begonia I had bought for company, and sat down and wrote to Penny. We had promised to write to each other every week, and now I had lots to tell her. I described the bakery, my room and Isobel. "She's a bit older than me," I wrote, "but I think we'll be friends. She's lived in London for five years and knows all the best shops. Some Saturday we're going to go shopping together.

There were three other girls at the bakery: Christine, Marcia and Donna. In the mornings when they arrived they immediately began to fuss over each other's clothes, asking where a blouse or skirt was purchased and how much it cost, while I took off my coat and put on my yellow overall in silence. I wished they would greet me with more than a "Good-morning," or a "How are you today?" Even when I wore my best blue skirt they said nothing.

We took our lunch in pairs, and as Christine and Marcia were best friends I ended up with Donna. If it was raining we went to the Wimpy Bar, otherwise we bought filled rolls half-price at the bakery and ate them walking up and down the Harrow Road, looking in shops. Sometimes we spent the whole hour in Boots or Woolworths, and Donna would make up my face with fuchsia eye-shadow and violet lipstick. Whenever an assistant asked in an icy voice if we needed help, Donna would say we were just looking. Every day she talked about what was happening with her boyfriend, Rob.

They'd been going out together for six months. One day we
met him in the street and he was utterly different from what
I'd expected: very thin with red ears and short hair. All the
time they were talking about which film to see that evening,
he kept wiping his hands up and down his trousers. When he
left I didn't know what to say, but that night as I sat in my
room eating fish and chips, I'd have given anything to be
Donna, sitting by his side at the cinema.

One of the first things I had noticed about London was that
people walked quite differently from at home. After a while
I understood why: no one expected to meet anyone they
knew; they hurried along minding their own business. In
Hawick I couldn't go out for a newspaper without meeting
half a dozen acquaintances. At first I was in love with the
endless, unstoppable mass of people. I could do whatever I
wanted and no one would care. But as the days passed, turning into weeks and months, I began to hate the way everyone
looked past me, as if I wasn't really there.

I had imagined that in London it would take a bit of time to
get to know people, but after three months I still did not have
a single person to whom I could say let's meet, let's go out.
No one. Donna was busy with Rob, and although Isobel
seemed glad enough in the evenings to share my cakes,
whenever I suggested doing something, like going shopping,
she had other plans. I always offered to work on Saturdays —
I needed the money and it was nice to have the other girls
thank me — but there were still Sundays.

Sunday waited at the end of each week like a huge dark
hole. I would get up late, go out and buy a *News of the World*
and read it over tea and toast in a café. Then I would go
somewhere famous, like the Houses of Parliament or the
Tower. These places were always swarming with tourists,
which made me feel that I too was a tourist, only skating on
the surface of the city. Occasionally a sun-tanned man would
smile at me and say hello in a foreign accent, but I was

careful never to do more than nod back. In the evening I would go to the cinema and come home filled with relief that I had somehow passed another day; that tomorrow I could go to work again, and be known, and noticed, and called by my name.

During the week I couldn't afford to go out but sometimes, if the weather was nice, I went for a walk in Regent's Park. I liked walking round the zoo. Occasionally the head of a giraffe appeared above the bushes or a huge bird flew from one side of the birdcage to the other.

One day when I was on my way there it started to rain, and I took shelter in a pub called The Blind Beggar. I'd only been in a pub twice before, once on my seventeenth birthday and once for a farewell drink with Penny. The room was full of people. As I made my way to the bar, I was sure everyone was wondering what I was doing there alone. A man standing next to me asked for a lager, and when it was my turn I asked for that too.

"Half-pint?" said the bartender.

I nodded. It was easy. I carried my drink to an empty table. Someone had left a newspaper; I seized it gratefully and spread it in front of me. I had finished the front page and was reading a story about an actress when half a dozen people came over to the next table.

"Are these chairs free?" a man asked, smiling at me.

I said yes, and he turned the chairs around.

A woman in a red dress told a joke about a parrot and everyone laughed. I felt embarrassed; I was sure they would think I was spying on them, or trying to pick someone up. Quickly I finished my drink and got up to leave. Their chairs barred my way, and I had to say excuse me several times.

Outside the rain was worse than ever. I walked along trying to avoid the large drops which fell off the awnings of shops. The manageress had offered me an umbrella that had been left in the bakery, but I had forgotten to take it. I was hurrying down Formosa Street thinking how stupid I was when I saw Isobel standing on the doorstep of the house. "Isobel," I shouted. Beneath her brown umbrella she half turned. I started to run to get through the open door. She disappeared inside. Just as I reached the top step, the door slammed shut in my face. I fumbled through my handbag for my keys.

In my room I took off my coat and hung it on the back of a chair with a piece of newspaper spread underneath to catch the drips. The room was freezing, and I had no coins to feed the gas meter. For a few minutes I walked up and down with my arms wrapped around my chest, shivering. Then I went across the hall and knocked on Isobel's door.

She had already changed into her pink furry slippers.

"Didn't you see me?"

"When?" She stood in the doorway, every curl perfectly in place. Over her shoulder I could see the gas fire glowing.

"In the street. I was right behind you."

"I have to wash my hair now," she said, moving back and edging the door forward.

I had intended to ask for change — Isobel kept a jar full of ten-pence pieces on her dressing-table — but instead I asked for my magazines back. She had borrowed every magazine I had bought since I moved in.

"Oh, I threw them out. The pages were so dirty I couldn't bear to touch them. I was sure you wouldn't want them back."

I said the first thing that came into my head. "My sister's in hospital. I need them to take to her."

Isobel took a step back while pushing the door closed. "Don't be silly. Hospitals have to keep things clean."

I went back to my room and climbed into bed to keep warm. As I ate the Bakewell tarts I had brought home from work I began to cry.

After that I went to The Blind Beggar almost every evening. Neil the bartender began to smile and say hello when I came in. If he wasn't too busy he would stop and talk for a few minutes. Sometimes as I sat reading the newspaper or a magazine, a man would offer to buy me a drink, and I would accept. But I would never let anyone see me home. These men weren't just strange in the sense of strangers, there was always something slightly wrong with them. And yet sometimes as I walked home along the dark streets I imagined the man I'd been talking to beside me, and I didn't understand why I'd said no.

Winter was coming. Every night I went home alone and climbed into my cold bed; I could have been dead. If I died no one would know. At the bakery they'd think I'd gone off and got another job. Probably Isobel would be the first to notice; she would complain about the smell. And eventually Penny would miss hearing from me. I always sent her a postcard of wherever I visited on Sunday; sometimes, if Donna or Isobel had told me interesting stories, I managed to write a letter too.

Penny's letters were mostly about her boyfriend. Several of the girls in our class were already married and I could tell she was going that way herself; she would never come to London and join me, as we used to imagine. She often asked when I was coming back, and I would remember the long afternoons we used to spend in her bedroom trying on each other's clothes. Penny was the only friend of whom my mother had approved. But if I went back I would have nowhere to live; there weren't any bedsits in Hawick. And all the people who had told me it was foolish to come to London would be able to say they had told me so.

Neil was talking about his wife. "She says I have terrible taste. Every year she gives me a list of exactly what she wants for Christmas, and where to get it."

As he spoke there was a sudden uproar. Someone had fallen over the big black dog which always slept in the doorway of the lounge bar. It was the man who had taken the extra chairs from my table the first time I came to The Blind Beggar. I had seen him several times since. When he had quieted the dog, he came over and apologised to Neil.

"Oh, she's used to it," said Neil. "She gets trampled on nearly as often as the doormat. If she didn't like it, she'd have learned by now." He moved away to serve another customer. The man turned to me. "What are you drinking? Lager?"

I nodded.

"Why don't you grab that table over there."

I did what he said. I groped in my bag for my compact, but the light was too dim. All I remembered was his short smooth hair and his bright brown eyes, but I liked everything about him. I sat up straight, and pulled my shirt down tight into the waistband of my jeans. When he put our glasses down on the table his looked like orange juice. Then I recalled the advertisements and realised that it probably had vodka in it; I didn't need to worry about drinking alone.

He sat down. "I'm Paul." He stretched out his hand and I shook it. There was a gold ring on his little finger.

"My name's Kathleen."

"What do people call you? Kathy? Kate? Katie? Kat?"

"Just Kathleen."

He must have caught my accent, because he asked where I came from.

"I lived in Scotland when I was younger," I said, trying to make it sound a long time ago.

"Edinburgh?"

"No, Hawick. It's in the borders."

"Maybe I've passed through it on my way to Edinburgh."

"Maybe," I said doubtfully; I had never been to Edinburgh. I told him that I had worked in a knitting mill during the summers and asked if he had any jumpers with "Made in Hawick" on the labels. He promised to look. Then he asked what I did in London.

I told him about the bakery. "It's only temporary," I explained. "What I really want to be is a secretary, like my

Aunt Irene. She works for British Caledonian. What do you do?''

"I work in advertising. You know those ads in the tube for Burton raincoats. That's one of our accounts." He was making it sound like nothing, but I could tell he had a good job. "Will you buy another round?" He handed me a ten-pound note and headed off in the direction of the Gents.

I had forgotten to ask what his drink was called, but Neil seemed to know. I decided to have the same. It did taste like orange juice, but I began to notice that if I didn't pay attention I missed the ends of Paul's sentences. Although I was afraid he might disappear, I excused myself. In the toilet I let the cold water run over my hands until they felt numb. I washed my face and patted on more foundation. When I came back he said, "It's getting so noisy here. Would you like to go to my place for a cup of coffee?"

We walked out into the street. "I parked just round the corner," he said.

It had not occurred to me that we might drive. For a moment I wondered if I should say no. What would I do if he pounced on me? How would I get home? Paul stopped beside a white car. He opened the passenger door and began to throw things onto the back seat. "Sorry it's a bit of a tip."

"No, it's fine." I squeezed in beside a large box.

It was only a few minutes before we drew up at the curb. I got out and stood waiting. I was so excited that I had to keep my hands in my pockets. Paul unlocked the door using several keys and led the way inside. We went into the living-room. The walls and ceiling were white and there was a large red and blue rug in the middle of the bare floor. It was the first time since I came to London that I had been inside a house, and it was the nicest house I had ever seen.

He put on a record. "Do you know this?"

I shook my head.

"Scottish folk songs. I thought they'd make you feel at home. What would you like? Coffee? Tea? Wine?"

"Coffee, please. If it's not too much trouble."

"It's no trouble, but won't it keep you awake? I'm having wine."

"Oh, wine is fine. I'll have wine."

I followed him into the kitchen. The sink was full of unwashed dishes, and there were a couple of pieces of burnt toast by the toaster. Paul poured two glasses of red wine, and we sat down at the table. He talked about the house. It had been a shambles when he'd bought it five years ago. Gradually he was getting it the way he wanted it. "Houses are a lot of work," he said. I nodded. He took off his ring and tapped it against the wooden table. I was sure he was bored. Not knowing what else to say I asked where he came from.

"I was born in Northumberland, but we moved to Croydon when I was six."

"Do you remember Northumberland?"

"A bit. Only the highlights. I remember me and my friend Nick getting caught stealing apples. Another time we got into terrible trouble for tying my sister to a tree and leaving her there. I remember running into a car on my bike. That's how I got this." He gestured to one of his teeth, and I noticed that it was slightly chipped. "My mother says I was a terror. What about you? Were you a Beryl the Peril?"

"No, not really." I couldn't think of anything to say. I saw Paul glance towards the newspaper lying on the table. I looked at my glass and said maybe I ought to go home.

"Yes, it's late." He yawned. "Come on, I'll drive you."

"I didn't mean that. I can walk."

"I have to move the car anyway. It's at a meter."

I had no idea how to find Formosa Street, but Paul said he knew the way. He put on a tape and music filled the car. I wanted to go on and on driving through the dark streets, sitting side by side, listening to the music, watching the lights. Much too soon I recognised the local launderette. We pulled up outside the house. Reluctantly I fumbled with my seatbelt.

The engine was still running. Paul touched my hand. "I'll see you soon," he said.

I thanked him for the lift and got out. As soon as the door clicked shut, he pulled away. I stood watching until he turned the corner. Inside the house I switched on as many lights as possible. It was against the rules to take baths after eleven, but I decided to anyway. As I searched my purse for coins for the meter, I found a wodge of notes: Paul's change from the drinks. I was aghast. What would he think, that I was a thief? No, he would understand; anyone could make a mistake. I didn't even know where he lived, but tomorrow as soon as I finished work I would go to The Blind Beggar and leave the money with Neil. I put it in an envelope which I placed in my bag. Then I ran the largest bath I could afford and lay in the steamy room until the water grew cold.

In the morning on the way to work I thought about paint-ing my room. I had been meaning to ever since I moved in, and now the thought of Paul visiting me made me decide to do it at once. Donna and I were working next to each other. I wanted to tell her about Paul, to say "Paul says" "Paul and me," as she did all the time about Rob, but I didn't dare. In-stead I told her about my room.

"My room's blue, sort of like this," she said, pointing at her sweater. "It's my favourite colour." She handed a cus-tomer four rolls and a Vienna loaf, then turned back to me. "Rob's room is black."

"Black?" I said, wondering.

"Yes. Everything, the walls, the ceiling, even the floor has a black carpet. At night you feel like you're going to float away. When you look out of the window you can't tell where the wall stops and the sky begins."

But when we went to the ironmongers at lunch-time it turned out that white paint was much the cheapest. You could never get tired of white, Donna said, and I thought of Paul's living-room. The man said I would need two gallons. For a moment I hesitated. It cost much more than I expected and Donna didn't have any money. Then I thought I could borrow some of Paul's change. As we walked back to the bakery I realised that now I needed to go to the bank to

replace the money. I would have to wait till tomorrow before
going round to The Blind Beggar.

After work I walked home carrying a tin of paint in each
hand, the roller tray under my arm. A note had been slipped
under my door. For a moment I thought it might somehow
be from Paul, but it was a sternly anonymous message about
taking baths in the middle of the night; I was sure that Isobel
had written it. I threw it in the wastepaper basket.

I put my oldest night-dress on over my clothes. Then I
pulled the furniture away from the walls and began to apply
the paint. The roller slid up and down the walls. I made
clumsy letters P A U, then painted them over. I was just
starting on the second wall when there was a sudden noise. I
turned. In the dark two men were looking through the window. Their faces squashed white against the glass seemed
huge.

For a moment I couldn't move. Then one of the men
pointed, his mouth opened. I ran to the door of my room,
and out into the hall.

I stood in the hallway, my knees shaking. After a few
minutes I knocked on Isobel's door. There was no answer. I
didn't know any of the other people in the house. I sat down
on the floor, leaned my head against the wall, and tried to
think what to do. Would the men ever leave? What would I
do if they stayed all night? I shivered. I had no idea how
much time had passed when I got to my feet and cautiously
opened the door: no one was there. I hurried over and pulled
the dirty green curtains tight together. In the bathroom I
scrubbed my hands until the last speck of paint was gone.
When I got into bed I left the light on and my transistor radio
playing.

All the time, as I put purchases in bags and took money and
talked with customers, I thought about Paul. I imagined us
driving down Oxford Street, having dinner by candlelight,
going to a discothèque. I saw us dancing amidst flashing

lights and glittering people and then going home to his white
house. At lunch-time I went to the bank. In the afternoon I
took off my watch and hid it in my pocket. Eventually six
o'clock came.

When I arrived at The Blind Beggar, it was still almost
empty. Paul wasn't there. I was sure he had been there the
night before while I painted; he would not come again
tonight. I would have to give the money to Neil. If only I
knew his phone number, or had paid attention to where he
lived, or even asked what he meant by soon. Perhaps I would
never see him again. My stomach ached.

Neil was behind the bar. "Been painting, have you?" he
said.

"How did you know?"

He smiled and pointed at my hair.

"I thought I'd got rid of it all." I was on my way to the
Ladies, to see how bad it was, when I caught sight of Paul. He
was wearing a red sweater and black trousers. He waved and
hurried towards me. "I'm going to see the new Clint East-
wood film. Do you want to come?" It started very soon: we
would have to run.

I forgot about my hair and followed him. In the daylight I
could see that the backseat and floor of his car were covered
with books, papers, clothes, a couple of squash raquets, an
umbrella. While he drove, I twirled the knobs of the radio
and fragments of music rippled through the car.

"What have you been doing?" he asked.

"Nothing much. How about you?"

"Oh, work, work. I'm trying to think up something about
fish."

"Fish?"

"Yes, how eating fish will make you into a Martini sort of
person." We stopped at a red light. Paul pointed to a low
blue car standing next to us. "If I get a bonus at Christmas,
that's what I'd like to buy. I do so much driving, I deserve a
nice car."

We drew up beside a zebra crossing. Paul took out his
wallet. Suddenly I remembered the money, but before I
could speak he handed me a note and asked me to buy the
tickets while he parked the car. As I crossed the street I saw
that he had given me twenty pounds. I waited in the black
and white tiled lobby, watching the people stream past, and
thought what if he didn't come. A few minutes after the
doors closed, he ran in.

"Sorry. I couldn't find a space." He took my hand and
hurried me inside. We climbed over half a dozen people and
sat down in the middle of a row. Already in the film several
shots had been fired. I kept sneaking glances at Paul, wondering if he would take my hand, but he sat with his elbows
on his knees, gazing at the screen.

After the film we went to a restaurant. A small, fat man
who was standing in the doorway led us to our table and
placed two menus before us. "Taverna — Greek
Restaurant" I read at the top of the page. I did not recognise
a single dish.

"What are you going to have?" I asked Paul.

"Moussaka, I think."

"What's that?"

He described it.

"Oh, sort of like shepherd's pie," I said, and he laughed.
The waiter took our order and brought our food almost
immediately. The wine was pale yellow; it had a bitter taste
which made me shudder. Paul asked if I'd ever been abroad.
I shook my head; I couldn't tell him that I thought of London
as abroad.

"Lucky you. You have a treat in store." He had been to
Greece last summer. "We flew to Athens and rented a car,"
he said. "Then we drove to Delphi." He did not say who
"we" was.

He poured himself more wine. "Wasn't that a great
film?" he said. I nodded.

After dinner we walked to the car. "Where are we?" I
asked.

"Hampstead," said Paul. "It's one of the poshest parts of London." He drove in silence down the long hill. I looked at him, wondering what to say, wondering what he was thinking. We stopped, and suddenly I saw we were outside his house. I had assumed that he was driving me home. He turned off the engine and put his hand over mine. "Would you like to come in for a while?" he said.

While he fussed with the lights, I looked at his collection of records. I was studying a picture of a man in a large white suit, when he came up behind me and put his hands on my shoulders. I turned and pressed myself against him.

Presently we climbed the stairs to his bedroom. Paul pulled me onto his large brass bed. Under the covers he took off my clothes, and his own. "You're lovely, Kathleen. You're so sweet," he said. He kissed my fingers, my ears, my face. I was amazed at the smoothness of his body; it seemed more feminine than my own, and I ran my hands up and down his back with delight.

After we made love, he fell asleep. I lay quietly, trying not to disturb him. Next to the bed there was a window. The curtains were open, and the lights and houses stretched out into the distance. I thought about how to arrange things in the morning. If I got up at seven I could easily be at the bakery by eight. No one would care if I wore the same clothes two days in a row. As quietly as I could, I took off my watch and put it on the floor.

"What time is it?" Paul asked, opening his eyes. "Oh, God, and I have to go to Colchester tomorrow. Come on, I'll drive you home."

As we turned into Formosa Street he suggested we meet at The Blind Beggar the following Tuesday. I looked at the house; every window was dark. I said that was fine. He kissed me on the cheek and I got out. Just as I was closing the door, I remembered his change. I bent down and leaned back in.

"Did you forget something?"

"Yes. I feel like an idiot. I kept your change. Both times, at The Blind Beggar and at the cinema. I'm awfully sorry." I

began to search through my bag. In the dark I could not find
the envelope.

"Forget it. Buy me a drink sometime," he said, reaching
across to shut the door. The noise of the accelerating car
echoed down the dark street. Perhaps it had woken Isobel. I
put the money on the mantelpiece next to the chestnuts and
the begonia. It made me feel sure that I would see him again.

Next day at work I told Donna about Paul. I said a friend
had introduced us. She asked what he did, and I could see she
was impressed by the raincoats and the fish. At lunch-time
we went to Boots and she helped me choose some make-up.
Remembering the women who had been with Paul the first
time I saw him, I bought grey eye-shadow instead of the purple Donna suggested.

"What are you and Paul doing this weekend?" she asked
as we walked back to the shop.

"I don't know. Nothing special." I shifted my bag to my
other hand and asked about her plans with Rob. They were
going to visit his aunt in Greenwich; she'd broken her wrist
and needed someone to do her shopping and to clean up. "I
must be a real mug," said Donna. "Imagine spending your
day off hoovering."

I stood waiting on the pavement while the manageress set the
alarms and locked up the shop.

"Goodness it's turned cold," she said, as she buttoned her
coat. "I don't know what I'd do without you, Kathleen. All
the other girls complain about working Saturdays."

"I really need to," I said awkwardly.

"Yes," she nodded, "everything's so dear nowadays. Well,
have a good rest tomorrow. See you on Monday."

I watched her walk away in the direction of the bus-stop. I
did not know what to do with myself. Since meeting Paul I
felt shy about going to The Blind Beggar. People were lining
up outside the local cinema and for a moment I was tempted,
but after the paint, I could not afford it. I turned in the
direction of Formosa Street, walking slowly past the familiar

shops. In the window of the travel agents there was a photograph of a man and a woman jumping hand in hand into bright blue water. I thought of Paul's stories of Greece and imagined being somewhere warm with him, somewhere where one hardly needed clothes.

There was nothing of interest in the windows of the post office, or the fishmongers, or the butchers. In the launderette an elderly man was standing at the window smoking a cigarette, and a couple of boys sat on top of the washing machines talking. Suddenly I remembered that I had two carrier bags full of dirty clothes. If I was with Paul I wouldn't have time to do my washing during the week. I looked at my watch and hurried towards home.

On Sunday I finished painting my room. I pushed all the furniture back into place, and decided to ask Isobel to take a look. I needed someone to admire my work.

"Do you want to come and see my room?" I said. "I've just finished painting it."

"So that's what the smell was," she said. She was wearing her dressing-gown.

"It'll only take a minute." I stepped back out into the hall.

"Well, let's see what you did with the dump."

In spite of herself, she seemed impressed. "What a difference. It always used to look so dirty. Now if you just got yourself some decent furniture."

I was so pleased by her praise that I offered her some malt bread. She took half a loaf back to her room.

In the coffee bar next to the post office I wrote to Penny. She had written that she was thinking of getting engaged; now I had something to tell her in return. I described Paul, his car, the film, the restaurant, how much the meal had cost. I had found an advertisement for Burton raincoats in a magazine and I enclosed it. The model was blond but he did look a little like Paul. The letter was the longest I had written since coming to London; by the time I sealed the envelope it was dark outside.

I went straight back to my room. For dinner I had several

fig newtons and a garibaldi square. I spent the rest of the evening sorting through my clothes. Even my best Hawick clothes seemed old-fashioned. As I stood looking at my reflection in the cloudy mirror it occurred to me that perhaps I could use Paul's money towards buying a pair of jeans to wear next time I saw him. It would just be a loan, for a week, until I was paid.

On Tuesday after work I went home to change. First I put on the satin blouse that Penny had given me when I left Hawick, then I thought I would feel foolish wearing it to the bakery next day. I changed into a shirt and my new jeans and put my toothbrush in my handbag.

Paul was standing at the bar chatting to Neil. When I came over he kissed me on the cheek. "I'm hungry," he said. "Let's go and eat."

We went to the Indian restaurant round the corner. I asked Paul what he'd been doing and he said he'd played squash and gone to a farewell party for someone at work. "We ended up going out for breakfast at four in the morning. I haven't done that in years, not since I was your age. I slept all day on Sunday. How about you?"

"Oh," I said, moving my fork through my rice, "I went out with Isobel. We went to visit her sister."

"That sounds nice." He signalled the waiter for another beer.

After dinner we went back to his house. He asked if I wanted anything, and when I said no, he took my hand and led the way upstairs. The bedroom was cold. "I'd better turn on the electric blanket," he said.

In bed it was soon warm. We made love.

I lay on my side watching Paul. He was faintly sun-tanned, and against the white pillowcase his face looked tawny. I wanted to touch him but was afraid he would wake. Then his eyelids moved. "Shall I switch out the light?" I asked.

"Sorry. I didn't realise how knackered I was. Let me call a taxi while I'm still conscious."

"I could walk to work in the morning."

"It's really easy to get a taxi." He was already reaching for the phone. I got out of bed and began to dress. I felt I had done something wrong, but I wasn't sure what. He hung up and reached for his wallet, which was lying on the bedside table; he handed me ten pounds. I protested that it was too much, but he said he had no change. Before I could argue, there came the noise of a car horn hooting.

"You'd better run. They don't wait. Will you come over on Friday?"

I said yes, kissed him and hurried downstairs.

I paid attention as the taxi drove along so that I would be able to find the house on Friday. On Friday Paul wouldn't be fretting about work. Tomorrow I would tell the manageress that I could not work this weekend.

Paul was wearing an apron when he opened the door. "I thought we could eat here," he said. He was making omelettes, and asked me to make the toast. "It sticks. You have to watch it like a hawk." As I stood with one hand on the knob, gazing into the glowing toaster, I thought that maybe tomorrow I could offer to make my speciality, toad-in-the-hole. I watched Paul ease the spatula round the omelette and divide it onto our plates. Just in time, I caught the toast.

We watched television while we ate; it was a replay of a football game. Paul commented between mouthfuls. When we had finished I carried the plates to the kitchen.

"Can you make us a cup of coffee, Kathleen?" he called after me. I put the kettle on, and while I waited for it to boil I washed our plates and the other dishes in the sink. When I carried our mugs back into the living-room the game was over.

"What a great game," said Paul. "Thanks for clearing up." He switched off the television, and took both mugs.

Upstairs he put his arms around me. "So what do you think, Kathleen?" he whispered. I buried my face against his neck. I wanted to say that I loved him, but I did not dare.

Later, as we lay quietly, I took a sip of the cold coffee and asked if he had any plans for the weekend.

"I'm going over to Pete and Sandy's. They just moved into a flat in Chiswick." He told me they were friends from work. Pete's parents had a cottage in Norfolk, and in the summer they often invited Paul to go sailing. "What are you doing?" he asked.

"I don't know. I thought maybe we could do something together."

"That would be nice," he said, "but I seem to have plans every minute."

I couldn't stop myself from blurting out that I had arranged not to work on Saturday.

"I'm sorry. Pete and Sandy asked me weeks ago. I tend to be busy at weekends."

He put on his dressing-gown and left the room. I heard him go downstairs. I burrowed down under the covers. I felt like an idiot for not asking him sooner; of course by Friday night he would have plans. But at least he would not be going to Chiswick at the crack of dawn. Suddenly I heard the muffled sound of his voice, from the hall below. A moment later he came back into the room, carrying his wallet.

"The taxi will be here in five minutes." He sat down on the edge of the bed. "Here," he held out some notes. "I want you to do something nice this weekend." He suggested we go to a film on Monday.

I wanted to ask why I couldn't stay, but I was afraid that if I tried to speak I would start to cry. Why did he think I had to go home? Didn't he realise that no one would care if I stayed out all night, every night?

Next morning I woke at seven. In the darkness I lay wondering whether to get up and go to the bakery. I thought of the bright neon lights, the smell of the bread, the manageress's stories about her dog. Then I thought how stupid I would feel if they didn't need me. Eventually I fell back to sleep, and when I woke again it was nine-thirty. As I dressed I decided to go shopping. There was only four pounds in my purse, but I had Paul's money.

I took the tube to Oxford Street and wandered through a maze of shops, looking at sale racks, trying on anything that took my fancy. At four o'clock I emerged with a shirt, a jumper and a belt. I felt a little guilty about my extravagance, but I reminded myself that they were presents from Paul.

As I walked along Formosa Street I found myself hoping that Isobel would be home. I wanted to show her what I'd bought, even though she was sure to point out something wrong. But when I knocked on her door there was no answer.

It was five o'clock. I sat on the edge of my bed. The rest of the day hung over me like a sword. On the bedside table my clock hummed; I watched the second hand go round and round. In my room it was the only sign of life. I stopped breathing for as long as I could: forty seconds. Then I took a deep breath and tried again: fifty seconds. Again, forty-five seconds. I got up and walked around and managed just over fifty. Whatever I did, I could not get up to a full minute.

It was the longest weekend of my life. Before Paul I had found a way to manage my time, to get through it somehow, but now, knowing him, knowing he was out there without me, I was lonelier than ever. On Monday, for the first time, I was late for work, and twice I gave customers the wrong change.

"Wake up, Kathleen," said the manageress.

Donna offered to take my place at the counter, and I spent the rest of the morning working in the back of the shop. At lunch-time, as soon as we were out in the street, she asked what was wrong. I told her about Paul always being busy at weekends.

She tried to cheer me up. "Rob and I are engaged and I only see him two or three times a week, if I'm lucky. That's

the trouble with professional men." We walked past Woolworths. "Do you mind going to the ironmongers. It's Mum's
birthday and I want to get her a kettle."

She chose a bright blue kettle with a whistle. It reminded
me of Paul's. On our way back to the bakery, she mentioned
that Rob's favourite group were playing on Friday. She and
Rob were going to hear them and had two extra tickets.
Would Paul and I be interested in going? I said I would ask
him when I saw him.

Donna talked about the concert all afternoon; she and Rob
had even bought new clothes for it. I had never been to a
concert; it sounded wonderful. But that night as I walked to
The Blind Beggar to meet Paul I imagined myself asking him
and already I could hear him saying that he was busy.

We went to a film in Leicester Square, and ate at a Bernies
Inn. Paul suggested we meet on Thursday, and there seemed
no point in even mentioning the concert. Next morning I
told Donna that we would not be able to go.

"Are you sure?" she asked. "It's going to be really good."

"Paul's busy," I explained, thinking that this would be the
end of the matter. But Donna asked what I was doing, and
when she discovered I was free, she insisted I come alone.

On Friday the manageress let us go fifteen minutes early.
We changed in the toilet and Donna sprayed my hair and
made it stand on end. I felt foolish but she said I would fit in
perfectly at the concert. It was true; the girl next to me was
wearing a jacket covered in hundreds of safety pins, and her
boyfriend had a plastic fish skeleton dangling from his ear. I
felt as if my eyes were jammed open, and the music was so
loud my seat shook. Afterwards Donna and Rob and I had to
shout to hear each other. We went back to Rob's and sat in
the black room, listening to records. Donna was right, it was
like floating.

On Monday I met Paul at The Blind Beggar. "I just ordered a
pizza," he said. "I'm too tired to go out on the town."

"Oh," I said. I was wearing my new shirt and the earrings I had bought to wear to the concert; I had hoped we would go somewhere exciting.

We ate the pizza in front of the television because there was a programme about advertising which Paul said he ought to watch. While they were showing pictures of different kinds of ice-cream, I told him about the concert.

"I had no idea you were going. Why didn't you tell me?"

"You said you were busy."

"Yes, but I might have been able to change my plans. It sounds great."

"If you were free, why didn't you get in touch with me?"

"I didn't say I was free. I said I might have been able to change my plans." He poured himself another glass of wine. "Can you remember what songs they played?"

I put down the slice of pizza I had been eating, and placed my plate on the floor. "It was too noisy to hear anything," I said.

When the programme was over, Paul made coffee and suggested we go upstairs. In the bedroom I sat on the edge of the bed. He began to undress, then came over and undid my blouse. We got into bed.

Before he could kiss me, I said, "Why don't you ever see me at weekends, Paul?"

"I'm always busy. It's the only time I have to see my friends."

"But couldn't you see me too?"

"Kathleen, I can't just abandon all my old friends because of you." He seemed irritated.

"That isn't what I meant." I sat up, struggling to explain. "I mean, why don't I ever meet your friends? I'm your girlfriend but the only person we ever see is Neil."

Paul reached up and kissed me. He pulled me down beside him and rolled on top of me. I felt as if all the air was being forced out of my lungs. I closed my eyes.

Afterwards I slid out of bed and carried my clothes to the

toilet. In the mirror, my cheeks were bright red. I got my toothbrush out of my bag and began to brush my teeth, back and forth, up and down. It was the first time I had used it at Paul's.

When I came back, fully dressed, he was still lying there. I stood in the doorway. "Are you leaving?" he said, his eyes closed.

"Yes."

"You're very sweet."

"Aren't you going to call a taxi?"

"Of course," he said, opening his eyes and reaching for the phone. "I didn't realise you were in such a hurry." He gave the address and hung up. "How about Thursday?"

I said I didn't know.

For a moment he looked surprised. "Well, how about Friday then?"

"I don't know. I'll let you know." I came to the edge of the bed and said quickly, "Aren't you going to pay me?"

"For the taxi. Yes, of course."

I looked at the money in his hand. "Oh, come off it. Fifteen pounds for a five-minute trip. You're not just paying for the taxi."

He was sitting up in bed, the money in one hand, his wallet in the other. "What's ten pounds between friends?"

"Nothing. If we were friends." I stood, looking at him. I was so close that I could see the pores in his skin. Nothing in his expression changed. In the mirror on the far wall, I saw myself standing next to a man lying naked in bed. He had paid for the clothes I was wearing.

"How about a little extra? Because I'm so sweet?" My voice sounded hollow, the way it did when I spoke aloud in my bare white room. I waited for Paul to tell me not to be stupid, to shake me. From the street below came the sound of a car horn.

He shrugged his shoulders, and picked up the cheque-book from the bedside table. "I've no more cash but I can give you a cheque. How do you spell your name?"

I stammered out the letters. I would have given anything to stop. Paul scribbled for a moment. Then, ignoring my hand, he leaned forward and tucked the cheque into the pocket of my jeans. The doorbell chimed.

"I loved you."

"I know," Paul said. He smiled.

I swung my hand as hard as I could against his cheek. Without looking back, I ran downstairs. In the hall I paused for a moment, took the cheque out of my pocket and dropped it on the table by the phone.

The taxi driver was standing on the step. He was West Indian and wore an enormous, coloured beret. "Where to?" he asked, looking over my shoulder.

Half turning, I realised that Paul had followed me in his dressing-gown. "As far as you can take me for fifteen pounds," I said, and strode down the steps.

The driver opened the door for me, then climbed in. He turned and smiled. "You must be going somewhere."

"Formosa Street," I told him. "But take me the long way round."

"What's the long way round?"

"You decide. I just want my money's worth."

"Anything you say, sister."

The taxi glided down the street. In the darkness I sank down in the corner, and put my feet up on the folding seat in front of me. I gazed out of the window. The pubs must have just closed, for the pavements along Oxford Street were filled with people. I noticed too that the shops were already decorated with lights. In Trafalgar Square there was a Christmas tree.

Learning by Heart

Learning by Heart

The summer Janey was born Robert Cumming let the house at Lackghie to the Spencers. The winter had been the worst in twenty years; the cattle were still gaunt in May, and the barns were so bare, Robert joked, that even the rats were leaving. When he saw the advertisement in the local paper, he jumped at the chance of getting some money out of the rich English. He wrote the Spencers a letter, offering Lackghie at a steep price, and they wrote back immediately, accepting his terms.

The day before they were due to arrive, the village cricket team was playing and Robert set off down the hill to watch. He was halfway across the field of cows when he saw Elsie toiling up the hill followed by their daughter, Netta. They were coming home from church. He watched as Elsie raised the skirts of her blue dress and clambered over the stile, then reached down to help the child. Elsie was eight months gone, plump as a pigeon and flushed from the climb.

She caught sight of him and waved her hand. "Look, Netta," she said, "there's your father." Even though she didn't think it was quite proper, she had squeezed in a prayer about Robert before the Our Father, and here he was, come to meet them. Perhaps they could have their dinner together.

As Robert waited the cows clustered around him. "Els," he said, when she was drawing close, "I've rented the house. We'll be staying in the bothy." He pushed away the most inquisitive of the cows. "Make sure the place is clean. They're paying a bonny price. Get the bairn to pick some flowers."

"What do you mean?"

"I've rented the house for the summer," he repeated. "The Spencers are coming tomorrow on the four o'clock train. Be sure to have their tea ready." Before she could reply he strode off down the hill.

Elsie stood very still, staring after him, then grabbed Netta's hand.

"What's happening?" the little girl asked. "Mama, what's happening?"

Elsie pulled herself together with an effort and looked down at her daughter. "Some people are coming to live in our house for the summer," she said. "And you and Daddy and I are going to live in the bothy."

After a hasty dinner, Elsie set to work. Although the house was already spotless she went from room to room, sweeping, scrubbing and dusting. She carried out the rugs and set Netta to beating them. By the time she'd finished, the place looked so nice that she ached to think of strangers living there.

Next day Netta picked big bunches of stock, sweet-william and cornflowers while Elsie made the beds with clean sheets. Then Syd, the farm-hand, brought the cart to the back door. He had put fresh straw in the bottom, and he loaded the few bits and pieces of furniture just as Elsie told him. When everything was ready he set Netta in one corner of the cart and began to lead the horse up the hill. Elsie walked behind.

The bothy was half a mile from the house. It was just one room, low, dark and dirty, with thick walls and a tin roof. The last person to live there had been the shepherd who had worked for Robert's father. Elsie set to cleaning it. Syd carried pail after pail of water up the hill until Robert told him to get on with the sheep.

As she worked, Elsie tried to smother the fear in her heart. It was eight years since Netta, but she'd not forgotten, and twice since then things had gone astray. To have a child in this desolate place seemed an invitation to bad luck.

Mid-afternoon Robert strolled in the door, all kitted out in a clean shirt and Sunday suit. He was off to the station to meet them. His face was stern; Elsie knew it must hurt him to rent the house he'd been born in to strangers. She went to put more peat on the fire. In spite of herself she waited for a word of praise, of acknowledgement for all she'd done, for the curtains in the windows, the neat row of beds, the freshly scrubbed table with three chairs, the kettle on the hearth. But he only looked at her critically and said "Tidy yourself. It's time to make their tea."

Robert had leased not only his house but his wife to the Spencers. She was to be their maid, taking orders in her own kitchen and serving people at her own table. "But what about the baby?" she asked. "It's not long."

"Syd's wife can take care of things for a few days. You'll tell her what to do."

Somehow his calculations made things worse. Sometimes she thought he was blind, didn't see or remember what was coming their way, but no, he did; it just made no difference. She found a clean blouse and went down the hill.

But it was not as she had imagined. Mrs Spencer was pleasant and unassuming. After tea she came into the kitchen and praised every aspect of the meal. She had no children of her own and on that first afternoon took an immediate liking to Netta, whom she found playing hopscotch in the yard. Mr Spencer was equally agreeable, a keen, hearty man. Mr Bell, Mrs Spencer's brother, was also very pleasant, but his health was poor. It was for his sake that they had rented Lackghie. They hoped that the Scottish air would do him good.

June the twenty-seventh was the hottest day of the summer. The gnats hung in swarms over the flower beds. Netta
went down to the river with Mr Bell. Elsie sat in the garden
under the beech tree, shelling peas and talking to Mrs
Spencer, who was knitting a shawl for the baby. Dark clouds
ringed the valley.

The Spencers had a cold supper. The rain started just as
Elsie cleared the table, and a few minutes later she felt very
odd. As she made the tea, she recognised the oddness as pain.
Mrs Spencer saw her face when she brought in the pot and,
before Elsie could say anything, turned to her husband and
said quietly, "Bill, would you mind fetching the doctor?"

He was on his feet in a moment, patting Elsie on the
shoulder and telling her not to fret, he would be back in two
shakes of a lamb's tail. Mrs Spencer helped her upstairs to
the spare room. Elsie protested. "I have to get home,
Ma'am. Once the pains start, I'll not be able to move."

"Hush, hush. What's wrong with this house that you don't
want your baby to be born here?"

"You don't know what it's like: the noise, the mess. You'll
get no sleep."

"I was with my sister when her children were born. I'm
not entirely useless." As she spoke, Mrs Spencer was untying
Elsie's apron and unbuttoning her blouse. Before she knew
it, Elsie was in bed.

She'd never been in the spare room before, except to clean
it, and now she looked around with pleasure. Mrs Spencer
pushed open the window and the curtains stirred gently,
promising coolness. Lightning came, briefer than the flashes
of pain. "Will you be all right alone for a moment?" asked
Mrs Spencer. "I'm going to take Netta over to Syd's. It'll be
better for her."

She left the room and Elsie lay watching the dark sky.

The crops were high in the fields, and in the Drumtochty
everyone was listening anxiously, with half an ear, to the
rain. Robert was playing dominoes when he heard his name
called. "Aye," he said, getting to his feet, fearing the worst,

that the byre had caught fire, or his cattle had been struck by lightning. But when he reached the door, he saw it was Ogilvie, the doctor.

"Mr Cumming," he said, "I just got a message about your wife. I'm off up to Lackghie to give her a hand."

Robert nodded and offered him a dram. Ogilvie refused sharply and hurried away.

Within a few minutes everyone in the Drumtochty knew the reason for the doctor's visit, and one after another, in anticipation of good news, they came and placed shots of whisky on Robert's table.

"Here's to your son," they said, raising their glasses.

Robert nodded and drank everything that was placed before him. "I'll call him Seamus, after my father," he announced. He was among the last to leave.

Next morning his head felt heavy. He had forgotten to bank up the fire, that was Elsie's job, but he blew up the embers and made himself a cup of tea. He drank it sitting on the doorstep of the bothy. The sky was clear and the air was fresh. From this vantage point he could see all the way down the valley, to the easternmost edge of his land and beyond that to the village church. The pale golden fields promised a good harvest. He threw the dregs of his tea onto a foxglove and stood up. He couldn't take the time to shave, but he dunked his head in a cattle trough and slicked back his hair before he went to ask for news.

The kitchen door was standing open. Mrs Spencer greeted him. She was wearing a brown dress, like a maid's; her sleeves were rolled up and her cheeks were flushed. "Elsie just woke," she said, leading him up the stairs. She tapped on the door and then went tactfully away.

Elsie was sitting up in bed, the baby suckling at her breast. He walked over to the bed and stood looking down. She smiled up at him. "I thought we could call her after your mother, Jane Elizabeth Cumming. Would you like that, Robert?"

* * *

Jane Elizabeth Cumming was born in 1904. She was married
to my father for twenty-seven years; he was dead for nine of
them. She died in 1984.

For me it was as if she died within a few hours, although
she was actually in hospital for eleven days; the course of her
illness was accelerated and compressed by the enormous distance between us, a distance not only geographical but emo-
tional. Since I had taken a job in Canada I saw her for only
an hour or two each year.

On the morning of July the sixteenth a letter came. A
friend wrote that my mother had broken her hip but there
was nothing to be concerned about, she was doing fine. It
was such a cheerful, reassuring letter that I took it to heart
and did not worry. Instead I was angry because I foresaw that
such an accident would inevitably bring changes in her life,
changes in which I would have to play some part. I went to
work as usual and planned to buy a get-well card on my way
home. Just after lunch I was called to the telephone. Without
any feeling, a voice read a telegram: "Mother seriously ill.
Little hope." The anger, which had a moment before filled
my head, vanished. I thought only of getting to her side. I
booked a flight, then phoned the hospital to say that I was
coming. The line was dim with three thousand miles of
static; I shouted into the receiver. Suddenly, as I was in the
middle of explaining for the second time who I was, the
roaring abated, and in the moment of calm that followed I
heard the nurse say, "I'm so sorry about your stepmother,
but really it was all for the best." Perhaps at the very moment when I was planning to come and see her, her heart
had stopped beating. Or perhaps it was a little earlier, when I
was angry.

My stepmother was almost always, during our life
together, referred to as my mother; to hear her given her
precise title was to receive additional confirmation of her
death.

Gradually over the months that followed I learned the

longer version of events. She had fallen while getting ready for bed. One of those idiotic falls when the legs suddenly give way or a small crease in the carpet is magnified into a huge obstacle. She did not lose consciousness. The television was on in the flat below, and she began to bang on the floor thinking that the neighbours would hear her. Eventually she crawled onto her bed. She was not found until two o'clock the following afternoon. She had lain there for sixteen hours.

In the hospital, they operated immediately. A few days later she was well enough to send me a birthday card. It had a picture of daisies on the front. Inside was a rhymed message: "Hope that this birthday/ is like all the rest/ with one big exception/ let's hope it's your best." On the left side of the card a nurse wrote that my stepmother was making good progress and that she had had a great number of gentlemen visitors. On the other side, above and below the rhyme, the writing is hers. There is my name in frail untidy letters and at the bottom she has signed it, "with love, M." The "M" stands for Mummy. For years she signed all her letters to me with that single initial, as if admitting the attenuated nature of our relationship. She enclosed a cheque for ten pounds. The card was incorrectly addressed, and arrived a week after she died.

The day after she sent the card, she developed an infection and was transferred to another hospital where she could more easily be kept in isolation. One week had passed since she had fallen. It was Friday the thirteenth of July.

On Saturday she was quite bright but not so well.

On Sunday she recognised people and could even answer questions, but her speech was thick. After some deliberation the telegram was sent. She died the following day.

A week later the funeral was held. The solitude and pride of my stepmother's life, with and without my father, led directly to that scantily attended ceremony. Fewer than a dozen people were present, and the minister, who had not

been acquainted with her, mouthed platitudes, speaking of
"our dearly beloved sister" and referring to the congrega-
tion as "those that mourn." It was an unusually hot day, and
whenever the minister fell silent, the buzzing of the bees
hovering around the wreaths of flowers was clearly audible. I
know all this only at second hand; I told myself that I could
not afford to fly from Toronto to Glasgow for her last rites,
when I would certainly have to go later to sort out her estate.
Now I wish that I had gone anyway. Perhaps if I had I would
not find myself still sitting down, twice a month, to write to
her.

There was no one present at the funeral who knew the
span of my stepmother's life, which began in a croft in the
north-east of Scotland and ended in a small flat in an ugly
market town a hundred miles to the south. The croft was
called Lackghie; it had been in the Cumming family for five
generations. When her father died it passed not to the older
son, Seamus, who had emigrated to Canada, but to the
youngest of the four children, Ian. In 1946 Ian gave up the
lease, and it was not until after my stepmother's death that I
heard the name: La-guy.

That my stepmother never mentioned Lackghie was not
surprising, for in the years I knew her she scarcely ever
talked about the past. The five decades which had preceded
her marriage were condensed into a few amusing episodes.
As she grew older, she also ceased to refer to the future,
which could only bring frailty and death. And I, when I talk
about her, can no longer use the future tense, nor the present; even the past tense seems presumptuous. I look back
through the years and a cloud of uncertainty forms, as if I
had pressed my face against a mirror.

My memories of my stepmother begin when I was four
years old. My father taught at a boys' boarding school which
was situated ten miles from the nearest town. Every morning, on his way to teach Maths and Geography, he dropped
me off at the house of Mrs Green to learn reading and writ-

ing. Mrs Green was a kindly woman with, from my point of view, one incomparable virtue: whenever she asked me a question, she unknowingly mouthed the answer. She lived next door to the school infirmary, and when lessons were over I often visited there. The year before I was born, Jane Cumming had taken the job of school nurse. I called her Aunt Janey; at this time I called almost all adults aunt and uncle as if the world was peopled by my relatives. She would give me biscuits and orange squash and, as a treat, allow me to flush the toilet. The cistern was high up on the wall and when I pulled the wooden handle the water rushed down with a loud, satisfying sound.

Like some oriental pasha, I accepted the universal kindness of adults as no more than my due. It did not occur to me that Aunt Janey was different from the many others who had taken an interest in me since my mother died. I remember in precise detail the day, shortly after my fifth birthday, when I was apprised of this difference. It was raining and I was playing house behind the kitchen door when the neighbour who was looking after me let slip the reason for my father's absence. He and Aunt Janey had gone off to get married. I was aggrieved that they had not asked me to be a bridesmaid. But when they came home from their honeymoon with a doll in a tartan dress I forgave them; I was delighted to have a mother again.

Almost thirty years later, I found among my stepmother's papers the letters she had received congratulating her on her forthcoming marriage. "You don't say what your new husband's like," one writer complained. "Is he tall or short? Serious or gay?" Not one of her correspondents referred to a stepdaughter. Perhaps she did not consider this aspect of the marriage worth mentioning.

Sometimes I used to imagine that my father had remarried in order to provide me with a mother, but I do not think I entered into his calculations any more than hers. I place the photographs of his two weddings side by side. The first was

taken outside a church. My father is almost fifty but the
bride is young, twenty years younger than he. She wears a
white, calf-length dress with a black bow at the neck and a
black hat. She is smiling out at their friends. My father, who
is holding her arm, teeters on the edge of the church step.
The second photograph was taken a few years later outside a
registry office. This time the bride and the groom are the
same age. She is wearing a suit. Her hat has a veil and beneath it her painted lips are clearly visible. She is paying not
the least attention to the crowd of well-wishers but is looking
up from beneath her veil at her husband; this gesture, the
first of her marriage, already suggests her proprietary attitude to my father, a sense of ownership so fierce that gradually it would exclude everyone else. These brides could
scarcely be more different, but the man in the two pictures is
identical. The joy in his face is so obvious and foolish that one
does not notice his baggy and ill-fitting suit. He is smiling not
for the camera, but for the woman.

My stepmother was fifty-three and this was the first time
in her life that she had had a home of her own. She kept
house with relish, complaining frequently about how much
she had to do. A cleaning woman was employed to come
once a week. I remember the smell of the bright orange wax
with which she had to polish the parquet floor until it was, as
my stepmother said, "clean enough to eat off," although I
was the only person who showed any inclination to do so.

Because the nearest shops were ten miles away, much of
our grocery shopping was done in the travelling vans which
came around the valley twice a week. There was Fitzgerald,
the butcher; Halley, the greengrocer; and on Fridays,
MacPherson, the fishmonger. I had no interest in Fitzgerald
or MacPherson, but Halley's van was an Aladdin's cave, full
of sweet smells and desirable treasures and best of all Halley
himself, a plump, rosy-cheeked, white-haired man who
looked like a cherub in brown overalls. When my stepmother
climbed in to do business, I would sneak in behind her. How

she enjoyed patronising these men, and how lucky she thought they were to have her custom. Their visits, like the cleaning woman, confirmed her new status.

It was not only her inferiors who provided this confirmation. The wives of other masters at the boys' school remarked frequently on how wonderful she was to rescue my father from domestic shipwreck and to bring up another woman's child.

My stepmother approached the task of bringing me up, like that of keeping house, with considerable vigour. Shortly after the wedding, she arranged for the removal of my tonsils. I have no idea if the operation was necessary, but it was at the time in vogue, and it gave her an opportunity to flaunt her area of expertise. For my part I was proud of the whole experience, of getting to stay in hospital for three days and to eat ice-cream, and I adored the enormous doll she and my father gave me.

During my recovery I was allowed to stay in bed and play with her mah-jong set. The set was kept in a small black suitcase. If the lid was lifted, the front of the case also opened so that one could see the coloured bricks and apparatus of the game arranged in four trays lined with green silk, layered one on top of another. The bricks were the colour of ivory and marked with curious red and green signs and symbols. I used them to build fortresses and roadways over my crumpled counterpane. I had no conception of how to play the game, but I loved the bricks, the suitcase and the name. They reinforced the sense I had that my stepmother was exotic. I never saw her play, but that may have been because she lacked companions.

Soon after the tonsillectomy I had my first and only birthday party. It was a sunny day, all the windows stood open, and a tribe of small girls ran in and out of the house. There was a pink-and-white cake and we were allowed to eat in the dining-room. What I remember best, however, is not the guests or the food but my father. As I was in the middle of

organising everyone to play a game of hide-and-seek, he
squatted down beside me and said, "Isn't this a lovely party?
Have you thanked Mummy for it?" I ran to the kitchen and
threw my arms around my stepmother's legs. "Thank you
for the lovely party, Mummy," I said, and ran back to continue playing.

Later, he sat next to me at tea. There was a pause after the
egg salad sandwiches, and my stepmother appeared in the
doorway bearing the cake topped with lighted candles. Amid
the chorus of oohs and ahs my father spoke. "What a splendid cake. Aren't you a lucky little girl?" I nodded and blew
out the candles. My parents' present to me was a children's
encyclopedia.

That summer the eaves of our house buzzed with wasps'
nests and the window-sills were lined with jam jars full of
beer; the sweet smell was meant to entice the wasps to their
death. The beer was made by my stepmother. She brewed it
in an old sink, and when it was ready I helped her with the
bottling. I would hold the end of the orange rubber tube
carefully in the neck of each bottle and tell her when it was
full. Once, when we had almost finished bottling a batch, we
discovered a drowned mouse at the bottom of the sink. She
fished it out by the tail and carried the dripping body over to
the dustbin. As she washed her hands she said, "Don't tell
anyone about the mouse. People are silly about these things.
We have to keep it a secret."

I nodded; I understood about secrets.

Years later I would hear her describe these events over and
over again, always with a chuckle. "Everyone said it was the
best beer I'd ever made," she would say.

*   *   *

It was Janey's job to help Netta gather the eggs. She followed
round behind her, carrying the white bowl with straw in the
bottom, and admiring the way Netta plunged her hand
under even the fiercest of broody hens and pulled out the

warm eggs. Janey was afraid of the hens, with their bright eyes and sharp beaks; she picked up only the eggs that lay abandoned. Coming round the end of the cart, she saw the two bantam roosters sparring; she stopped to watch them puffing up their chests, arching their necks.

"Janock," Netta called. "I need the bowl."

Janey turned and started running across the muddy yard. In a moment she tripped and fell. She began to cry. Netta ran over, an egg in each hand. She set them carefully on the ground.

"What am I always telling you, stupid? Never run with the eggs." She picked Janey up, and set her on her feet. There was so much mud that it was hard to tell if she was hurt. Netta carried her over to the water trough and washed her face, hands and knees. "Wheesht, wheesht, you're fine. Stop crying," she kept saying, as she patted her sister dry with the edge of her skirt. Only one knee was slightly grazed.

Janey had kept tight hold of the thick china bowl and it had survived her fall unharmed, but all the eggs were smashed. When she saw this, she burst into fresh tears. Netta picked up the bowl and tipped the mess of eggs and straw onto the ground. At once a dozen hens rushed over and began pecking away.

"I shouldn't have done that," Netta said. "It makes them eat their own eggs."

Somehow this made Janey feel better, that Netta too had done something bad.

"Now," said Netta, "we have to look awfully hard and find lots of eggs, to make up for the ones we broke."

Janey kept close at her heels and together they scoured the yard, gathering the stray, remaining eggs. Their mother was preoccupied with Seamus, who was only six months old, and dreamy with another pregnancy; she did not notice the scant supply of eggs, but only asked Netta to give her sister a good wash before tea.

* * *

My stepmother's job as a school nurse had given her very definite views as to how children should be brought up. With the exception of afternoon tea, I was not allowed to eat with the adults. Instead I sat alone at the kitchen table while she hovered near by, doing something at the sink and correcting my table manners. Breakfast was easy, cereal and toast, but lunch was almost always things that I hated: meat, boiled potatoes and boiled vegetables. She was firm that I must clean my plate; the starving children in India were invoked; I had a moral obligation. Many days I sat from lunch-time till tea-time, glaring at my cold food. Those were the longest afternoons of my life. Each moment was distinct and completely separate from every other, it seemed impossible that one should lead to the next. Occasionally I would be released, perhaps because she needed the kitchen table or had something else to do, only to meet again at supper the very same plate of food, now even less appealing than before. If it had not been for afternoon tea, when there were things I liked — egg salad sandwiches, Rice Krispies covered with chocolate and mounded into little balls — and when I was even allowed to eat with other people, I think I would have expired.

When lunch was finally finished, I had to go to the bathroom. Afterwards I made my report to her. Two days in a row without number two elicited a reprimand. If I answered satisfactorily, however, I was given a sweet: a tube of Smarties, a slice, nicely cut, of a Mars bar, or some kind of boiled sweet that came from a tin, like barley sugar. Occasionally I tried to lie, but she always seemed to know. "Did you really?" she would ask, and, shame-faced, I would have to confess. Then instead of a sweet I would get a scolding.

I ate in solitude because my stepmother believed that little girls should be seen and not heard. The constant admonition to silence rang through my childhood. Being noisy was the worst kind of crime, and only on very special occasions was I allowed to disrupt the polite conversation of grown-up life.

Whenever possible I was sent to play outside where I would be neither seen nor heard.

In line with this doctrine I was sent to bed early. Right after supper I brushed my teeth and changed into pyjamas. Then my stepmother would hear my lessons. Sitting on the edge of my bed she would ask me to recite my multiplication tables, or the kings of England. Often I forgot: what was six times seven, who came after Richard I. Inside my head I rushed frantically from place to place, looking for the lost item, in much the same way as I searched the house when I lost my mittens. Meanwhile she waited. Her silence drove me to speech; I guessed wildly. "I thought you told me you'd learned this," she said. In the morning I would not be allowed out to play until I was word-perfect.

When homework was over, as a reward, she would sing to me in her thin, sweet voice: "Good-night, Irene," "Oh, my darling, Clementine," "Sail bonnie boat like a bird on the wing over the sea to Skye." Then she would kiss me good-night, switch out the light and close the door. In summer, when the sun did not set until almost midnight, I lay for hours, fretful, wide awake, but not daring to get up and play with the toys which I could see on the other side of the room, nor even to open the book which lay beside my bed, in case she came in to check up on me.

When at last I fell asleep, I did not rest easily. Every night before I got into bed my stepmother bandaged my arms, but no matter how tightly she wound the strips of gauze, I always managed to burrow through and scratch the tender skin on the inside of my elbows until it bled. In the morning the bandages hung round my wrists like bracelets and I would narrow my hands and slide them off. My stepmother would sigh when she saw the bloody pile of bandages by the bed. "What a nuisance you are," she would say. "Didn't I tell you not to scratch?" She did not seem to understand when I tried to explain that it was not my fault. As long as I was awake I did exactly what she told me. There was no reason to do otherwise; the half-healed wounds were too painful to touch.

Being neither seen nor heard, I was easy to forget. One afternoon when I came home from looking for tadpoles I found that the front door would not open. With each attempt to turn the knob my terror increased. Too small to reach the doorbell, I pounded on the grey wooden door, hurling my whole body against it like a dog at a fence. At last, abandoning hope, I ran screaming down the hill to the neighbours. They tried to quiet me. While I sobbed they explained that everything was all right: my father and stepmother must have forgotten to tell me they were driving into town, they would be back for tea. I cried even harder. For some months after my mother died my father had answered my questions by saying that she had gone to town and would be back soon.

*   *   *

Netta was at school and Janey was sitting beside a bale of hay outside the byre playing with her dolls, Mrs Pyper and Mrs Matthew. She was telling them about India. Yesterday a missionary had visited the school to talk to the big girls and Netta had come home and told Janey all about it.

Out of the corner of her eye she saw her father coming around the hen-house. He was leading the two grey cart-horses out to the field. In furious tones, as if completely unaware of him, she began to lecture Mrs Pyper and Mrs Matthew about knitting socks for the little Indian boys and making aprons for the girls. As soon as her father was safely past, she jumped up and followed. If she kept well back he might not notice her, and she wanted to talk to the horses. She had learned from Netta to give apple cores and carrots flat on her hand to their soft whiskery noses; she loved their grassy breath. She skipped along over the ruts made by the cart-wheels, humming to herself. Suddenly, without turning round, her father said, "What do you want, bairn?"

Janey stopped short; she said nothing.

"A ride on the horse, maybe?"

Without waiting for an answer, he turned and picked her up. He set her on the larger grey horse and started walking again. She had never been on a horse before. When Syd offered her a ride she always said no. At first she held onto the mane in grim silence, but then as she felt the animal rock and heave under her and saw the ground miles below, she let out a terrified wail. Her father walked along with his hands in his pockets, chewing a stem of grass. Janey screamed louder and louder.

At last her mother appeared with Ian in her arms. Elsie did not say a word. She put the baby down on the doorstep, picked up her skirts and ran. She was a small woman but, in that moment, capable of extraordinary reach. Before her husband noticed, she had snatched the child off the horse and had her safe on the ground.

*   *   *

The beer that my stepmother made was used to entertain my parents' small number of guests. My father had several bachelor friends from before his first marriage whom my stepmother welcomed enthusiastically. She ordered them around and smiled flirtatiously when they told my father he was a lucky man. Occasionally one of the married school-teachers and his wife would be invited to drop in. In the company of the bachelors my stepmother drank beer like a good sport. When another woman was present, however, she always asked for sherry.

These people were primarily my father's friends. Whether my stepmother had any of her own is not easy to judge. I can think of two candidates: Aunt Agnes and Aunt Christine. Of course, they were aunts only in my sense of the word. Aunt Agnes lived in St Andrews, and my stepmother and I called on her on the very rare occasions when my father went there to play golf. During these visits neither woman paid the least attention to me, but I was happy gazing at the most wonderful lamp I had ever seen: a lady wearing a pink and black lacy crinoline, holding aloft a light bulb. While Aunt Agnes served tea she told long stories about her son, a naval officer. My stepmother, sitting in one corner of the sofa with her gloves and handbag on her lap, smoked cigarette after cigarette.

When it was time to say goodbye, Aunt Agnes hugged me several times. She smelled strongly of cosmetics. Even the four intricately folded handkerchiefs which she sent me every Christmas seemed to retain some of this smell. I always tried to avoid actually using them. Nevertheless I would write her a letter beginning "Thank you for the lovely handkerchiefs. They are just what I wanted," thereby sealing my fate for another year. Aunt Agnes did not live near by and we seldom saw her; perhaps this was what made the continuing relationship between her and my stepmother possible.

Aunt Christine had a face like a plate, round and flat, with each feature neatly painted on against a white powdery background She smelled exactly like Aunt Agnes and gushed terribly. She always gave me bath salts for Christmas, and I wrote her an identical letter. Although she was a near neighbour — she worked at the school as a secretary — I never saw her inside our house. I suspect she was deemed unworthy of the honour because she was a spinster who worked for her living. Nevertheless my stepmother maintained the connection, talking often of "poor Christine" and patronising her from afar.

From the letters my stepmother received on the eve of her marriage, it is apparent that she had made many friends and acquaintances during her years of working in hospitals, but somehow after she married my father they all disappeared. Perhaps she dropped them because they had known her as an old maid. Or perhaps, as sometimes happens, the relationships faded for no clearly explicable reason.

Although she may not have had friends, my stepmother was well endowed with relatives, and these played a large

part in our lives. Most prominent was her sister, Netta, who
with her elderly husband, Alex, paid brief visits for which
weeks of preparation were required. My stepmother's
younger brother Ian and Netta's stepdaughter, Lucy, were
less demanding and more frequent guests. With their
spouses they came often to tea. My main relationship with all
these people was a mercenary one. I soon discovered that
they had the endearing habit of slipping some money into
my waiting hand as they said goodbye; they became the
mainstay of my finances. I knew exactly what each of them
was good for and was disappointed on the rare occasions
when I received a mere embrace.

My father and I had only one relative, my great-aunt
Margaret. Every Christmas we went to visit her in Edinburgh. To get there we took a ferry across the Firth of Forth.
While we waited to get on the boat my parents sat in the car,
smoking and doing the crossword puzzle, and I ran around
looking at everything. High above us the intricately webbed
railway bridge stretched across the estuary. I had been told
that it was painted every year and that it took a year to paint,
so I always looked closely to see if I could find a group of men
nesting high up in the girders.

Aunt Margaret's flat was small, but we all squeezed in. My
parents had the bedroom, my aunt slept in the kitchen and I
had a little wooden truckle-bed in the front parlour. At night
the unaccustomed noise of traffic on the nearby street kept
me awake for a long time, and later I was invariably
awakened by the tremendous thump when my stone hot-
water bottle fell out of bed.

Aunt Margaret got a Christmas tree, which she and I
decorated together, and she always took me by bus to see the
Christmas lights in the centre of town. On the morning of the
twenty-fifth there would be a pile of presents at the foot of
my bed; I was not allowed to open them until after breakfast.
The tantalising packages rapidly turned into innumerable
socks, handkerchiefs and pieces of school uniform, with only

the occasional book or ten-shilling note. At one point I owned forty-nine pairs of school socks. As I opened the presents, my stepmother would make me keep a list of who had given what; all exclamations of joy were cut short by the command: "Write it down. Write it down." Straight after lunch I had to begin work on the thank-you letters.

One Christmas my father did not join us at dinner; he was ill. The doctor came every day and my stepmother and Aunt Margaret took turns nursing him. We did not go home until Twelfth Night. After this incident we always spent Christmas with Netta. I do not know how Aunt Margaret managed the holidays without us. She sewed very beautifully, and years later when I inherited a trunk full of her handiwork, I found, among the embroidered table-cloths and handkerchiefs, the clumsy place-mats and tea-cosys which I had made for her. Year after year she had exclaimed over them and made a point of using them first thing on Christmas morning.

*   *   *

Janey put a saucepan of water on the stove before she went to help Netta with the dishes from tea. They stood side by side at the sink, Netta washing, Janey drying.

"What's that new teacher like?" Netta asked. "They say she's full of fancy ideas."

Before Janey could think what to say, she heard a noise and, looking through the window, saw a cow burst into the yard; it was her favourite, Mirabelle. As soon as she found herself safely on forbidden ground, Mirabelle slowed to a decorous walk. When Seamus arrived, waving a stick, she was nosing unconcernedly at a pile of straw.

"Get a move on, you damned creature," Seamus shouted, whacking Mirabelle on the rump. His words carried clearly through the open window. Janey gasped and giggled, then stopped herself when she saw Netta's stern profile.

"I'm going to have to have a talk with Seamus, wash out his mouth with soap. Ever since Mother passed away, he's been behaving like a hooligan," Netta said sadly.

"He does an awful lot of work," Janey said. Although Seamus was a year and a half younger than her, only twelve as she kept reminding him, Father treated him just like Syd.

"That's no excuse for bad language. I'm on the go morning to night and you don't hear me swearing." It was true, Netta's strongest expression was "botheration." She started scrubbing the last of the saucepans. "Before we wash your hair, I want to cut it," she said.

"Can I have it like Mabel's?" Surreptitiously, Janey removed a piece of cabbage from the rim of the plate she was drying. Netta got awfully fussy if she handed anything back.

"Your hair will never be like Mabel's in a month of Sundays and you can thank the Lord. That girl's nothing but a trollop. Go and get the newspaper."

Janey fetched a paper from the pile in the scullery. Sheet by sheet, she spread it on the floor, taking care not to leave any gaps. then she undid her braids. Her fair hair was straight as a poker, but in spite of Netta's warning, she imagined it curling softly around her face like the notorious Mabel's. She placed a stool on the middle of the newspaper and sat down. Netta fetched the scissors and wrapped a towel around her neck.

"Oh," said Janey, starting up, "I forgot the mirror."

"Sit still," said Netta. "You'll see soon enough." Swiftly, she snipped away. "What's the text for this week?"

Miss Duff had set the Sunday school I Corinthians XIII. "Though I speak with the tongues of men and of angels, and have not charity," Janey began dutifully. Afraid that if she slowed down she would forget what came next, she raced through the first ten verses. Then the cold steel of the scissors touched her neck. She looked down at all the hair lying around her feet, and the words flew from her mind.

Netta prompted her. "When I was a child, I spake as a child, I understood as a child, I thought as a child." It seemed to Janey that the scissors clicked with extra fierceness as she stumbled through the last few verses. Netta was always drilling the children. She would ask them to recite not just

the present week's text, but also those from months before.
At last she untucked the towel, and Janey jumped to her feet.

"Mind the hair," Netta said. "Don't go traipsing it all over
the house."

"I'll be careful," Janey said, and ran to her bedroom. The
room was dim and for a moment, as she peered into the
mossy glass on the dressing-room table, she did not know
herself. Her hair hung, limp and uneven, to just above her
shoulders. She looked at it from every angle, then burst into
tears. In a few minutes Netta came in and found her lying
face down on the bed. "What's the matter?"

"You didn't tell me you were taking it all off. I look dreadful."

"Don't be ridiculous. You look fine. Wait 'til you see how
it is when it's washed. It'll be tidier and much more hygienic.
I don't have the time to fuss with your hair."

Netta steered her into the bathroom, fetched the pan of
water and gave her hair a good scrub. She rubbed it with a
towel and told Janey to sit by the fire until it was dry.

As she topped and tailed the gooseberries Janey stared at
the coals and prayed for a miracle. Maybe, just maybe her
hair would start to curl. She was in the middle of explaining
to the deity exactly what she wanted when Seamus came in
with a pail of milk.

"Blimey, what happened to you? Did you get caught in the
mangle? Hey, Ian," he yelled, "come and look at baldy."

"That's enough from you, young man," said Netta, coming in from the scullery. "There's nothing wrong with Jane's
haircut. She'll look fine when it dries."

But Janey was already in floods of tears when Ian came
charging in shouting, "Baldy, baldy."

Even their father remarked on it. "Good grief," he said to
Netta. "What's happened to the bairn? She looks like a shorn
sheep."

If only Mother was alive, Janey thought, this would never
have happened. In despair she heard already the taunts of

the boys in her class. No one would ever want to walk home with her now.

*   *   *

When I was eight we moved to a small village in the south of Scotland. My father was too old to continue teaching at the boys' boarding school where he had taught for almost forty years; he found a new job at a smaller school with a less stringent age limit.

It was at this time that I began to know what my step-mother looked like. Her nose was large, her mouth pinched, her eyes pale; but this lack of prettiness, which had marred her life when she was younger, became as she approached sixty almost an asset. She was not haunted by the shadow of lost beauty, and this made her seem ten years younger than she was. She wore her fair hair a little above her shoulders, curled somehow along the bottom; I often found her hair-pins on the floor, or down the sides of armchairs. Every few months she had a perm. Her figure, with the help of a corset, was still trim. Her best feature, as she often remarked, was her legs, which remained all her life fine-boned and elegant. I remember her telling me that she had once owned twenty-four pairs of shoes. From this same period she had a fur coat of which she was very proud. I found the bill among her papers; in 1950 it had cost one hundred and sixty pounds. The job she took at the school two years later had a salary of two hundred pounds a year.

Now that she had to keep house for all of us on my father's income, she was more frugal, but her clothes were always crisp and clean. She wore blouses and twin sets, skirts and dresses and almost always a piece of jewellery: a necklace or a brooch. I don't remember her wearing hats, but she did wear scarves and headscarves. At this time members of the Royal family were often photographed wearing headscarves.

My father, on the other hand, was oblivious to his appearance. Although my stepmother often bought him new clothes, he preferred his old ones. The suits in which he taught were rubbed down to the nap, and his raincoat, which he wore in almost all weathers, could have been part of the wardrobe of a tramp. Only by dint of my stepmother's efforts did he avoid outright shabbiness. I too was badly dressed, but not of my own choice. She claimed it was wasteful to spend money on a child who was still growing. My school uniform was so tattered that even my teachers complained. She did, however, the year I was twelve, buy me a dress for the compulsory school dance. It was made of a sea-green velvet in a style that would have suited someone of thirty-five; she made a point of getting it several sizes too large, so that it would last me for a while.

I do not know to what extent my terrible clothes caused the difficulties I encountered at my new school, but I was profoundly unhappy. As a farewell gift, my former schoolmates had given me a copy of *Robinson Crusoe*. Like Crusoe, in my loneliness, I explored the countryside for miles around, giving names to hills, streams, fields and trees in a futile attempt to make myself feel at home. I built bridges, and tree-houses, and dams. I tried to tell my stepmother how miserable I was, but she silenced me by saying, "I don't know how you have the nerve to complain. Daddy hated to leave the valley. We only moved here because of you, so that you could go to a good school."

The year after we came to the village my stepmother gave up brewing beer; instead she made sloe-gin. It was an expensive drink, and she made only a bottle or two of the lovely, amethyst-coloured liquid. This change in home brews paralleled the reduction in my parents' social life. When they had had something that resembled a circle of friends, beer, a beverage that can be made cheaply and in large quantities, had been appropriate. In the new village, however, where there was no one to be entertained, the sloe-gin was sufficient for their needs. Even the ingredients of the two drinks seemed to reflect this diminution. During the beer-brewing days my stepmother had given me every night before bed a spoonful of sweet sticky malt; the sloes, when I tried them, were so bitter that they shrivelled the inside of my mouth.

I did not understand why my parents had no friends. Living in a village, we were much less isolated than before; there should have been plenty of scope. But friendship failed to materialise. On one side of us lived a couple named Bob and Goldie. They were dark, plain people whose son, Brian, with his dimples and golden ringlets, looked like a changeling. He was too young to be my playmate, but often I would come home from school to find him sitting at our kitchen table, eating some kind of sweet. My stepmother's affection for him did not extend to his parents; Goldie crossed our threshold only to fetch him. Our other immediate neighbour, Miss Dawson, the village nurse, fared no better. Their common profession might have been the basis for a good relationship between the two women, but after a few occasions when my stepmother tried to share her expertise with Miss Dawson, a chilly silence fell between them.

The same kind of silence seemed to emanate from my stepmother when we went to the village shops. Unlike the van men who had travelled round the valley, the shop assistants were obdurately ignorant of her status. "What'll it be, dearie?" they would say in cheerful, ringing tones, impervious to her gentility. More and more she sent me in her stead. It was an agonising experience. I would wait patiently until it was my turn and then hand over her list like a magic talisman. But there were always questions: what kind of apples? what kind of bacon? I had never known the world was so full of choices, and whatever I chose was invariably wrong. On the way home the village children, with whom I was not allowed to consort, sometimes threw stones at me.

My father too was solitary. He made no friends among his new colleagues, but he did not seem to care; as far as I could tell it was all one to him, friends or no friends, as long as he had my stepmother. I think it is true to say that in almost twenty years of marriage neither of them made a single new friend.

To some extent people were replaced by animals. My step-mother developed a passion for donkeys. My father would locate donkeys in the neighbourhood and on Sunday after-noons and summer evenings take her to visit them. She would bring bread, carrots, and apples and feed the donkey over the fence. Just to look at these animals made my step-mother laugh, and when they threw back their heads and brayed she would fall into something resembling hysterics. This open and unbridled laughter was utterly different from the restrained way in which she laughed at jokes or humorous situations. Only the donkeys seemed to produce this in her, but perhaps there were other occasions, wit-nessed only by my father, when she forgot to be ladylike.

Besides the donkeys, there was our dog. Since he was a young man, my father had kept border terriers. Each suc-cessive dog was called Speckie, a reference to their brindled coats. The fourth one, the one I knew, was a pure-bred runt. Her teeth overlapped in such a way that she had tiny fangs, and her ears were uneven: one stood up while the other flopped down, no matter how hard she tried to prick it. She loved eating sweets and riding in cars, and, even more im-portant, tolerated being taken for bicycle rides.

Once, on our way to visit Netta, Speckie sat on my lap, and when we arrived my shorts were sticky with blood. My step-mother took me to the bathroom and cleaned me up. I tried to ask what was the matter; I worried that Speckie was hurt. "It's not something to talk about. Just try to be more careful in future," she said, as she scrubbed at me with a flannel. Later I dimly realised that there was some connection be-tween the blood stains and the fact that I was not allowed to let Speckie off the lead when I took her for walks.

This Speckie was the last of my father's dogs. She had to be put to sleep the summer I was thirteen, and our new dog was

chosen by my stepmother. He was a small black and white
mongrel terrier whom for some unknown reason she called
Bran. Although he was moody, greedy, erratic and irascible,
she adored him. Whenever he growled at me she said,
"Leave Bran alone," and on the one occasion when he actually bit me she asked angrily, "What on earth were you
doing to Bran?" My father sometimes referred to him as
temperamental, but, knowing that my stepmother took any
slight to Bran as a slight to herself, he maintained cordial
relations. In her collection of photographs, pictures of Bran
outnumber even those of my father.

Unlike my parents I did have one friend in the village, a
wall-eyed market gardener named Woody. I visited him
whenever I had saved enough money to buy flowers. I would
tell him how much I had, and together, followed by his two
creamy Pekinese, we would walk through the gardens making up a bunch of flowers: daffodils, anemones, freesias,
sweet peas, chrysanthemums. Generously, Woody always
gave me more than I could afford. My relationship with him,
however, was seasonal; in the spring I abandoned him to
pick big bunches of lilac from the bushes in front of an
empty house on the outskirts of the village. In my explora-
tions I had also discovered a marshy place where tall yellow
irises grew. It was several miles away; I bicycled there to
gather them and brought home as many as I could in the
basket attached to my handlebars.

Over the years I must have brought my stepmother
hundreds of bunches of flowers, but when it came to her
funeral I did not know what to send. Finally, I left it to the
florist to decide; he made a spray of pink and white carna-
tions and chrysanthemums. The most expensive flowers I
ever gave her, they were cremated with the coffin.

If I could have, I would have given her gentians. They were
her favourite flowers because they reminded her of the one
time she had been abroad. The year before she married my
father, she and Aunt Christine had gone to Switzerland, to

Lucerne. My stepmother often described the blueness of the
lake and the flowers. There is a photograph of her in a
restaurant by the water. She is sitting in the circular shade of
an umbrella, wearing a flowery dress and open-toed sandals.
The sandals look familiar. They are just like the ones that,
years later, she would ask me to clean with the same white
fluid I used for my school gym-shoes. More than any other
photograph of my stepmother, this one suggests a time when
a wealth of possibilities lay before her, so different from the
narrow crack of actuality in which I knew her.

She had a brooch in the shape of a gentian, which she
would show me when going through her jewellery box.
Sometimes, if she was in an especially good mood, she would
let me touch the rings and brooches, necklaces and earrings.
I regarded this as a great honour. Looking at her jewellery
always triggered a spate of stories about hospital dances.
These reminiscences culminated with her telling me in a
hushed voice that once before she had nearly been married.
We were even engaged," she said in solemn tones, but I sent
his ring back." She thanked her lucky stars that she had
waited and got my father, who was a gentleman, but she enjoyed the cachet of having had such a close escape.

In winter when there were no flowers, even at Woody's, I
bought her knick-knacks at a shop called Scotts. I remember
standing in the dim shop, losing all sense of time as I looked
at something I thought especially beautiful and wondered
how I could get the money to buy it. The village was too far
away for my stepmother's relatives to pay regular visits, and
I only got sixpence a week pocket money; in my calculations
the weeks seemed endless. From Christmas on I saved earnestly to buy her presents for Valentine's Day, Easter,
Mother's Day and her birthday.

Of all these occasions it was her birthday that excited me
most. When I was eleven, as a special treat, I was allowed to
take my parents breakfast in bed. I got up even earlier than
usual and went over everything a dozen times. If the toast

was burned or the tea stewed, I knew my stepmother would tell me about it later, saying with a sigh "If I want a thing done right I always have to do it myself." By the time I finally carried the tray upstairs, she and my father were sitting up in bed, side by side. I kissed them both and handed over her present.

"What a surprise," she said, smiling roguishly at my father. "I wonder what it is." "Open it," I begged. Briskly, she undid the paper in which I had wrapped the small blue vase with roses painted round the rim. "This is lovely, thank-you," she said, and gave me a kiss. My father smiled at me.

Then it was time to open his present. A pink spot appeared in each of her cheeks as she unwrapped his gift: a small Wedgwood goldfinch. She kissed him. After a minute or two she opened the envelope that came with the goldfinch. Every Christmas and birthday my father gave her a cheque; I never knew for how much. From the day of his death until the day of her own she carried in her handbag one of these envelopes, on the outside of which he had written: "Happy birthday to my Janey. Best love, Toby."

I had been waiting anxiously to see if everything was all right. Now she turned to me and said, "Off you go. We don't want the tea to get cold." And I went downstairs to have breakfast in the kitchen.

*   *   *

As she was changing out of her school pinafore, Janey looked out of the window and saw that, in spite of the drizzle, Netta was working in the garden. On the way home, she had been plotting how she might be able to get her sister alone, and here she was, without the slightest effort. Janey pulled on her work clothes and hurried outside. "What shall I do?" she asked.

Netta looked up from her hoe. The rain had darkened her acorn-coloured hair and her face was red with cold. "You're home already," she said in surprise. "I didn't realise the time. I started thinning the carrots but I didn't get them finished. You could do that."

Janey knelt down on the sack that Netta had been using to protect her skirt.

"Did you ever see the grass in such a state?" Netta said. "I'll have to get Seamus to do it the next dry day. Careful, you shouldn't take out so many. Here, use the trowel."

Janey took the trowel, cleared her throat and said, "Netta, I've been accepted into the nurses' college in Glasgow. I'll be starting in the autumn." She did not dare to look up at her sister; she saw the hoe pause for a second and then dig in more vehemently than ever.

"So that's why you've been like a cat on a hot tin roof every time the post came."

"I didn't think they'd accept me. I was certain they'd turn me down. That's why I didn't say anything." Janey had to force the air in and out of her lungs. All day in school she had been rehearsing this moment. There was no reason in the world why Netta should object, but every time Janey thought of telling her, she felt her tongue grow fat as a book in her mouth.

Netta was tall, much taller than Janey; she towered over her kneeling sister. "I wonder what father will say. I can't imagine he'll be too pleased at your sneaking off behind his back. If he can't trust you here, why should he trust you in the big city? Here give me the letter."

Before she knew what she'd done, Janey had reached in her pocket and handed over her precious letter. She hadn't let it out of her grasp all day. As soon as it was gone, she felt frightened. It was her only proof: what if Netta put it in the fire? "You're not angry, are you?" she pleaded, looking up at Netta.

"You should have spoken with me. I thought I could rely on you. Father's getting on, he can't manage as well as he used to."

"But there'll still be Seamus and Ian. All I do is help you, and you could easily get Annie to come in for a few hours a week. This way, I'll earn my own living, and if father gets sick, I'll be able to nurse him."

Netta was looking at the letter. "Do you think we're made of money?" she asked sharply. "You talk of having Annie as if we could pay her hand over fist, and what about your expenses, Madame, I'd like to know?"

"They'll pay me twenty pounds a year and board and lodging." Janey couldn't help sounding proud.

Netta did not acknowledge this point in favour of her plan. "It says here that you need your father's consent."

Janey gasped. She had not read the form closely; she had been too overjoyed.

"I suppose you thought I'd speak to him," Netta went on grimly. She wiped her hand on her apron, and pushed back her wet hair. "Well, I'll have to pick my moment."

The rain had been growing steadily worse. Even Netta was deterred. She slipped the damp letter into her pocket and headed off in the direction of the back-door. "Bring the hoe in with you, when you finish," she said over her shoulder.

In the twilight Janey sat there wondering what she would do if her father refused to sign. This was a terror that she had not even imagined. It was unbearable. Slowly, mechanically, she went on pulling out the tiny plants. The wet soil clung to their roots and her hands.

How could she make him realise how important it was? Ever since Mother died she had wanted to be a nurse. She remembered Netta leading her into the lamp-lit room. Her mother had raised herself off the pillow, taken her hand, and said, "Janey, you are my dear little girl. You must do your best to help Netta and to take care of your brothers. I want you to be good and kind and helpful. Keep the ten commandments and do what Netta tells you." Every day she remembered those words. She had read all the books in the Grantown library about nursing, she knew she'd be good at it. She'd gone with Netta to help a couple of women and she hadn't been scared. Everyone had praised her.

She tried, after tea, to talk to Netta, to tell her the good points she should mention to father, to tell her how important it was, but Netta shut her up. "For goodness sake, stop bothering me," she said. "Don't you trust me to know what's best?"

In bed that night Janey lay awake listening for the sounds of Robert coming home. If he was in a good mood perhaps Netta would ask him right away; she always waited up for him, more like a wife than a daughter. Janey lay there imagining him saying yes, him saying no. A little after eleven the dogs began to bark, the outside door opened and closed. Scarcely daring to breathe, she listened. Would he stop in the kitchen, or immediately climb the stairs to bed? There was silence. She counted to a hundred, once, and then again, and again. At last came the heavy sounds of her father ascending. As soon as he was safely in his room she slid out of bed and ran downstairs.

Netta was banking the fire for the night. "What are you doing up at this hour?" she asked.

Janey caught herself. Netta would tell her if she'd asked him. There was no point in provoking her unnecessarily. "I came to get a glass of water," she said, turning towards the scullery.

Next morning as she sat in the byre milking she tried to think of all the things she had to do today: cleaning her room, hemming a skirt, learning her lessons. There would be no opportunity for Netta to speak to Father until evening. Carefully she carried the full pails across the yard into the pantry. As she walked back to the byre she met Robert on his way to the barn. "So Netta tells me you're off to Glasgow," he said, without breaking his stride.

For a moment Janey stood staring after him, then she turned and ran back to the kitchen. Netta was standing at the stove stirring the porridge. "Oh, Netta." Janey flung her arms around her sister. "You did it. Thank-you."

"What are you talking about?"

"Going to Glasgow," Janey said. "Nursing." She could not see Netta's face; she hugged even harder.

"It wasn't easy to persuade Father," Netta said, extricating herself from Janey's embrace. "He's worried that I'll work myself to death."

* * *

After we moved from the valley the relationship between my stepmother and me seemed to undergo a significant change for the worse. She had always been strict but this strictness now seemed to grow stronger, embracing almost every aspect of my life and seldom alleviated by gestures of affection. She no longer sang me to sleep or made me birthday cakes. Worse even than the loss of these specific treats, which after all it could be argued I had outgrown, was the disappearance of any kind of complicity; we no longer shared secrets, even about dead mice.

Soon after we arrived in the village, I found in the long grass under the garden hedge a small, heavy saucepan. Proudly I carried it up to the house.

"Where did you find this?" my stepmother asked.

I told her.

"You're lying," she said. "How dare you lie to me."

As I started to protest, she slapped my face. My cheek burned. I turned and ran out of the kitchen, down into the depths of the garden. She had never hit me before. How could she think I was lying? Over and over I had been told that lying was wrong, that if I told the truth everything would be all right. It had never occurred to me that the truth might be unrecognisable. I wanted to die, to be eradicated, never to be seen by her again. I felt all at once my immense burdensomeness to her.

When I was ten I joined the Girl Guides, and my stepmother began to insist that I spend every Saturday morning cleaning my room. Part of being a Girl Guide, she reminded me, was keeping things clean and neat. When I claimed to have finished, she would come and check, running her finger along the ledges. Inevitably when she held it up it was grey with dust. "If a thing's worth doing," she said firmly, "it's worth doing properly." And I had to begin again. My enthusiasm for the Guides quickly waned as my membership became an argument for doing all kinds of unpleasant tasks.

She was also strict about my health. After we moved, I never saw the mah-jong set because I was never allowed to be ill. Whatever my condition, I had to go to school, although at this time school was such agony for me that I used to take apart my pencil sharpener and cut my fingers till they bled so as to have an excuse to leave class and visit the school matron. My stepmother's attitude to my father's health was quite different. He had only to clear his throat for her to urge him to stay at home. She nursed him untiringly through years of coughs and colds, asthma, bronchitis and pneumonia. There were at least two occasions, of which I was not aware until many years later, when her vigilance saved his life. In retrospect, the deaf ear she turned to my complaints is easy enough to understand; it would have been too much to have two invalids on her hands at once.

I do not remember her ever being really ill. Once she had a boil on the back of her neck. The question of how it should be dressed arose; my parents assumed that I would do it. When I expressed reluctance, my father was appalled. "How can you be so ungrateful?" he demanded. "Think of all the things Mummy does for you." Those words — all she's done for you — ran like a refrain through my adolescence. I was always in debt, constantly overdrawn.

Although I dreaded going to school, holidays were not precisely a relief. Now that we lived too far away for weekend visits, we always spent the school holidays at Netta's. Netta was a large, vigorous woman. She ran the local Women's Institute, organised the cleaning of the church, grew roses and vegetables, and kept her house spotless. Meanwhile her husband, Alex, several inches smaller and many years older, sat in his favourite chair by the fire. Netta had been his housekeeper before their marriage. During our visits my father had armchair number two, which was in a slightly inferior position, nearer the door. My stepmother for the most part used Netta's chair, for her sister was seldom motionless.

The days passed in an almost unvarying routine. Netta took me with her to the shops and allowed me to help her cook and weed the garden. Without her, I would have died of boredom. Meanwhile my parents smoked incessantly, did crossword puzzles, watched television, and discussed the various birds that came to the bird-table. Two or three times during the holidays my stepmother's brother Ian and his wife would drive over for the day. They lived in a village a half-hour's drive from Netta's. Netta's stepdaughter, Lucy, who lived at the other end of the town, came to visit more often. Her hair was the colour of eggshell, and, like all my parents' acquaintances, she was forty years older than me. It never occurred to me that she too was a stepdaughter.

Very occasionally while we were staying at Netta's there were outings. Several times we went to Loch Garten to watch the osprey nest. I remember the windy picnics by the shore, my father waiting anxiously, binoculars in hand, for one of the huge birds to sail into flight. What I never realised was that the loch was only a few miles from my stepmother's old home. We could so easily have driven over and taken a look at Lackghie, but she never even mentioned the proximity.

When we stayed at Netta's I had a whole new range of shops in which to look for presents for my stepmother, and at the same time my finances were much improved. Netta, in spite of my stepmother's protests, would pay me to do little jobs for her, and Lucy and her husband had not lost their pleasant habit of pressing half-crowns into my hand. This money was almost instantly transformed into gifts for my stepmother. These fruitless attempts to please her, which seemed to increase in direct proportion to the deterioration of our relationship, suggest how acutely I was aware of her increasing lack of affection for me.

Even now I cannot determine why, from year to year, she

liked me less. Perhaps I did something unforgiveable which I have long ago forgotten. Perhaps I did nothing. I was getting older and, gawky in my shabby clothes, must have been less appealing; she lavished attention on the neighbours' son, Brian, who was six years younger. In a new place where I had no friends I tended to hang around the house more, especially in bad weather. At the same time she was free, at last, to give vent to her feelings: in the village she was no longer living in the shadow of my father's first wife; there was no one to whom she needed to prove that his second marriage was a success. All these seem like possible reasons, yet none carries conviction. I have conjured them up in an effort to protect myself from the knowledge that, whatever the reason, she did not like me.

Wherever we lived, my real mother's photograph always hung over my bed. The black-and-white portrait showed a woman wearing a dark, high-necked sweater and a string of pearls. Her face was smooth and serious. She looked distant and romantic. I was taught to think of her as Eva; my step-mother was Mummy. Eva had been the school nurse before my stepmother. Her marriage to my father had created the vacancy which my stepmother had filled. As also her death. She had died of cancer when I was two and she was thirty-five. As far as I know my stepmother never commented negatively about her, and never displayed negative feelings on the very rare occasions when my father mentioned her. After his death she told me that Eva was very sweet, but she had a slight limp and a large, black birthmark on her thigh.

Any attempt to understand how she felt about Eva only brings me face to face with the limitations of imagination as a way of knowing. One has to imagine what is logical, what is reasonable. It would be reasonable to suppose that my step-mother resented this woman, her predecessor. But it is con-ceivable that she genuinely liked Eva and was grateful to her. Or, even more plausible, that she liked her and thought she was doing her a favour in marrying her widower and taking

care of her child. That it was Eva who was in her debt. It is
not so much that these ideas are unimaginable as that they
cannot be imagined into knowledge. Over and over I come
back to these things, the ones I cannot know.

*   *   *

"What ward are you on now?" Netta asked as she passed
Janey her plate of shepherd's pie.

"Geriatric."

"What's geriatric?" Ian said, with his mouth full. Janey
saw Netta glare at him. Although he was fifteen she was always after him to mind his manners.

"It's the ward for old people. It's a bit depressing because
you know some of them will never be going home. And they
often don't get many visitors. I'll be glad when I move to
theatre at the end of the month."

"What's theatre?" Ian asked, still chewing, and Janey
started to explain. Across the table Seamus ate swiftly without saying a word. As soon as his plate was clean, he got to his
feet.

Netta looked up at him. "Father wants you and Ian to start
the top field this evening. There's enough light, you could
get it scythed all the way round."

"If he wanted me to do the field, he'd have asked me himself."

"Don't be cheeky, Seamus," Netta said angrily.

Seamus said nothing. He reached across the table and took
a couple of slices of bread, then left the room. A moment
later they saw him bicycle past the window. Netta sat very
straight, her lips folded together so tightly that little puckers
appeared in her cheeks. Janey did not dare to comment; she
went on answering Ian's questions. Later, when she was
helping him water the garden, she asked what everyone had
been so mad about.

"Och," said Ian, "it's a big to-do. Netta doesn't want
Seamus to go off down the hill to see Bella."

"Bella? Bella Walker?" asked Janey, incredulous. Some of the water from the can she was carrying splashed onto her shoes.

Ian nodded.

The Walker family lived in a tumbledown cottage at the far end of the village. Bella's father drove a cart round the valley, buying milk from the crofts and farms, and Bella helped him. Janey had known her at school but not well; Bella had left at fourteen. She was plump and giggled easily and Netta had always said she was common. What could Seamus see in her? Besides, he was only seventeen, much too young to be courting.

*   *   *

Almost every day I prayed that I might somehow be rescued from my hateful school. After five years my pleas were answered; both the school I attended and the one where my father taught went bankrupt. It was a time when private schools were struggling to survive. The British colonies were shrinking and the parents of many of my school-fellows lost their jobs abroad and came home to retrieve their daughters. As an indirect result of the new-found independence of various exotic countries, my father, my stepmother and I moved back north, and rented a farmhouse.

The house was part of a steading, and the land around it was still farmed by the owners, who lived a few miles away. Tractors frequently rattled past our door, all winter long the yard was ankle deep in mud, and the cows lowed in the barn. This was the most remote place we had ever lived. My step-mother, who did not drive, was entirely dependent on my father for her comings and goings, and often she saw no one but him and me for days at a time. The house itself was cold and damp and had few conveniences. Ironically the mar-riage which had been meant to free my stepmother forever from the old, straitened life had brought her at last to a place remarkably like Lackghie, and I think she was happier there than she had ever been.

This farmhouse was not far from the boys' boarding school where my father had lived and worked for almost all his adult life; nevertheless he had little contact with his former colleagues. To me, dependent on my bicycle, the journey to my old haunts was huge, and I was even more lonely than before. Too old to play at being Crusoe night after night, I buried myself in homework.

At weekends, even though I was no longer a Girl Guide, I still had to clean my room. In addition there were other tasks. The farmhouse had a large garden, and my pocket money was increased dramatically, to half a crown a week, in return for cutting the enormous lawn. I needed the money; I had begun to have expenses of my own.

The summer we moved I was sent to stay with Aunt Margaret in Edinburgh. When I unpacked the suitcase, which my stepmother had packed, I found a bulky package of sanitary towels. Although I had never seen such things before, I did not go running to my aunt; I recognised them in some instinctive way. They proved a timely gift, and a unique one. From then on I had to use my pocket money to buy the necessary equipment, always with excruciating embarrassment. Sometimes it took several visits to the chemist's before the woman assistant was on duty and I could make my purchase. I smuggled the boxes home and hid them as best I could. My stepmother, as a former nurse, might have been expected to find the biological explanations fairly simple, but if it had not been for that first gift I would have assumed she had forgotten about such matters, or in some miraculous way been spared them, so absolute was her silence.

My father and I passed our days in adjacent schools, and at this time he began to take an interest in my school-work. He spent several evenings explaining to me why the result of multiplying any number by zero was zero. His speciality as a maths teacher was helping the slow and mathematically inept. My stepmother, although not pleased at his refusal to do the crossword puzzle with her until I had a thorough under-

standing of the problem, was tolerant. Her attitude changed
when my father and I embarked on more general discus-
sions: Hamlet's indecisiveness or Disraeli's attitude on
parliamentary reform. These conversations took place in the
living-room, at the hour when my stepmother was out in the
kitchen, preparing dinner. The rooms adjoined and the door
was always open; I could see her back as she stood over the
sink, peeling potatoes or scrubbing vegetables.

"I don't think Hamlet was weak-willed. He just needed to
get proper proof," I said.

My father was hard of hearing; I would have to pitch my
voice a little louder than usual, so that he could hear me.
What he could not hear were the comments my stepmother
made.

"Stupid brat," she would mutter, "what does she know
about it?" "Listen to her going on, little miss-know-it-all."
"What a lot of rubbish. I've never heard such a load of cods-
wallop in my life." I tried not to pay attention, to go on enjoying the unusual treat of my father's attention, but as the
weeks passed and her comments grew more scathing I fell
silent. My father continued, for a time, to ask me what I'd
been doing in school, but I began to answer briefly and
evasively. The only other chance I had to talk to him was
when he drove me back and forth from school, but the
journey was short and usually we were both preoccupied.

My stepmother's behaviour bewildered me. I knew I was
not really stupid — I dreamed about being Madame Curie,
or Dr Schweitzer, and I was always first in my class — but I
could not believe she was wrong. If I went out to help her in
the scullery, she treated me just as usual.

Now, when I would have preferred not to, I was allowed to
join my parents for meals. In fact I had no choice in the matter. "What's for supper?" I would ask as I placed the knives
and forks on the table. "Wait and see," my stepmother
would reply. Almost invariably it was meat: lamb, pork
chops, liver, roast beef, mutton. After all those years of sit-

ting at the table until I cleaned my plate, I had discovered I could eat meat if I cut it into small pieces and washed them down with gulps of water, thereby eliminating the need for chewing but eliciting a lecture about the unhealthiness of drinking during meals. For my father too, things were not always easy. If he refused a second helping, she would sigh and say, "I don't know why I bother, Toby. All this work and you've hardly eaten a thing." Manfully, he would buckle down and eat some more. During the meal, my stepmother would talk about what birds and animals she had seen that day and which van-men had called. My father would ask questions and sometimes volunteer some gossip from the staff-room of the rowdy school where he now taught. As soon as I had finished washing the dishes I returned to my homework.

There was fortunately some respite from our solitude. We now lived sufficiently close to Netta's to be able to drive over and back in an afternoon. Alex had died the year before we moved, and my stepmother now showed herself more eager than ever for her sister's company. At last she had something that Netta did not. "Poor Netta," she would say, just as years before she had said "Poor Christine." Of course the habits of a lifetime remained; Netta could no more refrain from ordering my stepmother around than my stepmother could keep from obeying, but at least now she could console herself in private by pitying her sister. She and my father began to go to Netta's not only for holidays but also most weekends. Sometimes, if I had enough homework, they would let me stay at home.

The move to the farmhouse also brought us closer to Aunt Margaret, and she began to pay us yearly visits. I enjoyed her company; she would talk to me for hours about her child-hood and show me how to crochet or to make flowers out of sea shells. I was allowed to take her a cup of tea in bed in the morning before I went to school, and she would often ask me to run errands in my lunch-hour. The year I was sixteen she prolonged her visit beyond the customary fortnight. I began to take her not only tea in bed, but supper too. Gradually, she ceased to get up, even in the middle of the day, but I thought only that she was tired and would soon be well again, and in fact I preferred talking to her in the privacy of her bedroom. I always went in to see her as soon as I got home from school. Then one day I came home and my father told me that I was going to stay with friends. My bedroom was next to Aunt Margaret's, and as I packed I kept sneaking in to look at her. She was lying back on the pillows with her eyes neither open nor closed. Her breathing was very loud, and her nose had become thin and pointed. She seemed to neither see nor hear me. I did not know that she was dying, nor why my parents sat downstairs, as if ignoring her. I asked what was wrong. They said she was not well and sent me away.

A few days after the funeral my father mentioned her will. "Poor Aunt," said my stepmother, in a full voice. "She was very grateful to me for taking care of her. She wanted me to have her money." As an afterthought she added that Aunt Margaret had also left me something. I am not sure how I learned that I was the sole legatee and my father was the executor.

For the next few weeks there was considerable confusion. My parents made several trips to Edinburgh, but they always went on school days and refused to take me with them. One evening when my father was outside working in the garden I complained to my stepmother. She turned and slapped me.

"Don't be impudent," she said. "You've no right to anything. Aunt was always saying what a terrible disappointment you were to her. If she had recovered, she was going to change her will." I stood and listened with my hand against my cheek. Whatever I did get, my stepmother made clear, was only a matter of courtesy on the part of her and my father. I could not argue; I was disabled by the sudden terrible knowledge that I had failed my aunt whom I loved.

After one trip to Edinburgh my stepmother talked bitterly about some friends of Aunt Margaret's who had helped themselves to various knick-knacks and pieces of furniture. These people were no better than thieves. And I too was a thief, hoping to take hold of what I had no right to. In the end out of all my aunt's possessions I inherited only four rosewood chairs and the trunk full of her handiwork which no one else wanted.

Looking back, I do not understand my stepmother's motives; very little money was involved, and she had never seemed to care for my aunt's favour. My father as executor of the will was putty in her hands. He did what she told him and believed that he was doing right.

Years later when he died I almost had my revenge. Among his papers the only will I could find was dated the year I was born and left everything to my mother. How insulted my stepmother would be to find that he had neglected to make a will in her favour. When I contacted his lawyers, however, I discovered that he had made a second will just before he remarried. At about the same time as he was writing this will, my stepmother was receiving the letters congratulating her on her forthcoming marriage. These documents have one thing in common: you would not guess from reading them that my father had a small child. I was invisible. He left everything to her.

After Aunt Margaret's death, I stopped asking my parents for things. I no longer asked if I could have music lessons, or play hockey after school, or have new clothes. I wore my ragged school uniform with contempt and stayed up doing my homework long after they had gone to bed.

* * *

Janey looked round the restaurant. It would be just like Seamus to be late, she thought. The place was nearly full but she spotted a table for two in the far corner and started to walk towards it. Suddenly, her brother was beside her.

"Come on," he said, "I've already got a table." As she followed him Janey caught sight of Sister Frazer with the new young surgeon and quickly looked away.

Seamus stopped beside a table where a woman was already sitting. Turning to Janey with a mock bow, he said, "Let me introduce you. Janey Cumming, Bella Cumming. Bella and I were married yesterday."

Bella smiled and stood up, but Janey stared at her, and she quickly sat down again.

When Janey finally spoke it was not to Bella but to Seamus. "You're joking," she said, both pleading and angry. Seamus had always been one for practical jokes; it was just like him to pretend to be married, and of course Bella invited a man to take that kind of liberty.

"No, I swear, twenty-four hours we've been man and wife. Look at Bella's ring."

Bella took off her glove and stretched out her hand. There was a thin gold band glinting on her plump finger. Seamus pulled out a chair for Janey, and carried along by his gesture, she sat down next to Bella. "I don't understand," she said. "Why didn't anyone tell me. I had a letter from Netta just last week and she never said a word."

"It was a secret," said Seamus. "There was no one there but the minister and Jock the post and his wife. I wouldn't even let Ian come. I didn't want him falling foul of Netta."

"Oh," said Janey. For a moment she thought about jumping up and running out of the restaurant, but before she could move the waiter came by to take their orders. He had the tiniest moustache she had ever seen. He smiled as he asked what she would like and Janey was reassured by the fact that he gave her precedence over Bella. She chose the haddock. While the other two were ordering she busied herself with taking off her gloves and looking at herself in her compact. "What about Netta?" she asked when the waiter had left.

"I left her a note. We stopped at the pub on the way to the station. Father gave us his blessing."

"You saw Father," Janey said in wonder. "I always thought . . ."

"I know, I know. He's a drunken sot but he's not as bad as we imagine." Seamus grinned cheerily. Janey could scarcely believe he was speaking about their father in this way. "No," he went on, "it's Netta who's the problem, not him. Come on Janey, don't be a stick-in-the-mud. What's done is done. You might as well get used to having a sister-in-law."

Janey stiffened in protest. Then Bella, who had been silent all this time, said, "This is a lovely place. I've never seen a chandelier before. And the china's nicer than our best at home!"

"Nothing but the best for you now you're a married woman," Seamus said. He pointed out the portrait of the King which hung over the fireplace. The waiter placed a pot of tea in front of Janey, and after a moment's hesitation she poured out for the three of them.

"Thanks," said Bella. "I've been dying for this all afternoon."

Seamus thanked Janey in his turn. Then he announced that this was their last meal in Scotland. They were sailing that night for Canada.

"For Canada?" Janey asked, as if she did not know what the word meant.

"We're emigrating, we're going to the New World," said Seamus jubilantly.

"But how can you? What about Lackghie?"

"They'll manage, somehow. Things are slack in the winter and Father can always get help in the spring. Ian will be off in a year or two, you mark my words. There's only room for one man there."

"And one woman," Bella added.

"Right enough," said Seamus. "No one will ever be good enough for Netta, not even the Lord himself." Bella stifled a giggle.

Common little thing, not fit to shine Netta's shoes, Janey thought.

While they ate, Seamus and Bella described their plans. Over the scones, Janey gazed at them in wonder. Canada was an endless distance away, almost the other side of the fat, blue globe which used to stand in the corner of the school-room. Somehow the news of their departure, even more momentous than the marriage, had made her forget her indignation, and when there was a pause, she asked about Bella's family. Weren't they upset that she was going so far away?

"They think I'm lucky," Bella said with a smirk at Seamus. He grinned back and patted her hand. Throughout the meal, he kept patting and touching her. Janey prayed that Sister Frazer hadn't noticed them; she did not dare to look round. When Bella went to the Ladies, Seamus mooned after her like a lovesick cow. "I can't believe my luck," he said. "I'm off to the land of milk and honey. Plenty of space, my own boss and Bella. I wish you knew her, Janey. She's a fine woman, not afraid to take a chance."

Right after tea Seamus and Bella had to take the tram down to the docks. Janey went with them. In the rain the grey ship, covered with lights, loomed above them. Suddenly Janey realised that her little brother, whose bag she used to carry to school, whom she had taken fishing in the burn and bird-nesting in the woods, was going to disappear into this huge ship, as surely as Jonah into the whale. She might never see him again. "You'll write," she said, clutching his arm.

"Yes. As soon as we get settled, I'll drop you a line. Do your best with Netta for us, lass."

He gave her a hug which almost lifted her off her feet. She hugged him back hard, and then she found that she was hugging Bella too, and wishing them both "Bon voyage."

*   *   *

A month after Aunt Margaret died my father finally retired. Without the last small bits and pieces of companionship which we had enjoyed on our way to and from school, silence fell between us. He now belonged entirely to my stepmother.

In the mornings I did not see them before I went to catch the bus to school. In the evenings I did endless homework. Dinner was a brief interruption, and if I was lucky my parents left the television on throughout the meal. As soon as I had washed the dishes I retreated to my bedroom.

When my father needed to communicate with me, he wrote a letter. He would bring these epistles into my bedroom and place them on the desk beside my schoolbooks. "Please read this," he would murmur, and turn away. He walked slowly and stiffly, as if at all times he was carrying a precariously balanced tea-tray. Some of these letters originated with my stepmother. These dealt with such problems as my impertinence and slovenliness. On his own behalf he wrote about my ingratitude to my stepmother. This correspondence was entirely one-sided. I did not reply to any of the letters, nor did my father ever mention them. If was as if once he had decided on this method of communication speech would have been a violation.

After I left for university he wrote me different kinds of letters, full of humour and small observations, but I could scarcely bear to read them and my replies were grudging and uninformative. It was one of these letters that brought me the news that Netta was ill. "You know what a dynamo she is," my father wrote, "so you can be sure something's seriously wrong when she agrees to let me make her a cup of tea."

No one had ever been able to persuade Netta to do anything she did not want to do, but now illness forced her to move in with Lucy. It was, of course, just a visit until the weather improved and her strength returned. I do not know why she did not come to be nursed by my stepmother. It would have seemed a more natural choice. But I suspect that my stepmother did not really want Netta. Her attitude to her elder sister's illness puzzled me. She seemed almost pleased. As the nurse in the family, she was the one who was in charge, who from a distance dealt with doctors and told Lucy what to do. Poor Netta," she would say, of course, there's nothing to be done''; the melancholy words could not wholly conceal a note of satisfaction. Perhaps she relished the prospect of at last being free.

Spring came and Netta could sit up only long enough for the sheets on her bed to be changed, but she was still convinced that she would soon be well. That summer I worked as a chambermaid in a hotel in the Channel Islands and my father continued to send me accounts of Netta's failing health. When I came home in September I visited her at Lucy's. The flowery pink wallpaper of her room imparted an unnatural glow of health to her cheeks, but as I came closer I could see how small she had become. Her hair had been shorn; the little white wisps that remained barely concealed the bones of her skull. It was one of those times when she felt better and, oblivious to the disease that governed her body, talked energetically about moving back to her own house. When I got up to go, she said she looked forward to seeing me at Christmas.

Two weeks later my father and stepmother drove over to see her. It was a beautiful autumn day and they took with them a bunch of russet-coloured chrysanthemums and a bottle of sloe-gin. When they arrived they went straight in to see Netta. My stepmother settled herself on the bed for a chat while my father, having paid his respects, fled to the living-room to watch horse-racing on television with Lucy's husband. Then Lucy made tea, and the two couples sat down together in the living-room. They were cheerful over their meal; my father told a couple of jokes which made them all laugh. In the next few weeks my stepmother described this day so often that now it almost seems that I too was sitting in the living-room, eating Lucy's cakes.

As soon as they had finished eating, my father insisted on leaving. He hated to drive in the dark and in winter never went anywhere after tea. While my stepmother was saying goodbye to Netta, he strolled out into the garden with Lucy and her husband to admire their Brussels sprouts. They were doing much better than his own crop, he said. He helped my stepmother into the car, started the engine, and let it warm up for a few minutes; generations of elderly cars had taught him not to begin a journey precipitately. Lucy lived at the top of a steep hill, and the car was already gathering speed when he announced that he felt ill, he could not breathe. My step-mother persuaded him to pull over to the side of the road and ran back to telephone for an ambulance. Wedged behind the steering wheel my father gasped for breath. By the time my stepmother returned, he was dead. He was se-venty-two; she was seventy-one. They had been married for eighteen years. Later she told me that he had said he would take prussic acid if she died before him.

＊　＊　＊

Janey had known Roddy all her life, he was a second cousin twice removed on her mother's side, but in the village shop she didn't recognise him until he said, "I see you've got too la-di-da to talk to your old friends."

"Roddy," she exclaimed. "I thought you were down south."

"No. I've been home all year." He told her he was work-ing part time as an electrician in Grantown and helping his father.

They stood chatting while Miss MacKenzie wrapped Janey's purchases. Then Roddy offered to accompany her on the rest of her errands. As they walked towards the manse she noticed that he had a limp. "Did you hurt your leg?" she asked.

"In the war. It doesn't bother me, I can still dance a fine reel." Raising his hands above his head, he danced a couple of steps right there in the road. "So how's the nursing?"

"I've almost finished my training. Exams in July. I came back to get some studying done. There's never any time in Glasgow."

"I shouldn't think you'd get much time here." He made a gesture encompassing her basket and her list of errands.

"Yes, there's always masses to do. When the weather's nice I go down to the old bridge to study. That way I get some peace and quiet." She shifted the groceries to her other arm, and Roddy reached over and took them.

At the bottom of the road up to Lackghie, they lingered awkwardly beside the mound of sand where years ago Janey had played as she waited for Netta to come home from school.

"Thanks for carrying my basket," she said shyly as he handed it over. Walking up the hill, she thought that Roddy must be the same age as Dr Anderson whom all the nurses were so keen on.

Netta was in the kitchen, peeling potatoes. "What took you so long?" she said, wiping her hands on her apron. "Did Miss Nicholson like the wine? Did you get the right shade of thread?"

"Miss Nicholson said thanks a million for the wine and she hopes she'll see you in church tomorrow and Mrs McLaughlin said she was awfully sorry you couldn't come to the tea and they'll have to struggle along without you, and it was grand of you to send a cake. And here's the thread."

She did not mention Roddy until they were out in the byre doing the milking and she could speak into the flank of her cow.

"He was wounded in the war. Did you notice?" Netta said. "People say he fought bravely, but now he just hangs around. No gumption, not like Seamus and Ian. He lives off his folks." As she spoke the jets of milk rang against the metal sides of the pail.

Janey sighed softly. She would never understand her sister. She scarcely ever had a good word to say about Seamus or Ian but here she was praising them in order to criticise Roddy. She thought of what Seamus had said: no one was ever good enough for Netta.

That evening as they sat by the fire sewing, Netta asked about Ian. She was convinced he was getting up to all kinds of

mischief since he had moved to Glasgow. "Why he wants to
be a mechanic is beyond me. I'd rather have a horse than a
car any day," she said, shaking her head. Janey did her best
to defend him. Where had Roddy learned to be an electrician, she wondered.

Next day it was fine, and in the afternoon, when she'd
finished doing chores for Netta, Janey carried her books
down to the old bridge. Roddy was sitting on the parapet,
gazing down into the fast flowing brown water.

He greeted her cheerfully and pointed to a fisherman
standing on the far bank. "There's Tyler," he said.

"Who's Tyler?" Janey asked, leaning over the bridge to
look.

Roddy stared at her in amazement. "You don't know?"

She shook her head.

"Tyler was Netta's beau. Last year he was calling on her
every weekend; people were sure they'd be married by Harvest festival."

Janey couldn't believe what he was telling her. "That's
impossible," she said.

"No, I saw them myself, walking in the evening when your
father was down at the Drumtochty. But apparently Netta
said they would have to wait 'til your father died and Tyler
wasn't prepared to hang around. He married Elma Smith
right after Christmas. Do you mean to say that Netta never
told you about him?"

Janey shook her head. She was amazed that something so
romantic and momentous had happened in her sister's life
— and without her knowledge.

"The sad thing," Roddy went on, "is that she's cutting off
her nose to spite her face. With Seamus and Ian both gone
your father needs the help. There's all kinds of fields he
hasn't touched in years."

Later, on her way home, Janey noticed the broken fences
and the unused fields. It must be true, her father was
slackening, losing his grip. A man in his late sixties, he'd

worked all his life, every day, in all weathers, and what reward had he ever had except more work and still more. No wonder sometimes in the evening he took a drop to drink.

*   *   *

When I arrived at Lucy's to organise my father's funeral, my stepmother met me at the door. She took hold of my arm and said in a voice thick with tears, "Netta's more like a mother to me than a sister. If anything happens to her, I'll be all alone." She joined Netta in a hopeless fantasy of the future. They would live together and my stepmother would take care of Netta as she had my father. Night after night she sat on the edge of her sister's bed recalling her eighteen years of marriage. And Netta, by this time almost beyond speech, would nod in confirmation of my father's virtues.

At this critical time, when my father's death brought the family members together, people began to tell me secrets. While I was washing up my stepmother told me that Alex's first wife, Lucy's mother, had committed suicide by cutting her throat. "And Lucy takes after her, poor thing," said my stepmother, drying a saucer. "I don't know what Alex would have done without Netta." As if she sensed these revelations, Lucy too confided in me. It was her father who had rescued the Cummings from financial ruin. After Mr Cumming died, Ian had come back from Glasgow to run Lackghie. Within a few months he married a local girl, and Netta went off to work as a housekeeper; she would not share the house with Ian's wife. As the years passed Ian got deeper and deeper into debt until at last Alex bailed him out and set him up in a grocery shop. But in spite of Alex's generosity the Cummings had always treated Lucy and her father like dirt.

Netta survived my father by a scant three weeks, and for the rest of her life my stepmother was, as she had predicted, alone. Ian did not want to be bothered with his sister. Within two years of Netta's death, the stiffness which had charac-terised his bearing had become a pronounced and fatal inelasticity of the lungs; his widow retreated into a nursing home. Seamus had been drowned years before in Canada, and in spite of repeated requests Bella had refused to bring home the Cumming heirs.

My father's death made me at least briefly an important member of the family. While my stepmother was nursing Netta with relentless zeal, I took care of the business of death. I ordered the coffin, I went to the registrar of deaths, I traced the will. Most important of all, I started looking for a place for my stepmother to live. For all kinds of reasons, she could no longer stay in the farmhouse, which was rented in my father's name for two hundred pounds a year. My father had left five thousand pounds, and with this money I organised the purchase of a small flat in the town where he had taught until he retired.

Although my stepmother had driven some kind of vehicle during the war, she had never bothered to get her driving licence. She claimed that she had an aptitude and could easily have passed her test but there had never been any need. For eighteen years she had been happy to let my father drive her everywhere. Now that he was dead, she kept saying that if only she had passed her driving test, everything would be all right. She could not accept that she must leave the farmhouse where they had been so happy.

Bewildered with grief, she moved into the flat. Bran, now stiff and elderly, was fetched from Lucy's to be her companion, and I went with her to help her settle in.

I slept on a camp-bed in one corner of a room stacked high with furniture; every night, in self-defence, I went to bed earlier than the night before. Gradually we unpacked boxes and arranged furniture, and daily my stepmother grew more querulous. At the height of her grief she had agreed to all kinds of things that she now denied. She became convinced that I had stolen from her, and blamed me bitterly for selling various things for too little money. She refused adamantly to give me any keepsake of my father; even in death she would not share him. At the same time her sorrow over Netta turned into anger; she felt entitled to her sister's possessions and could not reconcile herself to the idea that they had all passed to the long-suffering Lucy.

As a child I had stopped keeping a diary after my stepmother read it. Now I began to record the events that surrounded my father's death in a book which I called privately a death book. Unfortunately I neglected to hide it and my stepmother read a paragraph in which I recounted my fears that she might fall down the stairs of her new flat. She interpreted this as wishful thinking and threw my book on the fire.

The stairs were the big disadvantage of the flat, but they were balanced by a significant advantage: the proximity of neighbours who took a kindly interest in my stepmother and saved her from utter solitude. She became acquainted with a pair of sisters who lived in the building. Mrs Lang, a widow like herself, became her friend. She did not care so much for Mrs Lang's sister, Mrs Sutherland, who lived with her husband in the flat below; she thought the Sutherlands were common but set herself to tolerate their attentions with ladylike good grace. The two sisters had lived in the building for nearly thirty years and they welcomed newcomers, like my stepmother, as if receiving guests in their own home.

The flat opposite my stepmother was occupied by another newcomer, an elderly Englishwoman, Mrs Claypoole. Whenever Mrs Claypoole heard footsteps on the stairs, or Bran barking, she would pop her head out to see who was coming or going from my stepmother's flat. One day one of my father's bachelor friends, on his way to pay a call on my stepmother, saw Mrs Claypoole looking out. "I didn't know you had an old witch living next to you, Janey," he said in a loud, carrying voice. Mrs Claypoole never looked out again. Almost every time I visited her, my stepmother described this incident. She thought it was extremely funny. Part of it I suppose was the humiliation of her neighbour. Perhaps

more important, the story made a distinction between her
and this old woman who might otherwise have seemed so
similiar.

I did not mind the repetition of these stories on my visits.
Conversation was hard, and anything was better than
silence. On my way to see her I would rehearse topics that
seemed safe and innocuous — her neighbours, Lucy and her
husband, the Conservative government, local events — only
to discover that we had run through them all in the first ten
minutes. My stepmother had a gift for bringing any subject,
however distant, around to whichever of my crimes cur-
rently obsessed her. For several years she accused me of
stealing my father's golf trolley. Even when I produced it
from the cupboard in the hall, she was not convinced of my
innocence but claimed that I had substituted a clever forg-
ery.

Aunt Margaret and my father had been guilty of a certain
negligence in the making of their wills. My stepmother,
however, took the task of disposing of her possessions extremely seriously. Almost every month she wrote me a letter
threatening to disinherit me, and in the last three or four
years of her life she made perhaps a dozen wills. The final
version was dated six months before she died, and even it
had a small handwritten codicil reducing the amount she was
leaving to one of Seamus's children.

Whenever I asked her for something, a book of my
father's, an umbrella I had left behind on a previous visit,
she would always say, "You'll get it soon enough, when I'm
gone," in a resolute, quavering voice, killing several birds
with one stone. Although her flat was treacherous with furniture, she would not let me have the four chairs which,
along with the trunk of embroidery, were all that I had ever
received of my inheritance from Aunt Margaret. Finally, I
decided to take them. I brought a friend with me to help;
each of us picked up two chairs. My stepmother seized hold
of one and tried to pull it from my grasp. "You'll regret

this," she said fiercely as I walked down the stairs. When I
reached the car I was shaking and had to ask my friend to
drive.

*   *   *

Janey hardly recognised Roddy when she saw him standing
above the crowds on the steps of the church. Except for his
weather-beaten face, he could have been a doctor, or a
banker, or anything. She hurried towards him, and before
she knew what was happening he had bent and kissed her
cheek. "Where shall we go for our tea?" he asked.

"We could go to Mackies, but it's on the dear side, or
there's Browns, that's very near here."

"Janey, don't you see how I'm dressed? Today I'm a city
gent. Pick somewhere nice. Somewhere you'd go with one of
your fancy doctors."

She suggested the Victoria. She herself had never been,
but the other girls went there on special occasions; she could
already hear herself telling them all about it.

Five minutes later they swung through the revolving doors
into a huge cream and gilt room. A man in uniform took
Janey's coat, and she was glad she'd worn her blue silk dress.
Walking with her head held high she followed the *maître d'*
across the thick carpet. She was even more impressed with
Roddy when they reached the table and he looked around
and asked for a quieter one, further away from the
orchestra.

The waiter who brought their menus was so smartly
dressed that for a moment, until he bowed and called her
Ma'am, Janey thought he must be a customer. She stared
aghast at the prices. "Roddy, let's go to Mackies. This is
scandalous."

"Hush. This is perfect. Tonight I'm made of money.
Order whatever you want."

As they ate she gazed around the room, examining the
frocks of the other women. Roddy talked about the war. The
coffee came and he said, "There's something I want to ask
you." He paused and Janey had the brief sinking feeling that

he was going to consult her about some medical problem; he
seemed suddenly shy. His hands were resting on the table
and she found herself thinking how different they were from
the clean, soft hands of the doctors she knew.

"When you finish your training, why don't you come
home and marry me? I'm not such a bad bet, I'd take good
care of you."

She felt her cheeks burn. She looked down at the stiff,
white tablecloth and stammered out something about
scarcely knowing him.

"Nonsense. We've known each other all our lives. I
remember you being born. How could you know someone
better than that?" As Roddy spoke, the waiter dexterously
refilled their cups. "Will there be anything else, sir?" he
asked.

"Peace and quiet 'til we finish this and then the bill," said
Roddy.

Janey gazed at him admiringly. It was true, she trusted
him, unlike all these doctors and city people. All at once she
saw herself back at Lackghie, but everything different, no
longer a child but an equal. And as she pictured this she suddenly imagined Netta accusing her of wasting her training.
"But what about my training?" she asked. "I'd never get to
use it."

"There's always plenty of opportunities to nurse folks,"
said Roddy. "If you want to work in the wee hospital in
Grantown, that would be fine with me." He put a ring down
next to her coffee cup. "It was my grandmother's," he said.

The ring had a small cluster of sapphires and rubies. It was
much too big and Janey had to squeeze her fingers together
to keep it in place. "It's beautiful," she said.

"Now how about we go dancing," Roddy said. "I haven't
been in years."

Janey took him to the local Palais and, as he had assured
her, his limp was scarcely noticeable as they waltzed around
the room.

* * *

I could not bear to think about how my stepmother passed her days. On all sides life seemed to be leaving her behind. The nature programs on television which she had watched with my father were few, and between them were many things that she needed to avoid: "Nasty things." One evening when I was visiting her and desperate to get through the hours, I suggested that we watch *A Streetcar Named Desire* on television; I had never seen the film. After a few minutes she became uncomfortable. She said she wasn't interested in watching. I said that it was meant to be good. Five more minutes passed; Brando smouldered on the screen. Then she said, "This is just a piece of nasty rubbish. We're not going to watch this," and turned off the set.

Even books were growing scarce. She would read only certain kinds. She read with pleasure almost any book about animals. James Herriot and Gerald Durrell were great favourites; so were a number of popular books about a lioness called Elsa. She read travel books, if they were not too sociological in nature. With my father she had read all of Dorothy Sayers and Agatha Christie. Now she found these ladylike and innocuous writers hard to replace. The older she got the more she complained that modern books were nothing but filth and rubbish.

Bran too deserted her. At the ripe age of fifteen he developed a kidney infection and died. Now she was more isolated than ever. She no longer needed to leave her flat at regular intervals to take Bran for walks, and she resisted all but the most persistent of human overtures. When someone from the local church called she told him proudly that she was an agnostic and shut the door in his face. To the social worker who visited her at my request, she said that she had no time for busybodies. She became convinced that the doctor who called weekly was trying to kill her when he prescribed a controversial drug for her arthritis.

Her flat grew dirtier and dirtier. There were dust-balls in the corners and the cup in which she served my coffee was dark and grimy. When I went out to the kitchen to wash the dishes from lunch or tea I would scrub everything in sight, but after a few minutes she would come out and ask sharply, "What are you up to?"

I saw her only once or twice a year, and every time she seemed more frail. My father's watch dangled from her wrist. She shrank in height, grew hunched and walked with difficulty. Even her eyes grew smaller; the rims seemed more prominent and the pupils further away. Worst of all were her hands. Their joints stood out in knobs, and she could not stop them from shaking. They were a bluish purple colour and always cold; she rubbed them constantly. One Christmas I felt embarrassed because I had brought her so many little presents and it was an effort for her even to unwrap them. It took almost half an hour, her face fixed in concentration, her hands shaking over the awkward packages. And I realised as I watched that she would be unable to open the tins of food and the bottle of sherry and that there was no one to do it for her.

*　　*　　*

Roddy wrote that he had spoken to Janey's father and that Mr Cumming had said he would be glad to see at least one of his daughters safely married. The banns would be called next Sunday and they would be married in mid-August, three weeks after Janey finished her exams.

As soon as she heard that her father approved, Janey felt able to write to Netta. In the days since Roddy had proposed she had been having terrible attacks of anxiety; she would be imagining herself taking a sandwich out to Roddy in the fields, or sitting talking with him after tea, when suddenly her sister would appear, stern and furious. Now she wrote a long letter telling Netta in detail about the proposal, and about their plans to come home and live at Lackghie, how Roddy would help Father and she and Netta would take care of everything else.

A week later a letter from Netta was waiting for her at breakfast.

Dear Janey,
I can't tell you how grieved Father and I are. I've never seen him so upset. All the trouble and expense we've been to on your behalf, and you thinking of marrying someone like Roddy. He's a nice enough fellow and we all admire him for going off to fight but as Father says that's beside the point. He's in no position to get married, he couldn't support a wife, and where would you live? His parents' house is bursting at the gills and Father could never abide him here. If Mother were alive this would break her heart.

Netta

Janey was baffled. She could not disbelieve Netta; yet how could Roddy have been so mistaken? Why, he had even said that Dad missed her. Half a dozen times that day she was reprimanded by the ward sister. She forgot to give medicine, she lost track of what she was doing while feeding an elderly woman, she failed to answer questions and requests. In the middle of the night she got out of bed and wrote to Roddy saying maybe they should wait, not rush into things. She would come home in a couple of weeks and talk to Netta.

* * *

The last time I visited my stepmother was shortly before her eightieth birthday. The angry letters I got from her once a month made me think of her as indestructible, but when I saw her standing in the doorway I knew that time was short.

I plied her with questions about the past, which she answered grudgingly. After Glasgow, she had gone to a cottage hospital in Kent. During the war she moved to Portsmouth where night after night she worked through the air raids. The soldiers were all so good, so brave. They had

revived the name by which she had been known at school:
Janey Cumming-and-going. "That's when I started smoking," she said, and tapped another cigarette out of the
packet.

"What happened after the war?" I asked.

She had gone back to Scotland, she said, to stay with Netta
and Alex. She needed a rest. Then she had done private
nursing for a while before getting a job at the boys' school.
Suddenly she produced from her capacious handbag a piece
of paper; it was the letter she had received from the head-
master in 1952 offering her the job. She put on her glasses
and read, "I think the school nurse can have as much influence on the boys as any other lady in the community."

"And then what?" I asked, but further she would not go.

We had got through two hours; I got up to leave. "Bye-
bye. See you soon," I said, and kissed her. "Take care of
yourself," I said as she let me out of the flat, and she grim-
aced.

Outside, in the street, I breathed deeply as I walked
towards the car. When I reached it, I turned to wave and
there she was, at her bedroom window, holding the net curtain aside and waving till I was out of sight.

* * *

Netta was out in the garden, hanging up the washing, when
the post came. Janey opened the door, and Jock the post
beamed at her. He was red in the face from climbing the hill.
"Not long 'til the great day," he said cheerily, handing her a
large brown box. "I'll be glad when all the fuss is over, I
must say. Ever since the banns were called I've been lugging
presents up the hill twice a day."

"Presents," said Janey in a wondering voice.

"Aye, lass. Wedding presents for you and Roddy. They all
come here, even those from Roddy's folks."

Janey nodded dumbly. Holding the box in her arms, she
turned back into the house and went along the passage to the

parlour. The room was hardly ever used; she hadn't been in it since last Christmas. The blinds were down, but even in the dim light she could see a mound of boxes on the table. One by one she picked them up. They were all addressed to Miss J.E. Cumming, or Jane, or Janey Cumming. She sank down onto one of the chairs. What could it mean that Netta was silent in the face of these boxes? Why did she act as if the wedding would not take place?

Janey heard the sound of the back door opening. She jumped up, but Netta was already coming down the corridor, blocking the only possible escape. Janey stood helpless, the doorknob in her hand. She knew she should take the initiative, ask what was the meaning of not telling her about the presents, but her throat was jammed. Instead of anger she felt an unreasoning, terrifying guilt, as if she was the one who was in the wrong. Netta said nothing. She reached past Janey, closed the door, and turned and walked back to the kitchen. Slowly, Janey followed.

Netta was standing at the stove, stirring a pan of rhubarb.

"Jock had a parcel," Janey said. She fretted the material of her skirt back and forth between her fingers. "He told me about the others."

Still Netta said nothing, but stood with her back to the room, stirring. At last she turned and sat down at the kitchen table. She began to twist their mother's wedding ring round and round her finger. "Father never wanted you to go away. He said the house was too much work for me but I told him I'd manage somehow. I was desperate for you to have some kind of life outside Lackghie. I knew it was what mother would want."

The smell of rhubarb filled the kitchen; Janey remembered helping her mother make rhubarb jam. All by herself she had knelt on a chair at the table and stuck labels on the jars. Mother had given her a scone with warm jam.

Netta put the ring down on the table. "You don't know what hard work is," she said. "To be always on the go —

milking the cows, feeding the animals, tending the garden —
and running the house on no money, always scrimping and
making-do. That's what I wanted to spare you. That's what
mother died of. She was too delicate to be a farmer's wife.''
Netta got up, came over to where Janey was standing, and
took hold of her hands. "It's not too late. Everyone will understand. People don't know what you see in him. They think
you feel sorry for him because he's a cripple, they make
jokes about Nurse Cumming and her sick fiancé.''

Janey stood mesmerised. Netta's eyes were her own eyes,
her mother's eyes. On the verge of decision, she pulled away.

"I'm going for a walk,'' she said.

* * *

She has been dead two months when at last I make the long
journey from Toronto to her flat in Scotland. In the street
outside the building two men are fixing the pavement. There
is a thick wooden plank straddling the fresh cement so that
the occupants of the building can come and go. As I walk
across the plank the workmen nod cheerfully to me and I
remember the many bridges I built as a child. Today, in a
sense, is the end of my childhood. I climb the stone stairs —
no dogs bark, no neighbours appear — and for the first time
I do not knock and wait to be admitted. I put the key in the
lock and open the door for myself.

No one has been here since she died; everything is as she
left it. In the kitchen, her breakfast tray still sits ready for the
following morning. The napkin curled into the napkin ring
is dusty, and there is mould growing in the marmalade jar
beside her plate.

At first I cannot settle to anything; I flit from room to room
in a disorganised way. Then I choose a simple task, something small that I think I can manage. I go into her bedroom
and begin to unpack the suitcase that was sent home from
the hospital. Most of the clothing I put directly into a rubbish
bag, without looking at it, but I cannot help noticing the

smell. It is unique and indescribable and I would recognise it anywhere: it is the smell of her.

At the bottom of the suitcase is her pink sponge-bag. I empty the contents onto her dressing-table. There are several tubes of lipstick which I try out on my wrist. The colours are brilliant, with names like Firebrand and Mandarin red. And there are face powder and rouge. I imagine her using these things in hospital, powdering and painting for her gentlemen visitors, and I admire her unyielding vanity.

I move around opening everything, pulling out drawers and opening doors. The room begins to look as if it has been ransacked. Perhaps I should honour the dead by proceeding in an orderly way, but somehow this is beyond me. At the bottom of her wardrobe, still wrapped, are the presents I sent her for her eightieth birthday. She has torn a hole in the paper of each one, to see what was inside, and then put them away. Not only my gifts have been treated in this way; there is a big pile of such presents, dating I imagine over several years. I look through them and find endless bars of soap, as if her acquaintances had thought she would be washing her hands till doomsday.

The top drawer of her dresser is full of gloves. There are maybe twenty pairs, all kinds, clumsy woollen ones, big fur mittens like bear paws, lace gloves, but by far the greatest number are evening gloves made of the softest leather. They are pink, white, dusty grey. I try on a pair made of ivory kid. By narrowing my hands, I can just squeeze them in up to the knuckles. I remember her swollen hands. Fifty years ago they must have been fine and slender.

To match the gloves there are shoes, a small remainder of her extensive collection. I can still see the shape of the living foot in them. I throw a couple into a rubbish bag, then I get them out again. Perhaps tomorrow.

Noticing that it is already two o'clock, I decide to visit Lucy and deliver the silver Georgian candlesticks. They belonged to my father's parents, and in the final version of her will my stepmother left them to Lucy and her husband.

I am driving along the narrow road over the hills, with the candlesticks on the seat beside me, when the car in front of me hits a sheep. The sheep flies through the air, like a piece of laundry. The other car stops and so do I. The sheep is a black-faced ewe, and her eyes are very dark. As I kneel down beside her, she raises her head for a moment and blood oozes from her mouth. The man who hit her is examining the damage to his car. I would like to bury my hands in the rough greasy wool, so that the ewe will know she is not alone, but the touch of a human might, I think, be frightening, rather than consoling. I get back in my car.

I drive up the hill, past the place where my father died, to Lucy's house. She makes tea and we sit together in the kitchen. She says, "It's not easy, not easy at all being a step-daughter. It's a very odd relationship."

With her words, the old, hard facts fall into a new pattern, and I realise the full scope of Netta's accomplishment. Not only did she prevent Janey from marrying until she herself was safely wed, but such was the strength of her influence that when her sister did get married it was to a man as much as possible like Netta's husband: a widower with one daughter.

Lucy offers me more shortbread and I ask questions, trying not to be too obsessive, too relentless. She tells me that the Cumming family farmed a croft called Lackghie — she pronounces it La-guy — near Boat of Garten. There were four children, Netta, Janey, Seamus and Ian. A couple of miscarriages, also twins who died. Mrs Cumming died. Netta brought up her sister and brothers. The father took a drop to drink. Janey was engaged to a distant cousin but Netta broke up the engagement and Janey collapsed. Unable to complete her training, she went to work in a cottage hospital in Kent. It was 1948 before she sat and passed her exams.

In two days I empty the flat. I sell some things, store others, and throw out most. Hour by hour I harden myself to get rid of the many things that have no use or value. The shoes that I cannot bring myself to consign to a rubbish bag one day, I manage to stuff into a dustbin the next. And all the time it is as if I am throwing out my past. The second morning I wake up sad because I have let the pink milk jug go to strangers who will smash it or sell it for a few pence. During the summer it stood in the scullery, covered with a little net to keep out flies.

All day I run in and out with bags of rubbish, boxes, cups of coffee, and I never leave the building without looking back at her bedroom window, where the net curtains still hang. However badly my visits to her had gone, she would always come to that window to watch and wave, and I would wave back. One time, for a moment, it seems that there is someone standing there, but it is only the breeze moving in the net.

As I work, the neighbours drop in with offers of cups of tea. My stepmother left a hundred pounds to Mrs Lang, the ladylike sister with whom she was friends, and nothing to Mrs Sutherland, whom she considered common. The Sutherlands do not seem to feel slighted by this opinion; they offer me endless help. It is they who live directly underneath her flat.

I meet Mr Sutherland on the stairs. He is being tugged along by a black Labrador, whom he introduces as Hamish. They are going out for a walk, but already Mr Sutherland is out of breath.

"How are you?" I ask.

"My rheumatism's bad, awfully bad," he says, "but I try to keep active."

I say something sympathetic and explain that I have been to various shops looking for boxes. Half an hour later, while I am in the midst of packing books, I hear a knock. The door is wide open; somehow the further I get with dismantling the flat, the less the normal protocol applies. Mr Sutherland comes in carrying several cardboard boxes.

"I thought you could use these," he says, panting. "They're whisky boxes, the best kind."

I am kneeling beside a box, filling it with books. He stands awkwardly; there is nowhere to sit down.

He says, "It's sad, it's awfully sad. You know I was home when it happened. My wife was away but I was home. I was watching television. I had the set on loud, because my hearing's not that good." He pauses. "Maybe if I had heard her, it would have made a difference."

His face is red, and as he speaks, he stares down into the box of books.

I answer very carefully, making my voice loud. Over and over I have wondered whether she might have recovered if she had been found sooner, but I am desperate to reassure this man. When I finish speaking, he shuffles his feet and says nothing. I say, "Is there something you and Mrs Sutherland would like?" I gesture around.

"No, no," he says.

"I mean a keepsake."

"Oh, yes, we'd like a keepsake, but you should choose." He says if there is anything he and his wife can do to help I mustn't hesitate to ask, then announces that he has to go to work.

Later Mrs Lang comes and invites me to take a cup of tea with her and Mrs Sutherland. Mrs Lang is slim and pale. She must be close to seventy; she wears her hair like my stepmother's, curled under just above her shoulders in a limp perm. I follow her downstairs. I have chosen keepsakes for the Sutherlands — a heavy cut-glass bowl and two little painted china dishes. When I put them down on the kitchen table, I am embarrassed. Somehow I seem to have become infected by my stepmother's attitude towards the Sutherlands. I have chosen in a spirit of meanness, things that are not worth much, as if these people are not worthy of a better gift.

The two sisters talk about my stepmother. Mrs Lang used to call on her every day. And often she would come downstairs to have tea at this very table.

"Sometimes she'd be down in the dumps," says Mrs Sutherland, "but we'd cheer her up and then we'd all have a good laugh." She is like her husband, stout, red-faced and breathless. She laughs as she speaks, as if to show me that her words are true. Together she and her sister describe how in the evenings my stepmother would get out her suitcases and show them all her old photographs.

"Really," Mrs Lang says, without quite meaning to, "I hate snaps."

I want to laugh and yet I feel a pang of envy; she has shown these women the souvenirs which she would never show to me. And I would have listened, and paid attention, and remembered. Instead I have inherited hundreds of unidentifiable photographs.

Next time I see Mrs Lang I ask if she would like a keepsake. At first she says no but then, when I press her, she bursts out with some embarrassment, "You know what I'd really like is her china donkey. She loved donkeys and I do too."

I had forgotten all about the donkey. It is a holiday souvenir, in terrible taste, of which my stepmother was genuinely fond. One leg has been broken and clumsily glued back together. That this woman should want it, and that I have not given it a second thought, makes plain the huge distance between my stepmother and me. Something of my feelings must show in my face, because Mrs Lang begins to apologise for her effrontery in choosing something so personal. It takes me several minutes to convince her that I would be happy for her to have the donkey. When I touch the ornament, I realise that it is filthy. I scour it with a Brillo pad before I give it to Mrs Lang. I also pick out for her a small silver brooch, with shiny pebbles.

She demurs and then accepts it. "She was very fond of her brooches," she says. "You know I shall miss her. She was an odd lady."

I put my arms around her and my lips against her cheek.

For one brief moment I hold my stepmother. Then she is gone.

*   *   *

She slid her cigarettes from under the cushion where they were hidden and tipped one out of the packet. Using both hands, she squeezed the lighter several times until a flame shot out. It was only nine in the evening, the sun had not yet set, but after this last cigarette she would go to bed. She remembered how sometimes in the summer they had all gone up the hill after tea and worked on the harvesting until nearly midnight and still the days were much too short.

Slowly she got to her feet, went to the kitchen, and began to lay the tray for breakfast. She put out marmalade but not the butter; it was too warm to leave it uncovered over night. She filled the electric kettle so that in the morning all she would have to do would be to switch it on. As she performed these tasks she could hear the faint sounds of the television from the flat below. The Sutherlands watched indiscriminately all evening long.

She cleaned her teeth, washed her face and took her pills. Mrs Lang had loosened the lids of the bottles so that now she could easily slip out the tiny blue-and-white capsules by her-self. As she swallowed them down, she looked at herself in the mirror and said sternly, "No lying awake for you tonight, my girl." She was reading a book about the tribesmen of the Gobi desert; she would draw the curtains tight and prop her-self up in bed to look at the pictures of endless sand dunes, but only till ten o'clock. Then it was lights off and time for sleep.

In the bedroom she turned to put her cardigan on the chair. Suddenly the floor shifted; in an instant she was lying with the dusty, floral carpet pressed against her cheek. There was a sharp pain in her hip. She heard the television clearly. Using one fist, she began to pound slowly on the floor.

Nothing happened; no one came. After a long time, when the television was silent, she made one last, desperate effort to attract attention. She lay waiting. If only Bran were here now, he would bark and bring help.

As long as she lay still she had the illusion that at any moment she would get to her feet and finish undressing, but as soon as she moved, even a little, a red hot bit drilled into her bones. Still no one came. Outside, it had grown dark.

Very slowly, she began to manoeuvre towards the bed. It took a hundred tiny, separate, painful movements, but finally she lay there under the quilt, safe after a fashion. The lamp on the bedside table was on and the ceiling was soft with light. She closed her eyes. She was down by the old bridge with her mother. She had written a message to the children of Africa inviting them to visit Lackghie, and she and Mother had gone down to the river to send it. They put it into a bottle and threw it far out into the stream. Mother said, "It will be washed ashore on a beach with big palm trees and some little naked boy or girl will find it." On her honeymoon with Toby she had seen palm trees. While she gazed at the long skinny trunks he explained how it was that these trees came to grow here, in this one spot on the west coast of Scotland. Far out in the ocean a part of the Gulf Stream for no obvious reason swung north; although it was still hundreds of miles away from the coast, it created this unexpectedly balmy climate. Once for Geography she had drawn a map showing the Gulf Stream as a red arrow thrusting through the blue ocean; Netta had helped her to write in the names: America, Atlantic, Europe, Scotland.